UNDISCLOSED

PUBLIC RELATIONS BOOK 1

LIZA GAINES

Edited by
RHONDA MERWARTH
Cover Art by
CROCO DESIGNS

CHAPTER 1

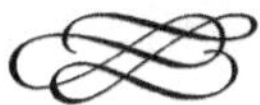

MAC

"This is the last one, Mac. You can do it."

My personal assistant, Cece, is giving me a bright smile and an encouraging pat on the shoulder as she nudges a crisp sheet of cream paper toward me with one expertly manicured aqua fingernail. Not for the first time, I wonder if she's ever considered leaving me to teach. She'd be good at it. With her warm brown eyes and supportive smile, she has the right demeanor, and her reassuring, cheerful attitude would be just what a kindergartener having trouble with their letters needs.

"Have you ever thought about teaching?" Slouching further into my chair, I peer briefly at the ceiling, deliberately ignoring the resume she's trying so hard to get me to look at.

"What?" Cece raises both brows, her lips parted in confusion. But before I can answer, she narrows her eyes and shakes her head, her auburn hair swinging about her shoulders. She's the picture of disappointment. "You're procrastinating."

I am. I've spent the last two weeks conducting interviews, even coming into the office to meet with prospective candidates on New Year's Eve, and I've reached my breaking point.

It's been an endless parade of recent graduates with stellar resumes but the personality of a houseplant. I'm sure they're all lovely people, but it's impossible to get a read on that when they're so fucking formal. I'm going to kick some career counselor's ass for convincing all these poor kids that being professional means being bland and absolutely uninteresting. Especially if they want a job in public relations.

PR is about charm. It doesn't matter how well you did at Harvard if you can't sell your client's reputation, and so far, none of the candidates have been able to sell me on themselves, let alone convince me they could do it for someone else. It's not an encouraging sign.

After more than two dozen interviews, there are only two applicants I would consider calling back for a second meeting. Either of them would probably work out fine. They're certainly qualified. Ivy League educations. Impressive internships and community involvement. Glowing references from professors, peers, and supervisors. But they just don't *feel* like the right fit, and I'm running out of options.

"All right, let's get this over with." Sitting up in my chair, I straighten my tie and smooth my shirt in an attempt to look...well, not bored to death before turning my attention to the resume Cece's left on my desk.

Gwendolyn Pierce. She graduated high school more than a decade ago, but she didn't earn her bachelor's degree until this past June from the University of Michigan. Not the main campus in Ann Arbor, where I'd gotten both my bachelor's and master's degrees though. Ms. Pierce attended the satellite campus in Flint which, yeah, is still the University of Michigan, but let's face it, it just doesn't carry the same cache as a degree from Ann Arbor. Not even close.

But this is the first resume to cross my desk that stands out from the others. Granted, that's because she lacks the Ivy League education and prestigious connections the others all boast of, but I'm not so sure that's a bad thing, given the project she'd be working on.

Cece returns, Ms. Pierce in tow, and my heart seizes in my chest. I know this woman. Or I did, when she was fresh-faced out of high school and I was getting ready to start my master's degree. We'd spent one crazy summer in Ann Arbor together, and then she'd simply vanished. I never thought I'd see her again, and now here she is, nearly twelve years later, standing in my office for a job interview.

Holy fucking shit.

She's changed since I knew her. Her face is thinner, her tits bigger —or maybe that's just the perfect fit of her silk blouse. Her honey-blond hair, which had been shoulder length then, is now much longer and pulled into a neat braid, a few loose strands framing her face.

She looks older, more mature, but she's still the most beautiful woman I've ever seen. Over the years, I tried to convince myself that she wasn't actually as gorgeous as I remember. That I fabricated an idealized version of her in my memories. But no, my memory hasn't been playing tricks on me. Not this time, anyway.

"Gwen?" It's not really a question. I know it's her, and I can see recognition amid the flurry of emotions flashing in her blue eyes. She remembers too.

"You know each other?" Cece asks, eyes wide and lips parted, her gaze bouncing between us.

"Yes," I say.

"No," Gwen says at the same time.

"Well, I'll let you get to it." Cece smothers a laugh as she lets herself out of my office, giving me one last glance that says we'll-talk-later-and-I-want-all-the-gory-details before closing the door behind her.

Gwen immediately fills the silence, stepping toward my desk, one hand extended as if we're going to shake. "It's a pleasure to meet you, Mr. MacKenzie. Thank you for seeing me today."

I don't rise from my chair and I don't reach across my desk to shake her hand. Rude, I know, but honestly, I'm fucking stunned. Both by her presence and the fact that even now that we're alone, she's persisting with this charade.

My world has turned upside down and I can't even tell how I'm feeling. Angry. Hurt. Happy. Confused. Numb. A kaleidoscope of emotions, and I don't know what to do with a single damn one of them.

"This is how you're going to play it, Gwen? You're just going to stand there and pretend we've never met?" I tip my head to the guest chair and wait for her to sit and get settled. But once she has, she still doesn't answer, instead staring at me, stone-faced and unblinking, her hands knotted in her lap. "Really? So, you're going to pretend I haven't had my dick in every hole in your body? That you didn't disappear without so much as a goodbye?"

She's still staring at me blankly, but her knuckles have gone white in her lap. The woman must have a fucking titanium spine, though, because she forces a plastic smile and says, "I'm sorry, I'm afraid you have me mixed up with someone else, Mr. MacKenzie."

"Mac. You damn well know my name is Mac. But that's fine, Ms. Pierce. You've at least answered one question for me. I wondered what happened to you. I worried about you. I couldn't understand how you could walk away like that when I was crazy-mad in love with you. Fucking crazy, Gwen. But I get it now. None of it ever meant a damn thing to you. That must have made it pretty easy to go."

She's noticeably paler now, and I could swear she flinched on the word "love," but that might be wishful thinking. I should be able to handle this situation with a little more class, but apparently not. I don't know if it's just because I'm an asshole or if it's because even after more than a decade it all still feels too fresh and raw, but I can't play this game with her.

"You know, I don't think there's much point in continuing this interview, so I won't waste your time, Ms. Pierce. Have a nice afternoon." I slide her resume off my desk and drop it straight into the trash before turning to my computer, making my point as clearly as I can.

We're done here.

~

GWEN

WALKING in to find Mac sitting behind that desk was one of the biggest shocks of my life. If I was thinking clearly, I would've turned and left without a backward glance, but I was too dazed, stupefied into inaction.

It's understandable, really. Though he's older than the last time I saw him, he's just as handsome with thick, dark hair and soulful brown eyes, the chiseled planes of his face so sharp you could probably cut granite with his jawline. Although seated behind his desk, in a suit that probably—definitely—cost more than my entire wardrobe, it's clear he's no longer the lanky young man I'd known. Still fit, yes, but he's filled out and grown into his tall, broad frame. For a split second I got distracted, wondering if he's still all muscle and sinew under his fancy clothes or if he'd gotten a little soft in his thirties. Hoping he did. No one has any right to look as perfect as he does.

And then he said my name, in that still-familiar deep voice, and panic overrode whatever good sense I normally possess. But still Mac's presence is as magnetic as it ever was, and I couldn't just run away. So, I did the only thing I could think of to survive this encounter. I pretended I didn't know him.

It's almost funny in a morbid sort of way, because despite our time together a dozen years ago, we really didn't know one another. Until about five minutes ago, neither of us even knew the other's last name. No, actually, it's worse than that, because if the nameplate on his office door is correct, I didn't even know his real first name.

William Z. MacKenzie, Jr.

He's right, it would be a disaster if we tried to work together. This painfully uncomfortable reunion is evidence enough of that. But I need a job. Badly. And now that I've stumbled into Mac again, there's something else I need to do too.

One thing at a time, Gwen.

Removing another copy of my resume from my portfolio, I lean forward and slide it across Mac's desk. I'd like to say my hand isn't shaking, but that would be a lie. All I can do is hope like hell he doesn't notice and if he does that he'll be kind enough not to mention it. "I'd like to continue with the interview, Mr. MacKenzie." Unlike my hand, my voice is steady, so I've got that much going for me.

Turning back to me slowly—so, so slowly—Mac's expression is impressive in its absolute lack of emotion. Cold, unfeeling, uninterested. As if his face were carved of marble. It's intimidating as hell, but I lift my chin, determined not to let him get to me. Well, not any more than he already has, anyway.

"You want to continue the interview." He repeats my words flatly, although I think I detect a glint of disbelief in his eyes. When he was younger, Mac had a scary hot temper, but it seems he's mellowed some with age, because while this detached response is uncomfortable, maybe even frightening in its own way, it's nothing like the way young Mac would have responded.

"Yes. I'm qualified for this job and I want it. Besides, after the way this started, I figure if I can survive an interview with you, any other interview should be a piece of cake. It'll be good practice." I add the last part in an attempt to lighten the mood, but Mac isn't amused.

"Okay, let me ask you this. The position we're trying to fill will be very intense, and whoever gets the job will be required to work closely with me. There will be significant travel involved. A lot of long days and stressful situations. Do you really think you're prepared to spend that much time with me? Because I'll be honest, Ms. Pierce. We have unfinished business, and the fact that you won't even acknowledge that doesn't give me a lot of hope for a cordial working relationship."

He's not wrong. I've only been in his presence a few minutes, and my skin itches. I might even be starting to break out in hives. But I've done my homework, and knowing what I do about this agency, the job he's describing sounds like a political campaign. Depending on the candidate, I'd put up with a lot for an opportunity like that. "Who's the candidate?" I ask, ignoring everything else he said and cutting to the chase.

Mac pauses, rubbing his lower lip with his thumb before saying, "Kimberly Dunn."

Slapping my hand over my mouth to smother my excited squeal, I lose my grip on my portfolio and it slips off my lap, falling to the floor and spilling sheets of cream-colored linen paper on the carpet. "Oh, shit," I mumble, scrambling to pick everything up. When I've gathered it all and zipped my portfolio closed—something I should've done in the first place, live and learn—I look up to find Mac watching me, the corners of his mouth twitching with barely suppressed amusement.

I'll be damned. Nobody enjoys making a fool of themselves, but the tension between us had been unbearable, so I don't really mind this once if it's cleared the air a little.

"I take it you're a supporter?" he asks, and though he's locked his expression down again, his tone isn't so brusque.

"You could say that, Mr. MacKenzie. It's not just that I agree with most of her policy goals, though I do. She's an inspiration. Did you know she got pregnant when she was only sixteen? She was on scholarship at an elite prep school here in DC and got kicked out because of some ridiculous morals clause. So, she got her GED and waited tables to put herself through school and support her daughter. She was dealt a really shitty hand, but she worked so hard. She didn't let anything get in her way." I'm rambling, not because I'm nervous but because everything I've said is true. I've admired Kimberly Dunn since her first appearance on the national scene some eight years ago when she ran for, and won, a seat in the House of Representatives. Now she's running for President, and I'd do almost anything to get a job with her campaign.

"I knew that, yes." Mac smiles faintly, the only indication he's noticed my hero worship, but there's something else in his tone, something intimate, that makes me wary.

"Are you in a relationship with her?" I blurt before I can think better of it. Representative Dunn is probably fifteen or twenty years older than he is and, by all accounts, happily married, but I'm uncertain either of those things would matter to him.

"No," he says with a clipped voice, his fingers drumming on his desktop as he adds, "but if I were, I don't see how that would be any of your business, Ms. Pierce."

"Well, you're wrong. If my employer and the client were involved in a secret affair, I'd have to be prepared with strategies to deal with the situation when it inevitably broke in the press, because obviously the employer and the client would be too close to the situation to handle the fallout with clear heads." I just totally made that up, but it sounds pretty good, right?

Mac rolls his eyes and gives a slight shake of his head, clearly not buying it, but he lets it go, his gaze dropping to my resume. That's a step in the right direction, so I wait quietly while he reads it. When he finally speaks, he doesn't raise his head to look at me. "You just earned your bachelor's last spring. What took so long?"

Wouldn't he like to know. Answering that question in detail would tell him exactly why I disappeared all those years ago and what's happened since then. I'm not prepared to do that right now. Hell, I can't even handle thinking about it right now. It's too surreal and, even as unexpected as this reunion is, guilt and regret gnaw at me.

Yes, there are things I need to tell him, but this isn't the time or place.

"Family obligations and monetary limitations prevented me from going to school full time." Not a lie, but I can do better than that. I'm applying for a job with a PR firm—I need to give him spin. "I suppose that's why I admire Ms. Dunn so much. Like her, I've had to work very hard to get where I am. Sometimes it seemed impossible, but no matter how difficult it was, I never gave up. That tenacity is one of my strongest assets as an employee. Furthermore, I expect much of my competition for this position is several years younger than I am, probably with better educations than mine. But I bring real-life experience to the table, and none of them have that, not like I do. I come from a blue-collar town. I've lived and worked and put myself through school in that environment. Those are some of the same voters Ms. Dunn needs to win over if she wants to be the next President of the United States. I can help her do that in ways that a bunch of Ivy League Trust Fund kids never could."

Mac looks up, his eyes narrowed as he studies me, weighing my words. I can't tell if he's impressed or indifferent. "Speaking of family obligations, do you have a significant other? Children? Pets? House plants that require frequent watering?"

"You can't ask me that in a job interview," I point out. It's both illegal and inappropriate. Not as inappropriate as ten minutes ago, when he was whisper-shouting about having his dick in me, but we've moved past that, I hope, and I'd like to keep this on track.

"The pets and houseplants are fair game, but you're right about the rest. I'm asking anyway, and if it puts your mind at ease, I discussed this with all the other applicants as well. This position will be very demanding. I have no objection to hiring someone with a family at home. I want the best person for the job, full stop. But I want to make sure you understand precisely what you'll be getting yourself into if you're hired."

It almost sounds reasonable, and to some extent I believe him. But Mac's counting on me not catching the difference between asking and discussing. He would've warned the other candidates it would be a challenging position and urged them to carefully consider how they'd balance that with their personal lives before accepting an offer. And then he would've moved on to another topic, not even giving them the opportunity to volunteer their personal details.

With me, it's different. He's asking, and damn the consequences, because he wants to know. Am I presumptuous to draw that conclusion? Not even a little. It's been a while, but I still know Mac.

He's made a mistake, though. Not because I'll sue him if I don't get the job. There's already too much ugly history between us to worry about improper hiring practices. No, his mistake is underestimating me. I'm no longer the same naive, gullible girl I was in Ann Arbor.

"Mr. MacKenzie, I assure you that whatever family obligations I have, they won't impact my job. Nor would the job, should I get it, impact my personal life." It's super hard to keep my smile from splitting my face. I've laid to rest his concerns without giving him the information he wants. I just hit a homer and, if the irritated clench of his jaw is any indication, we both know it.

Honestly, I'm making this interview my bitch. The ludicrous parts only happened because this is me and Mac, because of what we once were to each other and how that ended. If the interviewer were anyone else, none of that would've happened and I'd be feeling fantastic about my chances right now. But it is Mac and no matter how well I do, he'll never give me the job. Knowing that is kind of freeing too. I'll own this interview and use it to build my confidence. The next one, which couldn't possibly be this fucked up, will be a walk in the park.

Mac glances down at my resume again. "A dual major in marketing and psychology is interesting. What was your thought process there?"

"Understanding how the mind works helps me better understand how best to market a product."

"But you're applying for a job in public relations instead of marketing?" He's leaned back in his chair, relaxing into the conversation. It's almost encouraging.

"It's the same thing, isn't it? A marketing firm is trying to sell you the new and improved razor with five hundred thirty-seven blades for a closer, smoother shave. You're trying to sell a person's character or reputation."

Rubbing his jaw absently at the mention of shaving, Mac chuckles and nods. He gets it, but his unconscious gesture distracts me. He's clean-shaven today, but I haven't forgotten the sting of his whiskers when he went a day or two between shaves. Sometimes it was rough enough to leave my skin pink and—

"Ms. Pierce?"

My cheeks burn when our eyes meet, and he gives me a crooked smile, one brow arched in taunting question. He couldn't possibly know precisely what I was thinking, but he's aware of the general direction my mind wandered.

"Hmm?" Not a great answer, but I'm too busy trying to will blush away to bother with a better response.

"I asked if you're currently employed. I don't see anything on your resume?"

Pull yourself together, Gwen. This is an easy question. "I'm not, actually. I just moved here in August." What I don't say is it's been almost six months and if I don't get a job that uses my degree soon, I'll have to go back to waiting tables. The cost of living around here is no joke and, even with my sister's help, my meager savings won't last long.

"And here is..." Mac glances down at my resume again. "Alexandria?"

"Yes. Our apartment is only three blocks from the King Street metro. If I were to get the position, it's convenient that your office is metro accessible."

Mac tilts his head, both brows raised as a smile plays about the corners of his mouth, and it takes me a second to realize what's happened.

Fuck. I said "our."

"You don't have a car?" he asks, and I sigh with relief, because I expected him to poke and prod at my slip like a sore tooth. He would have when he was younger.

"I sold it when I moved. To be honest, the traffic around here is pretty intimidating." "Intimidating" is an understatement. "Gut-wrenchingly terrifying" is more like it. And I needed the money more than the car.

"You'll get used to it if you stick around."

Was that a jab about me disappearing? I can't tell, and his expression gives nothing away. "You're probably right."

"Do you have any questions about the position?"

"No, I don't think so." I have a million questions, but he's humored me this long and I'm not going to waste any more of his or my time when we both know I won't get the job.

"Well then." He leans forward again, palms flat on his desk. "We'll be making a decision fairly quickly. Cece will be in touch if you're chosen."

"Thank you. I really appreciate your time, Mr. MacKenzie." I stand so I can look down at him with what I hope is a saccharine smile. "It's been a pleasure meeting you."

He sighs and mutters something I don't catch, but the corners of his eyes are crinkled with amusement and his mouth is tugging up in a reluctant smile. All things considered, this doesn't seem like such a bad way to leave things between us.

At least for now.

CHAPTER 2

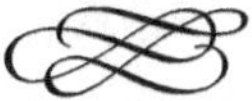

MAC

OVER THE YEARS, I've tried to put all my memories of Gwen in a lockbox and throw away the key. It hadn't worked all that well, but dammit, I tried, and seeing her again has weakened my already fragile defenses. I can't stop thinking about her. Remembering how soft and serious she could be, how fun it was to coax her out of her shell. How she infuriated me, drove me crazy, made me want her more than I'd ever wanted anyone.

We never talked about our families back then, but I got the sense that someone in her life had burdened her with their unreasonable expectations, just like my dad had me. But unlike me, who cheerfully gave my dad and his plans the finger, Gwen lived inside the box she was put in, obedient and accommodating to a fault. She played by the rules and bent over backward to meet expectations. Except when it came to me.

With a groan, I pour another scotch and glance at my watch as I flop down on my couch. It's after ten here, which means it's after seven in Seattle. Jake should be home from work now. Maybe he'll have some brilliant advice for me. Or not. He's a little bitter about how things went down with Gwen too, but maybe that's just what I need to hear. After grabbing my cell off the coffee table, I place the call.

"Hey, Mac, what's up?" Jake answers on the third ring, his voice strained. There's a loud crash in the background, followed by Jake's wife Heidi yelling that she has it, whatever it is.

"Uh, I was hoping you had a minute to talk, but it sounds like this might be a bad time." It's often a bad time to call Jake. He and Heidi have three kids under six, two dogs, four cats, and a parrot. I'd make the usual joke about their house being a zoo, but it's a little too close to reality to be funny.

"No, no, it's fine. Meredith and Autumn are already in bed, but Levi's being a little shit. Teething, you know, man?"

Nope, no fucking idea, and every time I talk to Jake, I'm reminded I like it that way. "Sure, sure. Otherwise, everything good with you guys?"

"Fucking fantastic. I was in Napa last week checking out this new winery. I really think it will be big and we're getting in on the ground floor. Super exciting. And Heidi's all but got her promotion locked up. We expect the announcement to come in the next few weeks. I'm really proud of her. Except..." He trails off, his voice muffled when he continues, "She's started talking about having another baby, man. I...I don't know if I can take it."

"I'll keep an eye out for the Facebook announcement." There isn't a doubt in my mind baby number four will be on the way before the year is out. He sounded just like this before the first three too, but when it comes right down to it, he adores his wife and is flat-out incapable of telling her no. What Heidi wants, Heidi gets, and Jake is always happy in the end.

"You know, someday you'll be knee-deep in this shit, and I'm not going to have one damn ounce of sympathy for you," Jake threatens, but there's humor in his tone too, like he's looking forward to it.

"Nope, not a chance. You're an after-school special for happy bachelors."

Despite the occasional whining, Jake loves his wife and kids and the life they've built together. I'm happy for him, I really am, but that life isn't for me. I can't blame him for forgetting now and then, though. The guy hasn't had a solid night's sleep in more than half a decade. I probably wouldn't be able to remember my own name if I were him, let alone my friend's plentiful and unpleasant baggage.

"You know you're not him, right?" Jake asks, and I know exactly who he's referencing.

I hold the phone away from my face long enough to scowl at it before tucking it between my ear and shoulder again. "Jesus Christ, not this again. Why did I call you?" We've had variations of this same conversation a thousand times, and I'm really not up for it again tonight.

"I don't know, you tell me." Jake chuckles across the phone line.

"You'll never guess who I saw today." I should just come out and say it, but I'm delaying the inevitable lecture. Telling Jake that Gwen is back in my life, in any capacity at all, will go over like a lead balloon.

"Kyle?" It isn't a bad guess, all things considered.

"No, a woman." I figure he needs the hint, or we might be here all night.

"Nat?" Jake asks, his tone laced with confusion.

"I see her all the time. You know that." Loosening my tie, I lean back into the couch cushions and close my eyes, waiting to see if he'll figure it out.

"Then you might as well tell me. It's not like there's a long list of women you've had meaningful relationships with. You haven't... Oh, shit. Don't tell me. I don't think I want to be having this conversation anymore." As he speaks, his words come slower and slower, heavy with dread.

"Yeah, me neither, to be honest." I sigh.

"So, it was her?"

"Gwen?"

"Yeah."

"Yeah, it was definitely her."

"How? Where? Why? I mean… Jesus, what the fuck? After all this time?"

"She came in for a job interview. We're hiring a social media specialist for Kim's campaign. She spent the whole interview pretending she had no idea who I am." It pissed me off at the time and still does every time I think about it, but I have to admire her commitment. Once she chose her strategy, she never wavered.

"She came in for a job interview," Jake repeats slowly, trying to understand, and I wonder if he heard anything I said after that.

"Yes."

"I…" He's at a loss for words, a somewhat rare occurrence, which is gratifying. At least I'm not the only one dumbstruck by this development.

"Now you know how I feel."

"What happened?" he asks cautiously.

"Like I said, she acted like we'd never met before and I might have yelled a little." An understatement, because I totally lost my cool. If I wasn't still so busy licking my freshly reopened wounds, I'd probably be embarrassed about that.

"No wall punching?"

Once. I did that once when Gwen vanished into thin air, but Jake will never let me live it down. "I've matured."

"Uh-huh. So, you okay?"

"Yeah. That was a long time ago, you know?" I try to play it off, but the truth is if I were okay, I wouldn't have called him.

"Sure, but you were kind of a mess when she took off."

Ah, so I'm not the only one into understatement tonight. "There was a lot of shit going on back then, and I thought I loved her. You can't blame me for being a little shook up she just disappeared like that." At the time, I was crushed, but as the years passed my hurt was replaced by anger and resentment, though that never overshadowed missing her.

"And what do you think now?"

"I think she might be bug-fuck crazy, man. Who goes into an interview with an ex whatever-the-fuck-we-were and acts like they don't even know the person?"

"Ex-boyfriend. You are her ex-boyfriend and, yes, her reaction is unusual, but she was probably as surprised as you were. She panicked." I can hear the shrug in Jake's voice, and it's not a bad theory, except...

"I'm not her ex-boyfriend. And I don't see what she has to freak out about. She isn't the one who was left with no explanation."

It had been frustrating as hell. Our only source of information clammed up. Lindsey might have been Jake's girlfriend, but she was Gwen's best friend, and whatever else I could say about her, Lindsey's loyalty to her friend was unbreakable. No matter how hard I begged, she wouldn't say a goddamn word. Ultimately, it cost Jake and Lindsey their relationship too. Her loyalty to Gwen and his to me became an insurmountable divide too great for them to bridge.

"So, you're not going to hire her?"

"Why would I?" It's irritating he seems to know I've been considering it. Hadn't she shown me she was made for this job? Sure, she fed me a lot of bullshit in that interview, but wasn't that the point? Even when I knew my questions got to her, she was quick on her feet and gave plausible answers. If I didn't know her so well, she'd have had me fooled.

Not only that but just like her resume, she stood out from the pack. She has a different perspective from the trust fund kids she scoffed at, and when it comes right down to it, that's exactly what I am, or at least an older version of it. Her point of view would be useful.

"Because you want to get in her pants again?" Jake suggests. The know-it-all smile I can hear in his voice is annoying.

"I really, really don't." I'm a damned liar. She is as gorgeous as ever, and my dick doesn't seem to care about what happened before or that Gwen very well could be crazy. Hell, my dick is making a credible argument that crazy is good, but I'm not listening because I can't. "And even if I did, it could never happen. Not if I hired her. I'd be her boss, for fuck's sake. That's skeevy as hell."

"I know you think that and maybe even want to believe it, but I was there, remember? You two were like hollandaise sauce and—"

"Excuse me?" I interrupt, sitting up a little straighter because, seriously, what the fuck is he talking about?

"You've had hollandaise, right? It's fucking amazing on pretty much everything. Anyway, the ingredients are simple, just eggs, lemon juice, and melted butter, and if you do it right it becomes this incredible creamy sauce. But if you fuck up, the sauce breaks and it's greasy and clumpy and vile."

"Have you started watching the food channel?" This doesn't sound like Jake at all.

"Meredith likes it. She sees this crazy shit on TV and then wants me to make it with her." Jake is distracted for a minute, and I can hear Heidi in the background, followed by the soft gurgle of a baby. Apparently, Dad is in charge of Levi now. When he's settled again, he goes on. "My point is, when things were good between you two, they were great. Then one of you would do something stupid and break the sauce. But no matter how fucked up the two of you were, you always, always went back for more, because hollandaise is that fucking good. And I'm telling you right now, if you hire her, you will fuck her, regardless of your intentions, because you two can't not."

"You probably shouldn't say 'fuck' that much in front of Levi," I say, buying myself time to process what he said. Filtering out all the food channel bullshit, I get his point; maybe he's right about how things used to be, but a lot has changed since then. I've changed and odds are, she has too.

"All I'm saying is, if you hire her it'll be just like old times. Mark my words."

"I'm not going to hire her," I insist because I can't hire her.

If I do, there's an excellent chance one of us will be dead and the other in jail on murder charges before the first primary is held. She can't keep up this farce forever that she has no idea who I am. Or worse, maybe she can, and I damn well know I can't deal with that.

"Great. Then you can find out where the hell she went and fuck her."

"That's not happening, either."

"Which part?"

"All the parts. I don't care what happened anymore. It's in the past and better off left there." Maybe saying it out loud will convince me it's true, because even though I wish I didn't, I still want to know what went wrong. Did I finally run her off, or did something else take her away? If I'd known what was going on, could I have changed anything? Would I have, even if I could? None of it matters anymore and some of it is unknowable now, but I can't stop myself from wondering.

"So, let me get this straight. You're not hiring her, you're not using your newly acquired contact information to find out why she took off, and you're not going to jump her bones."

"Right."

"Then why did you call me?"

"If she were anyone else, I would've hired her on the spot."

"You feel guilty," Jake says with a sigh, finally catching on.

It's like a reverse casting couch where she isn't getting a job she's qualified for because she slept with the boss. How am I supposed to feel good about that? "It seems pretty shitty to deny her a job opportunity for personal reasons."

"Then hire her."

"You make it sound so simple."

"It is simple. You have three choices. Hire her, don't hire her but go talk to her, or pretend this never happened. You've said you're not hiring her, except you feel guilty about it. You also said you don't care about what happened in the past, so—"

"No, you're twisting my words. I said I don't care about finding out the specifics. That doesn't mean I don't care that something *did* happen. I can't hire her and coexist with her in some kind of shared delusion that we're strangers to each other."

"Then don't hire her."

"You're no help at all," I complain, dropping my head against the back of the couch.

"That's hurtful, Mac." Jake clucks at the baby before continuing.

"I'm very helpful, but I'm not going to tell you what to do. I'm not exactly unbiased when it comes to Gwen, and you wouldn't listen to me anyway. You'd do the opposite of whatever I said just to be contrary, and I'm too tired these days to figure out how to reverse psychology you into doing what I think you should be doing."

"But I don't know what to do." It comes out whinier than I'd like, and I hate admitting it but if there's anyone I can be that honest with, it's Jake. He's known me for exactly what I am since the day we met in second grade.

"You'll figure it out." Jake says this with a confidence that seems wholly unwarranted before asking, "Is the campaign swinging out this way any time soon?"

"I'll check the schedule and have Cece call Raven and see if they can schedule a dinner or something." When we were kids, we had to ask our mothers for permission to have play dates. Now we have to ask our personal assistants.

"Sounds like a plan. If it's convenient, you can crash here while you're in town."

I'll crash at Jake's house even if it isn't convenient. I might not want a family of my own, but I love spending time with his. He's my best friend, Heidi is fantastic, and the kids are a blast. Being the fun uncle who breezes in and out of town a couple of times a year definitely doesn't suck.

After we hang up, I stare across the room at the dark TV. When Gwen walked out of my life, she left turmoil in her wake, and now her unforeseen return is just as tumultuous.

What the hell am I going to do?

CHAPTER 3

GWEN

I frown over the rim of my wine glass at my sister, Willa. She's right, I know she's right, and judging by the disapproving slant of her brows, she knows it too. But I don't want her to be right, and that has to count for something. "I mean, maybe I don't. He's not going to give me the job, so I'll never see him again." Except I know how to find him now so I could see him again. If I wanted to. Or needed to. Whatever.

"Right, but—"

"Mom!" Tristan's high-pitched call from down the hall interrupts Willa.

"I'll be back." Ignoring the meaningful look she's giving me, I push away from the table and head for Tristan's room. "What's up, tiger? Did you have a bad dream?" I ask from the open door. He doesn't have nightmares often anymore, but from the firm line of his lips, tonight might be an exception.

"No, but I can't sleep." That's probably really a yes, but he's reached the stage where he doesn't like admitting he's afraid.

"Would you like me to stay for a bit?"

"Yeah," he agrees with an almost imperceptible nod, pulling the blankets tighter under his chin.

Moving to the edge of his bed, I sit down and put one hand on his chest, softly rubbing it. Ever since he was a baby, that's soothed him, and it still works, although I imagine the day is fast approaching when it won't.

He's growing up so fast.

Studying Tristan's face as he eases back into sleep, I'm struck, today of all days, by how much he looks like his father. Over the years, I've convinced myself that a lot of the resemblance was in my imagination. Otherwise, it was too painful to see so much of the man in the boy. But after seeing Mac today, there's no denying the obvious.

Tris has my blond hair and, I think, my cheeks, although as he's getting older and the baby fat melts away, I'm not so sure of that. The rest of him is all Mac though, especially his dark brown eyes, such a stark contrast to my own blue irises. He has Mac's nose and eyebrows. Even his eyelashes, long and thick on his cheeks in sleep, came from his father. And he's going to be big like Mac too, because he's always been taller than most of the other boys in his class.

The resemblance is uncanny, especially taking into account the mannerisms Tristan got from the father he's never met. The way he arches his left eyebrow skyward when he thinks I'm being silly or unreasonable. The way he rubs his bottom lip with his thumb when lost in thought. The way his smile—not the one he plasters on for school pictures, but his real, genuine smile—always kicks up one corner of his mouth higher than the other, in a lopsided grin that makes my heart hurt with how much I love him. My son...Mac's son...is a walking, talking endorsement for nature over nurture.

"Stop staring at me, Mom," Tristan demands with a sleepy whine, his eyes still closed.

Biting my lip to contain the laughter bubbling up in my throat, I redirect my gaze to the Captain America poster on the wall and consider my conversation with Willa.

She's right, of course. I have to tell Mac about Tristan, but after all these years I don't know how, and I'm terrified of his reaction. But even if Mac didn't have a right to know—and he does—Tristan deserves to know who his father is. Every Father's Day, birthday, Christmas…it always comes up, especially as he's gotten older and can see the relationships his friends have with their fathers. Until now, I've never had much of an answer for him because even if I wanted to, I didn't know how to find Mac, although at one point I tried. Now I finally have answers and I owe them to Tristan.

It can wait a little longer though. Mac has a lot on his plate right now with Kimberly Dunn's campaign, and he'll be traveling with her as long as she remains in the race. If she loses in the primaries, I'll tell him once she drops out. If she doesn't, I'll wait until after the general election in November. That way, if he wants to meet Tristan, wants to have some kind of relationship with him, he'll be around enough to make it happen.

There's the possibility too that he might try to take Tristan away from me. It's hard to imagine the Mac I used to know doing something like that, but as implausible as it might be, I can't ignore the possibility. I can't—won't—risk losing Tristan, and I can't afford an enormous court battle right now. Especially not with someone like Mac, who'd probably hire the most expensive attorneys in D.C. Until I tell him, I'll stash every spare penny I can in case I need to hire a lawyer of my own.

If Mac doesn't want to be in Tristan's life…well, if he wants nothing to do with our son, I'm not sure what I'll tell Tristan. Knowing Mac, this is the most likely scenario, and I need more time to figure out how to deal with it.

When Tristan's breathing has slowed down and evened out, I lean over and kiss his forehead before slipping out of his bed and heading back to the kitchen, leaving his door cracked behind me. Willa's still waiting for me, our wine glasses refilled and a plate of cookies in the center of the table. She expects me to argue with her, so I cut her off at the pass as soon as I sit down. "I'll tell him. But not yet."

"Why wait?" She gives me a dubious look and reaches for a cookie.

"As long as he's working on a presidential campaign, he isn't going to be around much. It seems unfair to tell him—to tell them both— when he'll be gone most of the time. When that's over, they'll have time to really get to know each other. I mean, if that's what Mac wants."

Willa isn't convinced, her blue eyes narrowing with suspicion. But then her expression softens, her teeth catching her lower lip and she sighs, setting the cookie back on the plate, uneaten. "I hate this."

"You and me both, sister, but I said I'd tell him, and I will. Just not yet." Turning the stem of my wineglass, I watch the red liquid crawl up the sides in waves, unable to look at Willa because I'm afraid I know what she's about to say.

She hesitates but finally blows out a loud breath and says, "I feel like it's all my fault."

"How is it your fault? You were eleven when I was off being stupid with Mac."

"Not that part. Even at that age, I'd have told you to use a damn condom." Willa laughs and waves one hand before saying more quietly, "No, I mean, just the way it all turned out. Who knows what might've happened if you didn't have to take care of me and Liv?"

"You're being ridiculous, and we've been over this before. It wasn't your fault. What do you think would have been different, anyway? You think Mac would have married me?" I scoff and lean back in my chair, shaking my head. "He wouldn't have, you know. He really wouldn't have. He wasn't like that. Things would've ended up exactly as they have...you and me and Livie and Tris against the world. And maybe Mac would've drifted in and out of our lives visiting Tris now and then and maybe he wouldn't have, and maybe that would have been worse, at least for Tristan. But it wouldn't have made anything better."

"How can you be so sure of that?"

"Because Mac is...sometimes I thought he was contrary just for the sake of it. I still think that was true some of the time. But it was more than that too. You know how I am, right, Willie? Always following the rules. Always worried about what people think of me. He didn't care about any of that—he thought rules were made just so he'd have something to break."

"You're smiling," Willa points out quietly.

Shit, I am.

I guess I shouldn't be surprised. For someone as anxious as I was back then, it was so easy to get caught up in Mac's devil-may-care attitude. It was fun. "The point is, Mac would've felt no obligation to marry me just because I got pregnant. The very suggestion that he should feel that way would've pissed him off," I say, taking care to force my face into a neutral expression.

"Leave it to my straight-laced, perfectionist, prude of a sister to fall for a rebel," Willa laughs, shoving her white-blond hair over her shoulder and reaching for the cookie again.

"I'll give you straight-laced and maybe perfectionist, but I'm not a prude and I didn't fall for him," I huff, indignant.

"I just want to make sure I'm clear on this," Willa says with a sarcastic smile, breaking off a piece of her cookie and eating it before continuing. "You lost your virginity with Ted because you thought you loved him and you'd get married and live happily ever after, right?"

"Yes..." I answer warily.

"The very next guy after Ted, you have a one-night stand without even sharing names. And then, when you run into him again at a party, you start a torrid affair, regularly having sex without a condom."

"Occasionally," I correct her, wishing I never shared any of the details with my sisters. I meant it as a cautionary tale so they wouldn't make the same mistakes I did and so far, it worked. But now it's being used against me, and I don't like that so much.

"Gwen, this is ridiculous. Yesterday, you refused to go through the twelve items or fewer line because you had two tomatoes and if you counted them separately, that made thirteen items. But you want me to believe you repeatedly had unprotected sex with a dude you didn't care about? It was just this casual thing, as if that's a thing you do?" Willa is incredulous now, and even I have to admit when she puts it like that it makes sense. But she's wrong.

"I didn't fall for him. I didn't," I insist a little too stridently.

"Then how do you explain it? You broke all the rules for him, and if that doesn't sound like a good girl falling hard for a bad boy, I don't know what does." Willa crosses her arms triumphantly over her chest but then quickly drops them again to break off another piece of her cookie. In the Pierce family, quality baked goods always take priority over gloating.

"It wasn't like that. He just… I don't know. He made me stupid. I couldn't think when he was around. It's like I was someone else." With a sigh, I steal a piece of her cookie, wishing I could explain it better, because Willa has it all wrong and I can't seem to make her understand.

"Do you even hear yourself?" She's struggling not to laugh now.

"What?" I ask defensively, cookie crumbs spraying the front of my shirt.

"I know you're basically a nun now, but that's what falling in love is like. It turns everything upside-down."

"I'm not a nun," I correct her as I shake out the front of my shirt to dislodge the crumbs.

I'm really not. Granted, my dating life has been pretty bleak ever since Mac. But it isn't like there hasn't been anyone else. A lot of guys aren't interested in single mothers though, and I was so busy, there was little time for the few who weren't scared off by my other responsibilities.

We're both quiet for a minute, stuffing our faces with chocolate chip cookies and thinking our own thoughts. Finally, when I'm just about to call it a night, Willa nudges the plate of cookies away and frowns at me.

"What?"

"I was just thinking. What will you do if he does offer you the job?"

"Don't be ridiculous. That'll never happen." I push away from the table, laughing quietly to myself. Despite all my other problems, this one is actually funny, because it isn't a problem at all and it's cute that Willa thinks it could be.

There's no way in hell Mac will offer me that job.

CHAPTER 4

GWEN

"I'm bored," Tristan announces, flopping down on the couch with a dramatic sigh.

"Then come help me," Olivia says from her place on the floor. She's just finished painting her fingernails and she sticks one foot up in the air, wiggling her toes at him.

"I'm not painting your toenails." Tristan glares at my youngest sister, but we all know he'll end up doing it.

"Oh, come on. You always say that but—"

"Has anyone seen my scarf?" Willa asks, rushing out of her bedroom.

"No," Olivia answers absently. She's waving a bottle of blue nail polish in Tristan's direction.

"What do you need a scarf for, anyway? It's warm here." Tristan isn't wrong; January in Northern Virginia is warm, at least by Michigan standards. But it's not lost on me—or Willa—that he didn't answer her question.

Suspicious.

"Where's Aunt Willie's scarf, Tris?" I ask in my best Mom voice, which evidently isn't very good, because he ignores me, conveniently overcome with interest in the fashion magazine Olivia left on one of the couch cushions.

"Ugh, I don't have time for this. I'll be late for work," Willa groans and pulls on her coat. "If I get pneumonia while I wait for the bus, it'll be your fault, Tris."

"But you're on your way to work. What better place to get pneumonia?" Olivia points out, sharing a giggle with Tristan.

Willa is an RN and started a job at the nearby hospital just before Thanksgiving. It's a huge relief to have one of us working, but I really need to find a job too, and soon. The move from Michigan was expensive. Living in the D.C. metro area is expensive. Olivia will start college in the fall, and even with the in-state rate—one of the big reasons we moved—the tuition is outrageous. We can't last much longer on Willa's income and my nearly depleted savings. And we need to get out of this cramped two-bedroom apartment. It isn't enough space for all of us. Tristan has his own room, Willa and Livie share a room, and I sleep on the couch, a fact my back is regularly starting to complain about. And that's not even taking into account the horror of the four of us sharing one bathroom.

"You know, Livie, being a nurse and all, I could beat the crap out of you, and no one would ever have to know." It's an empty threat. Willa's already grabbed her purse and is headed for the door.

"Ohhh." Olivia rolls her eyes and shivers in mock horror. Her sudden movement results in Tristan inadvertently leaving a streak of blue polish across half her foot. Turning her attention back to him she frowns and grumbles, "Hey, watch it!"

"I might be late tonight. Dr. Neuhaus is working too, so we might grab a coffee or something after our shift," Willa calls before slamming the front door behind her.

Is it wrong that I dream about my sister marrying a doctor? A young, good-looking, kind doctor. A rich doctor. A doctor who wants to help her and her hapless family. Yeah, that's probably wrong. I'd never do that. But still...

"Mom!" Tristan's distressed squeal yanks me from my thoughts. I'm not sure exactly what happened, but Olivia has him pinned to the floor and she's holding the bottle of nail polish just centimeters from his forehead, precariously tipped on its side. A flick of her wrist, and she'll dump the whole thing on him.

You'd think at seventeen, Olivia would be more mature than this, but you'd be wrong. Most of the time she's a smart and poised young woman, but with Tristan…well, all bets are off.

"Let him up, Olivia. If you blind my son with nail polish, even Willie and her doctor friend won't be able to help you." It's another empty threat, just like Willa's, but it does the job anyway and Olivia releases him. Tristan scrambles away, still complaining.

Thank God it's Friday. Two more days, and Christmas break will be over, and they'll both be back in school.

I can't fucking wait.

"Hey, Mom, can we—"

Tristan's request is interrupted by my ringing cell phone. Holding up one finger, I glance down at the cracked screen. The caller ID says The MacKenzie Agency, and I almost choke on my own tongue. "Be quiet," I hiss before connecting the call. I force what I hope sounds like a professional tone. "Hello?"

"Hello, this is Cece calling from The MacKenzie Agency for Gwendolyn Pierce." Cece is shockingly chipper, her voice light and airy, and it's hard not to smile.

"Hi, Cece, this is Gwen." I'm struggling to maintain a calm and even tone. Why is she calling me? What does this mean? Did I forget something at their office yesterday? Is she offering me the job? If she does, should I accept?

My mind is whirring with all the possibilities I should've considered before. Even if I didn't expect Mac to offer me the job, I should've decided what I'd do if he did, just to be safe. That I hadn't… well, let's be honest. It's unlike me not to thoroughly scrutinize a situation and all its potential outcomes, but it's also par for the course where Mac is concerned.

"Mac asked me to call you and see if you'd be available to start work on Monday."

"I... That's... I'm sorry, what?" I babble, staring across the room at Livie and Tris, who are having a thankfully quiet disagreement about something.

"I know it's short notice and I'm sorry, but the job is yours if you can deal with that," Cece elaborates as Tristan reaches up to pull Livie's hair. Glaring at them both, I stab a finger in his direction, and he subsides with a lift of his shoulders, as if to say, *what did you expect, Mom?*

"I'm so sorry, Cece. What were you saying? I'm a little distracted at the moment." I understood her perfectly fine, but I need more time to process what she's said, because this can't be happening. The job is mine if I can handle the short notice?

What the fuck?

"If you're still interested and available to start on Monday, we're offering you the position." Cece doesn't sound annoyed at having to repeat herself. If anything, she sounds like she's really enjoying this conversation.

"Can I have some time to think about it?" I already know what she'll say. It's nearly noon on Friday, if they want me to start Monday there's no time for me to mull this over.

"Maybe I should put you through to Mac," Cece suggests, far too delighted with the idea.

"No, no, that's not—" I start, but I'm already on hold, so I take the opportunity to get rid of my audience. "Go to your rooms."

"Who is it?" Livie asks, already up and heading for the hall.

"I'll tell you when I'm done, I'll just be a minute. Now get." I'm out of my chair, herding them both down the hallway.

Their bedroom doors have just slammed behind them when the line connects again. "This is Mac." Even over the phone, his gruff voice does things to me it shouldn't after all these years, and there's an awkward silence while I pull myself together, which is no small feat given the circumstances.

There's something surreal about Mac's voice rumbling in my ear while his son is in the next room. Never have they been so close to the same place at the same time, and it makes my secret that much heavier. For a fraction of a second, I'm paralyzed by the guilt that's been slowly unraveling me ever since my interview.

With a deep, settling breath, I finally say, "Mr. MacKenzie, thank you for speaking with me. I'm sure you're busy and I'm sorry to bother you but—"

"Do you want the job or not, Gwen?" he asks curtly. That's Mac, never one to beat around the bush.

"Could I have some time to think about it?" I repeat the question I already asked Cece, though this time I cringe at the croaky sound of my voice.

"No," he answers without giving it a moment's consideration.

"I see." Even though it's the response I expected, I thought he might be a little more diplomatic about it.

"Well?" he presses and his irritation crackles over the phone line.

Anger swells in my chest and I heave a harsh sigh, resigned to what I'll do, even before I really realize it. The son of a bitch wants me to reject the offer. I don't know what kind of game he's playing, and I don't care. All I know is, if he doesn't want me to take the job, I'm taking it. Screw him and his stupid games.

Besides, I really need a job, and at this point I can't afford to be picky. People depend on me, need me, and I can't let them down. Not that I expect the spoiled playboy on the other end of the phone would understand that.

"I'll see you Monday, Mr. MacKenzie."

"I'm looking forward to it." His tone suggests otherwise. Mac transfers me back to Cece to make the arrangements for my first day, and then I'm off the phone and staring across the room, dumbfounded.

I have a job.

With Mac.

But still, I needed a job and now I have one. That's the most important thing, isn't it?

"Come on, you two. Get showers and get dressed. We're going out for lunch," I call down the hall when I've shaken off my disoriented stupor.

"What's going on?" Tristan asks through his cracked bedroom door.

"We're celebrating. Your mom just got a job," I answer with a beaming smile that hides the turmoil I feel inside. I can worry about Mac later. For now I'm focusing on the fact I've finally found work. That's worth celebrating, isn't it?

CHAPTER 5

MAC

I THOUGHT I'd found the perfect solution to my problem. Offer Gwen the job in the most demanding, unaccommodating way possible. She'd refuse, and I wouldn't have to feel guilty. Except she didn't refuse and now, in two short days, I'll be Gwen's boss.

Fucking fantastic.

"I'm so excited," Cece gushes, her brown eyes dancing with mischief as she practically bounces into my office.

"About what?"

"Gwen accepted the job, and I like her." She collapses into one of the guest chairs across from my desk and beams at me.

"You don't even know her."

"True, but I was afraid you'd hire that boring dude, Trevor or Trent or whatever the hell his name was, and then all these trips with Kim would be a giant sausage fest and I'd have no one to talk to."

Generally, I'm glad Cece and I get along so well, that we're friends even. It makes life a lot easier when you have a good relationship with your PA. But right now? Not so much. "Now you'll have competition for Alex's attention. Are you sure that's what you want?" Cece's crush on my brother is a secret to no one. Well, except my brother, who's as clueless as they come.

"I don't think that's true at all." Cece gives me an appraising look before adding, "Come on, tell me how you know her. You know you want to."

"There's nothing to tell," I insist, not for the first time since Gwen's interview. No doubt it's all going to come out eventually, but I won't be the one who airs our dirty laundry.

"Have you put your cream in her donut?"

"Super-inappropriate question to ask your boss," I point out, trying not to laugh.

"Has she peeled your banana?" Cece persists.

"And that's some super-disturbing imagery, right there."

"Have you swept her chimney?"

"Cece…" It's becoming increasingly difficult not to laugh, but I really can't encourage this, partly because it's inappropriate at work, regardless of how close Cece and I are, and partly because if she wins and I laugh, or even give her so much as a begrudging smile, she'll never, ever stop. If Gwen and I are going to work together, I need to forget our past, which already seems like an impossible task. Cece's relentless badgering, begging me to recount our history for her gossip hungry ears, isn't helping.

"Mac, what I'm asking is—"

"I know what you're asking." I hold up one hand to stop her. "I'm just not answering."

"So that's a yes. God, I can hardly wait. This is going to be so fun."

"Don't you have work to do? Because I'm pretty sure I don't pay you to be a pain in my ass."

"You kind of do. And speaking of pains in your ass…" Cece sobers. Not a good a sign. "Your dad is here, so if you and Alex are planning to ambush him, now would be a good time."

This is good news, even if I'm not excited about confronting my old man. At least Alex and I are a united front this time. That should make it easier. Unless he crumbles like a sandcastle at high tide. That's always a risk with Alex.

As if they sensed we were talking about them, my dad and Alex stroll into my office, Dad looking confident as ever, my brother less so.

Great.

"No need to ambush me," Dad says, pinning Cece with a disapproving frown. "I'm right here."

"And that's my cue," Cece mumbles. Popping out of her chair, she beats a hasty retreat.

Dad takes the seat she abandoned but Alex doesn't sit, instead pacing behind Dad's chair. Another ominous sign.

"What's this about, boys?" When we both remain silent, mostly because we hate the "boys" bullshit, Dad turns his sharp eyes on me. "William?"

Without intending to, without realizing at first that I'm doing it at all, I sneer at him, distaste and irritation written in my every feature. Not that I can see myself now, glaring my anger at him, willing him to spontaneously combust in the flames of my hatred, but I've seen the look enough before, in every family picture ever taken, and I'm intimately familiar with the feel of my face when forced to deal with my father.

It's the only way I've ever looked at him, as a boy or a man. I've hated him for as long as I can remember. So long that sometimes I think it's written in my DNA. And it's in moments like this one, when he's called me "William" or, worse, the despised "Junior," that I hate him most of all.

"We know you've been talking to Brett Whitaker," Alex finally says to Dad, breaking the tense silence and giving weak-willed voice to the accusation. All it'll take is a few confident words from our father to smooth the frown lines between his brows.

Dad laughs. He actually laughs, shaking his head and waving one hand dismissively. "What of it? Brett and I have been friends since before either of you were born. Why shouldn't we talk?"

"Because he's running for President, and this firm has been hired to represent Kimberly Dunn," Alex explains, but I can already see he's second guessing himself when he casts a darting glance in my direction.

"So it has," Dad agrees, his voice flat.

"Then you'll stop?" Alex asks, his eyes lighting with hope. It seems he'll never learn.

"No," Dad says, leaning back in his chair and crossing his arms over his chest. "No, I won't stop. I've allowed you to commit this firm to Kim's campaign, but that doesn't mean I'm committed to her campaign." He says this as if he's a benevolent king, indulging our interests even when they run counter to his own. It's the sort of thing that always works on Alex, that blend of authority and confidence and certainty that Dad is so good at, like he knows what's best and he's giving us the freedom to catch up in our own time.

Alex stops his pacing, standing behind Dad's chair and spreading his arms, palms up, asking for my help.

"This has implications for the firm beyond your friendship with Whitaker," I point out. Dad already knows this; he doesn't need me to point out it's a conflict of interest for the CEO to be informally assisting a candidate running opposed to a client. He'd lose his goddamn mind if either of us did what he's doing.

"Don't be ridiculous. We are the premier PR firm in D.C. Top three on the east coast, top five in the country. Nobody gives a shit if I offer a little casual advice to an old friend."

"It has implications for the family too," I try again, even though I'm certain this line of attack won't be any more successful than the last.

"Your mother understands," Dad blusters, and for all I know, she does.

All my life, my parents have rubbed elbows with Presidents, congressman, governors, and career government officials, not to mention celebrities and wealthy businessmen. It was a result of Dad's job and Mom's family connections, and in the environment I grew up in, with prep schools and lacrosse and condos in the city and country estates in Virginia or Maryland, it seemed perfectly natural to me.

As I got a little older, it didn't take me long to figure out that no, most families didn't have the wealth and privilege we enjoyed. But instead of feeling lucky, I was jealous. I'd have happily traded the money for Jake's father, who took him fishing and camping and on long, wandering road trips with no particular destination in mind.

"I'm sure you're right," Alex concedes, and Dad gives me a smug smile, his eyes sparkling with secrets only he and I share. Not for the first time, a slew of angry words crowd my throat, demanding I set the record straight so Alex will understand. Instead, I ball my fists under my desk and swallow the temptation.

"Thank you, Alex," Dad says while giving him what appears to be a genuine smile. By the time he's turned to me, his smile has become cold and sharp. "You could learn a thing or two from your younger brother about what it means to be a family, Junior."

"My name is Mac."

I know what your goddamned name is, son. I gave it to you. That's what he would have said if we were alone. Since we aren't, Dad shakes his head and sighs, as if I'm the problem, and leaves the room with one last smile for Alex.

When he's gone, my brother turns to me, frowning. "You know, he isn't entirely wrong. I don't understand why you go balls to the wall with him on every single little thing. If you would—"

"Been there, done that. Maybe you don't remember, but I have fucking tried. Besides, things would go better if you didn't fold like a cheap suit."

"Low blow, Mac." Alex fusses with one sleeve of his suit coat to avoid meeting my gaze.

It was, but it's also the truth.

CHAPTER 6

GWEN

WITH A DEEP BREATH, I kick my shoes off under my desk and sink into my chair. Twenty minutes, and my first day as an employee of the MacKenzie Agency will be behind me. Aside from Mac very obviously ignoring me, it's gone well, but I'm exhausted. A year ago, I was going to school and working full time and caring for Livie and Tris, and I was tired all the time. A single day of work, one where I didn't even do any real work but rather spent the day with HR and IT, should not have worn me down this much. Apparently, a few months of unemployment was all it took to make me soft.

A glass of wine and a few quiet moments to myself will turn things around, though. Assuming a few quiet moments are attainable, which seems unlikely. It reminds me of when I was a girl and Dad would come home from his factory job and flop into a chair with a can of beer in hand. It's a bittersweet memory, his weary sigh and the satisfied groan that followed his first gulp of the ice-cold brew. I was a petulant, spoiled little girl, and I used to pout and whine when he was too worn down to entertain me, but now...now, I get it. I've been tired since the day I left Mac in Ann Arbor, crushed under the weight of school and work and responsibility, and sometimes I just want a few minutes to be me.

"Ms. Pierce."

Glancing up at the sound of my name, my eyes widen when I realize it's Mac's dad. He's standing next to my desk, looking down at me with a warm, welcoming smile, and my heart pounds in my chest. His professional reputation is so legendary it's a little like meeting a rockstar. I hadn't dared to think a lowly new hire like me would have the opportunity to interact with him. Extending my hand, I rise. "Mr. Mackenzie."

"Please, call me William, and don't get up," he insists, only taking my hand once I've settled in my seat again.

As we shake hands, his coffee-brown eyes are sparkling, and I blink, unsettled by his sudden resemblance to Mac. In his mid-sixties, I would guess, Mac's dad isn't as fit and trim as his son, but he's in better shape than most men his age, and the gray that's filtering into his otherwise dark hair gives him a distinguished air. "It's a pleasure to meet you, Mr. Ma— William. It's an honor to work with you." My cheeks prickle with heat as soon as the words are out of my mouth. *Work with him?* What a stupid thing to say. This will probably be the only interaction I ever have with him.

"We're glad to have you, and I'm sure you'll do fine. Junior has terrible taste in women, but he has an excellent eye for employees," William chortles and gives me a playful wink.

Struck speechless by the inappropriateness of it, it takes me longer than it should to figure out that Junior is, in fact, Mac, and a bolt of panic zips down my spine. Has he told his father about our history? God, if so, has he told everyone? Does that mean his dad is taking a dig at me when he mentions Mac's bad taste? Or is he unaware of our past and this is his way of warning me about his son? And what did it mean when he said Mac has an excellent eye for employees? Was that a genuine compliment, or was it a roundabout way of telling me his son makes a habit of sleeping with his staff?

No, stop. I need to get a hold of myself. William is still giving me a jovial smile. It was a joke, that's all, and I'm letting my paranoia and anxiety get the better of me.

Except I know Mac and William aren't close, or at least they didn't use to be. I don't know any of the details, though. Maybe they've mended fences. And even if they haven't, surely William wouldn't be so rude and unprofessional as to drag their family conflict into the office? Still, it niggles at me.

"Well, I hope I can live up to your expectations, sir," I finally stammer with what feels like a weak smile.

"Never doubt it." His own smile widens, and for a fraction of a second it's almost wolfish before settling into the benevolent expression of a kind patriarch. "I understand you fly out Wednesday to meet up with the campaign. Perhaps we could have lunch sometime between your trips to discuss your strategy for Kim's social media."

"Of course. I'd appreciate any advice you have," I say, hoping like hell I don't sound as giddy as I feel. I could learn more from him in the space of one lunch than I did in all my years of school.

"You misunderstand." His brows draw together in a pinched frown, and I hold my breath as he leans closer, his expression now grave. "I'm the one hoping to learn from you in this exchange. I am, regrettably, no longer at the top of the game. My sons handle much of the day-to-day operations, and technology has long since outpaced me. The only way to keep my toe in the water in this rapidly evolving business is to learn what I can from the fresh, young people who join us."

Whoa. William MacKenzie, Sr. thinks he can learn something from me?

Until now it hadn't occurred to me how much this business has probably changed since he was a young man getting his start. It makes sense that social media might not be his forte, and I'm flattered that he'd want to discuss it with me. "Oh, well, in that case, I'd be happy to but only on one condition." That came out flirtier than I intended, and I force myself not to cringe or start babbling in some incoherent attempt to gloss it over. That would only make it worse.

"What might that be?"

"You're the PR genius. I'd like the opportunity to pick your brain too."

"That's a deal, Ms. Pierce." He grins and raps his knuckles on my desk before turning to leave.

He's only three steps away when my new company laptop chimes. My initial excitement over my first work email evaporates when I open the app to find it's from Mac. The body of the message is empty, the subject line a terse command.

My office. Now.

Digging my nails into the palms of my hands, I squint across the bullpen toward Mac's office. The door is open, but the blinds are drawn, and I can't see him. That doesn't lessen my burgeoning anger though. The jackass went out of his way to ignore me all damn day and now, a few minutes shy of quitting time, he demands my presence. I must have misjudged him during my interview, because it seems he hasn't mellowed over the years after all. He's the same entitled dick he's always been, and unless I want to get fired on my first day, I have no choice but to accommodate him.

Mustering my strength, I slip my shoes back on and stride toward his office, mentally preparing for battle. His message might have been light on details, but I know him well enough to be certain that's exactly what this is going to be.

When I pause in his open door, hand raised to knock, he looks up from his laptop with a scowl before my knuckles contact the wood. He's seated on the leather couch in the conversation area to one side of the room, his feet propped on the coffee table and the laptop balanced on his thighs. His jacket is across the room, draped over the back of his desk chair, and his tie has been loosened, the top button of his shirt undone.

Jesus Christ, he's still a sexy bastard.

"Close the door behind you." There's nothing warm or inviting about his tone, and it cuts through my inappropriate thoughts, reminding me of my anger.

It takes a great deal of self-control to close the door without slamming it. As soon as I turn toward him again, Mac gestures to the chair adjacent to him, but I'm done cooperating, at least until I know what this is about. "I'm sorry, Mr. MacKenzie, but I'm in a bit of a hurry. I have somewhere I need to be this evening. What can I help you with?" I've advanced to stand across the coffee table from him, but that's as close as I'm going to get.

"You could start by calling me Mac, like everyone else around here does. Like you used to do."

"We've been over this, Mr. MacKenzie. You've mistaken me for someone else." It's probably silly to continue with this charade but for now, it feels safer. Because I'm scared, and my guilt is already eating me alive. Once I acknowledge our past, I'll have to tell him, and I'm not ready to face the consequences of my long-ago choices just yet. Waiting only makes this harder and it will be worse when I do eventually tell him about Tris, but it's still the only thing I can do until I've replenished my savings enough to hire a lawyer, if it comes to that.

Watching me, Mac sighs and rubs his thumb across his lip, as if he's trying to figure out what the hell he's supposed to do with me. I hope he figures it out. At least one of us should be clear-headed about our reacquaintance, and it isn't going to be me. "I saw you talking to my dad," he finally says, changing the subject, but he's still giving me that wary look.

"Yes." There's no point in denying it. What does it even matter?

"You should avoid him." Mac raises both brows in expectation, waiting for me to agree.

Whatever unresolved issues Mac still has with his father, it's got nothing to do with me. I'm a grown woman and I can handle myself just fine without his interference. Honestly, it's insulting that he thinks I'm so...I don't even know. Foolish? Weak? Helpless? Whatever it is, it's unwelcome. "Is this why you called me in here?"

"Just stay away."

His word is final, at least in his mind, and he's turning back to his laptop when I say, "Why?"

Mac's head jerks back and he repeats the question like it didn't make sense. "Why?"

"Yes, why?" It's a legitimate question. Sure, Mac is my boss and he's a big fish in the company pond. But his dad is the biggest fish of all. Why should I limit my opportunities within the company without being able to judge the situation for myself?

Mac stares at me for a long moment. So long that it's uncomfortable, and I think it must be uncomfortable for him too, because he's sitting perfectly still, frozen like a statue, his expression giving nothing away. It makes me anxious, my skin prickling and stomach clenching. I would give almost anything to know what's going on in his mind right now.

"There was a time, Gwen, when I'd have answered that question if you'd asked. I don't think I will now." He doesn't give me the chance to press him further, tersely adding, "Have a goodnight."

CHAPTER 7

GWEN

BY THE TIME I get home, I've come to terms with the fact that I'm not going to get any peace and quiet tonight. Olivia and her friend Harper are at the kitchen table, working on a project for their physics class. Something about building a bridge from toothpicks, which seems to involve a lot of glue and even more giggling. And as loud as two teenage girls can be, they've got nothing on Willa and Tristan, who are in the living room playing *Dance Party*, although in their case, dancing is more like uncoordinated flailing while Willa takes every opportunity to tickle Tris until he squeals.

In some ways, all the chaos and confusion is better than quiet time anyway. If it weren't for their boisterous distraction, I'd probably spend the evening replaying my brief interaction with Mac. There was something about it, besides his overbearing *stay away from my dad* bullshit, that unsettled me. A certain unfamiliar vulnerability in him I don't remember from our first acquaintance. Replaying the conversation in my mind, I want to comfort him. To pull him into my arms for a warm hug and soft words, much like I might with Tristan. Of course, that would be wildly inappropriate. Mac is my boss now, nothing more, and his emotional wellbeing is none of my business.

"Hey, how'd it go?" Willa asks when she notices me hovering in the space between the kitchen and living room. She's out of breath and collapses back on the couch with a groan.

"We're still dancing," Tris protests. He grabs his aunt by both hands, trying to pull her back to her feet.

Willa relaxes into the couch, making herself dead weight to thwart Tristan. "Today was your mom's first day of work, so we need to fuss over her and ask her how it went. You know, like she does for you on the first day of school."

"I hate that." By no means shy, Tristan thrives on being the center of attention, but only on his terms, and his terms do not include boring talks about school. Part of the problem is that he's a good student, but unlike me, who spent hours upon hours hunched over textbooks, he doesn't have to try. Without the challenge, it's just another thing he has to do, like going to see the pediatrician or cleaning his room, and he doesn't see the point in talking about it. I worry sometimes what it means for his future, what will happen someday when he comes across something that finally challenges him. After everything has come so easy for him, will he know how to conquer it?

"It's polite, Tristan." Turning to me, Willa asks again, "Well, how was it?"

"It was fine. I'm exhausted." There isn't really anything else to say and certainly not in front of Tristan.

"Did you see—"

"Hardly," I interrupt with a glare before she can finish her question. Mac is the last thing I want to talk about. At all. Especially with Tristan's eager ears listening.

"And?" Willa prods with a sly grin.

"He was a j-e-r-k." I don't know why I don't just say the word. Tristan's been able to spell it for years now. Old habits die hard, I guess.

"Who was a jerk?" Tristan asks, both brows flying up in curiosity.

"No one, and you know you aren't allowed to use that word."

"You did."

"Technically, she spelled it." Willa has one hand over her mouth to hide her smile.

"Can I say it if I spell it?" Tristan asks, excited to have found a potential loophole.

"No." Willa and I respond in unison and then she adds with a tilt of her head toward the kitchen, "Why don't you go see if Livie and Harper need your help?"

"We definitely don't!" Olivia calls from the table, which has the opposite of her intended effect, encouraging Tristan to turn his attention to tormenting them.

As he skips into the kitchen, Willa gives me an expectant look.

"What?"

"Now that he's gone, you can tell me all about it." She flinches when angry teenage squeals erupt from the kitchen. "Was I that annoying?"

"You are, yes."

"Present tense?"

"Present tense," I confirm and take a seat next to her on the couch. Then, before she can ask again, I volunteer a little information. "It went fine, and there is nothing to say. He seems pretty determined to avoid me and, honestly, that's probably for the best."

"Well, I'm glad it seems to be working out. For now, anyway."

"You don't have to sound so cryptic about it." I lower my voice. "I know things could get dicey when I tell him about Tris, but it'll be fine." I don't actually believe it that. Telling Mac he has a son will be a disaster, and the longer I wait, the worse the nuclear fallout will be.

"Actually, that's not what I meant. It's easy enough to avoid someone around the office, but traveling with the campaign..." Willa lets her sentence hang, her blue eyes narrowed with skepticism.

"We'll find out soon enough, I guess. We leave on our first trip Wednesday. Are you sure you can handle everything here while I'm gone?"

"Yes, I've got everything under control. I promise."

It isn't the logistics of the situation I doubt. Between Olivia and our next-door neighbor, Mrs. Murphy, someone will be available to watch Tristan after school on the days Willa works, and I'm incredibly grateful for their help. I've always been grateful for the help I've received over the years. None of us would have survived after my mother left without relying on the kindness of others, sometimes even complete strangers, and I had to learn early to swallow my pride.

This is different, though. Asking Willa to be responsible for him and our seventeen-year-old sister while I'm gone just compounds the already near-crippling guilt I feel about leaving Tris in the first place. Does it make me a bad mother? Will he resent that I accepted a job that took me away from him so much? Should I find a different job that doesn't require travel? Even if that means waiting tables again?

And what about Willie? She's only twenty-two. She just finished college and started her first real job. She should have the carefree experiences all young adults deserve, and instead I'm dumping my responsibilities on her. Sometimes it feels like after all these years of struggle, I'm still a failure.

"I know you do. But...I feel like I'm abandoning you guys, like Mom did, and I just don't know if—"

"No." Willa interrupts me with that one abrupt word and, based on the length of time she glares at me before she continues, she's angry. Really angry.

It's intimidating because it's so rare. Olivia is the one with intense and wildly fluctuating emotions. But Willie? She's calm and steady and not prone to dramatics.

"How many times have you said the four of us are a team?" Willa finally asks, her voice thick with emotion. "How many times did you work extra shifts so we could afford Liv's dance classes or my piano lessons? How many days did you work ten hours, then go to night classes, then stay up all night studying, just to do it again the next day so you could make all our lives better?"

"I didn't have a choice," I murmur when she takes a breath, and it's the wrong thing to say because it only makes her angrier.

"But you did," she insists, her hands balled in fists in her lap. "You always had a choice, and you always chose us. Now you have your dream job, in a field you love, working for a campaign you really believe in. You deserve it, and Team Pierce will support you just like you've always supported us. And I know what you'll say next too, but I don't want to hear it. It will be good for Tristan to see his mother happy and fulfilled instead of tired and exhausted from working too hard at a job she hates. Who knows, maybe when you get off your ass and grow a spine, this will bring his father into his life, and that will be good for him too."

Tears sting the corners of my eyes and I swallow around the lump gathering in my throat, but still, my voice croaks when I ask, "How did you get to be so smart?"

"Pfft." She waves one hand dismissively and rolls her eyes, but her voice is tight too when she says, "Genetics. Everyone knows I got all the brains. It's really too bad there wasn't much left over for you and Liv."

"What about me?" Livie calls from the kitchen, a lull in their own discussion apparently having fallen at just the right time for her to hear her name.

"Oh, nothing! I was just telling Gwen how sad it is that neither of you are as smart as I am," Willa teases.

A playful argument about who is smarter follows. Tristan and Harper get in on it too, and before long the tears are forgotten as we all bicker and laugh together.

~

MAC

I'M the world's biggest asshole.

Gwen was clearly pissed I warned her away from my dad, and who could blame her? I should have explained myself, told her why I wanted her to steer clear of my old man, and then left it to her to make her own decision, because she's a grown-ass woman fully capable of doing that. Instead, I made what from her perspective must have seemed like unreasonable and inexplicable demands. I treated her like a fucking child, and she didn't deserve that.

My only excuse, and it isn't a very good one, is that I lost my goddamn mind when she waltzed into my office with her fake smile and her farcical determination to pretend we don't know each other. It's maddening. If I were a better man, I wouldn't let it get to me, but it's still prickling under my skin an hour later when I let myself into my parents' house.

I'd rather be anywhere else tonight. Australia, maybe. I think I read somewhere once that Perth is the farthest city in the world from Washington, D.C. Even that wouldn't be far enough from my dad, but it would be better than this.

"Will!" Mom exclaims, popping out of her chair with a warm smile and bubbling joy the moment I step into the kitchen. This, I remind myself, is why I came. She doesn't deserve to suffer for my dad's sins.

I manage to mumble a greeting before she's smothering me in hugs and kisses, as if I were still a boy. When I was younger, this sort of thing embarrassed me, and I often pushed her away, but now I've come to accept that it's just part of being her son. If I were being really honest, I might even admit I like it. Besides, the stark contrast between her cool and aloof public persona and her exuberant affection for her children amuses me. No one outside of our immediate family would ever guess she behaves this way.

"Where's Alex and Dad?" I ask when she releases me.

"Not here yet." She herds me toward the island and the seat she vacated. "Chop those onions for Ruth. She's making your favorite for dinner—the least you can do is be useful."

"And what are you going to be doing?" I ask, frowning at the half-diced onion in front of me. It's not that I mind helping, especially if we're having Ruth's trademark French onion burgers and homemade French fries, but I'm clearly being roped into taking over Mom's chore.

"Staring at you," Ruth answers tartly as she bustles out of the pantry, a stack of plates in hand. No doubt she's speaking for herself and my mother. "You haven't been here since Christmas, and we've forgotten what you look like."

"It's been two weeks." I'm barely able to resist rolling my eyes.

"Alex comes over at least twice a week," Ruth reminds me, carefully setting the plates on the granite counter. She's worked for my family—first my maternal grandparents, and now my parents—since before I was born. She's more family than hired help, and sometimes it's a bit like having two mothers.

"Speaking of Alex," Mom chirps, elbows on the counter. She leans toward me, her green eyes sparkling with mischief. "Your brother tells me you're seeing someone, and that's why you haven't been around."

That little asshole.

I know exactly what happened. Mom was badgering him about his dating life—or rather, lack thereof—and he threw me to the wolves to save himself. Typical. On the bright side, there won't be any need for me to feel guilty when I return the favor at the first opportunity.

"I am *not* seeing anyone," I reply.

It is true I've been having sex with the same woman for several months now. But as lovely as Stef is, it is not a relationship, at least not by any definition my mother needs to know about. And now that Gwen's back, I don't know what that will mean for me or my casual arrangement with Stef.

Probably nothing.

Maybe nothing.

Possibly *something.*

"I'd like to have grandchildren before I die." Mom sighs, chin in hand.

Arching one brow, I tilt my head to the side and frown. She's sixty-three and probably in better health than I am. With glossy salt and pepper hair and few wrinkles—thanks to good genetics and an active lifestyle, not a plastic surgeon—she hardly appears to be knocking on death's door. But that won't stop her from pretending she's thirty years older if the guilt might motivate one of her sons to start a family.

There's no point reminding her I don't want kids, though. She knows, and she knows why too. My relationship with my dad has left me wholly unprepared to be a father. Hell, my parents' relationship with each other leaves me wondering why anyone would even get married, let alone have children. I've never considered the possibility. I do rather like kids, though, as long as they belong to someone else. Someone like Jake.

Or Alex.

"You should talk to my brother about that," I suggest without diverting my attention from the cutting board. As uncomfortable as this conversation is, it's not worth slicing off the tips of my own fingers.

"She has. Why do you think I told her about Stef?" Alex asks from the doorway, announcing his arrival.

I will kill him. Someday, I will kill him, and there isn't a jury in America that would convict me. At least not if it was composed entirely of older brothers.

"She has a name?" Mom chimes, perking up.

"No," I snap over Alex's laughter. "I mean, yes, obviously everyone has a name. But there is nothing going on with Stef."

"Stefanie Clark?" Dad asks, strolling into the kitchen to join us. *Great. He'll definitely make this conversation better.*

Mom straightens, turning to look at him, but her warm gaze has turned cool. "You know her?"

"She's a reporter at the *Observer*," Dad explains with a nod. "Why?"

"No reason," Mom lies without missing a beat. "The boys were just telling me about work, and her name came up."

Dad grunts and turns his attention to Ruth. "When will dinner be ready?"

"Forty-five minutes. Why don't you and Mac get out of the way, and Alex will help us finish."

Giving Ruth a narrow-eyed glare because she isn't even trying to be subtle, I follow my dad from the room. Although they share the same goal, she doesn't waste time on emotional appeals like my mom. Ruth just creates opportunities, forcing me to spend time with him. I guess she figures we'll work our shit out eventually if we spend enough time alone together, but she's destined for disappointment.

"I met your new hire this afternoon," Dad says as soon as he's settled in his chair by the fireplace in the den.

Still irritated by the earlier conversation about Stef, I'm not prepared to lock horns with my dad yet, which makes it difficult to ignore the impulse to shout at him and tell him to stay the fuck away from Gwen. I can't let him know that she matters to me. It would be like waving a red flag in front of a bull. "Okay," I say, forcing myself to keep my voice even and taking the chair across from him.

"She's a pretty girl," he muses, leaning back and crossing his legs.

"Is she?" I ask, shrugging and hoping he won't notice the way I'm white-knuckling the arms of my chair.

"You'd have to be dead from the waist down to miss those tits, son." His lewd chortle is like nails on a chalkboard. It's sickening to hear him talk about Gwen like that and, because the apple fell closer to the tree than I'm comfortable with, I can't help but remember the way her breasts felt in my hands. How her nipples tasted when I sucked and bit them until she screamed. It's been more than a decade, but the memories are so fresh it could have been yesterday.

"Stay away from her, Dad." I'm barely able to pull it off but I think my voice is steady enough he'll take this for the general "stop fucking the staff" warning I've given him dozens of times instead of anything particular about Gwen.

"Do you want this one for yourself?" He leans forward in his chair, his brown eyes bright with interest. If I could lower myself to indulge in these conversations with him, it would probably improve our relationship, which is a pretty fucking sad state of affairs.

"Why is it so hard for you to understand none of them are for any of us? They are employees. They are professionals. They should be able to do their jobs without the lecherous CEO and his sons getting handsy."

He's leaned back again and slouched down in his chair, one hand raised, opening and closing it as he rolls his eyes. Somehow, I've become the scold in the family, a role I am neither suited for nor enjoy. Which is probably why I'm not very good at it, judging by what little success I've had with him. "Get off your high horse. I know for a fact you've always got a piece of ass on the side."

"Sure, let's talk about that, because you're right. Unlike you, though, I'm single, I don't mess around with employees, and I fuck women who are both my age and well aware of the terms of our arrangement." I pause, waiting to see if any of that is sinking in. He glares back at me, so I play my last card, the one that, in my view anyway, is worse than all the others. "And I've never asked my son to pressure a woman I took advantage of to get an abortion so my wife won't find out what a shitbag I am."

"Who gives a fuck now, after all these years? You didn't do it, did you?" He waves a hand dismissively, because in his mind, the fact that I didn't do as he asked makes me the shitbag in this scenario.

"Just stay away from the employees. Can you do that for the next few months while Alex and I are away?" Somehow, my younger brother is still oblivious to just how creepy our dad is, and for reasons I will never understand, that matters to Dad. Having both of us on the road means he doesn't have to worry so much about getting found out if he dips his pen in the company ink. No lectures from me, no hiding from Alex. It's a win-win.

"You worry about Kim's campaign. Things will be just fine here."

It isn't an answer, but before I can press him, which would be a pointless exercise if ever there was one, Alex joins us and Dad resumes the mantle of wise patriarch.

CHAPTER 8

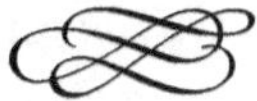

GWEN

"I am going to kill Mac." Cece wiggles around in her seat in a desperate bid to get comfortable. She should give up. I already know that's impossible in economy class. I am willing to entertain her thoughts on Mac's early demise though.

This is only my third day on the job. If Mac and his PA aren't getting along, that's not something I want to get in the middle of, especially since I'd really prefer to stay as far away from him as possible, at least until I'm ready to tell him about Tristan. But you know what they say about curiosity and cats. I just can't help myself and, despite my misgivings, I ask, "Why?"

"Because he's being a dick." She gives me a look that suggests she shouldn't have to explain this. "We always fly first or business class. All of us."

That is interesting, because while Cece and I are currently crammed like sardines in economy, both MacKenzie brothers are lounging around in first class, probably drinking champagne and eating caviar or whatever it is rich people do on cross-country flights. "Honestly, I kind of expected them to have a private jet."

"Eh, no. The MacKenzie's have money, but not private-jet kind of money. Do you have any idea how expensive those things are to maintain?" Cece whistles, and I shake my head, because I've never considered it. "Anyway, being stuck back here isn't all bad. It's easier to gossip this way."

That seems like a bad idea. Mac is ignoring me and, until I find the right time to tell him about Tristan, I'm happy to return the favor. So far, keeping our distance is making things much easier, if a little awkward. Cece is my primary contact, relaying messages between us so we don't have to talk. Childish and not the way it works with everyone else, judging by the parade of people in and out of his office. Even the receptionist has unfettered access to him but not me. Cece is a friendly but impenetrable wall. Fortunately, she's polite enough not to mention it, but I can't risk alienating her.

She must sense my reluctance, because she goes straight for the jugular. "How do you know Mac?"

"I don't."

"You know that schtick is driving him up the wall, right? That's at least half of the reason we've been relegated to economy." Cece sounds positively delighted, as if driving Mac crazy is one of her favorite pastimes. I'm definitely getting a little-sister vibe here and I ought to know, because I have two of them.

"And the other half?"

"He's pissed at me because I keep asking him how he knows you."

I can't help it. I laugh. "Aren't you afraid you'll get fired?"

"What? No," Cece scoffs. "Mac would never fire me. Well, I mean he would if I was embezzling or fucked up something huge for a client or something. But never just for giving him shit."

"It sounds like you two have a good relationship." When we were younger, Mac didn't always play well with others, but it seems that's changed.

"Mm-hmm. Mac's a good guy, but you know that." She gives me a sly, sidelong look, checking for my reaction.

She's persistent, I'll give her that much, but I won't be baited into revealing our history. If Mac wants her to know, he can tell her. "Is this the first campaign you've worked on?" I ask, hoping for a change of subject.

"No, I've been with Mac six years now, and he's worked on a bunch of campaigns since then. Mostly local, state-level stuff, and he really encouraged me from the start to jump in where I felt comfortable. Mac and Alex are the kind of bosses who really support their employees, you know? No one is *just* a personal assistant or receptionist or copy editor. If you have a talent or interest that leads in another direction, they try to foster that. Not like their dad."

It's tempting, so, so tempting, to ask Cece to elaborate on her obvious dig at Mac's dad. But it feels a little sneaky to pump her for information. Although, Mac gave me that cryptic warning about his dad. Surely she knows what that was about.

"Mac told you to stay away from Senior, right?" Cece asks, bringing my dilemma into sharper focus. If I'm going to ask, now would be the perfect time. But I've barely had the chance to nod before she's talking again. "The old goat is a lech. Fortunately, he isn't around the office much these days. He's sort of semi-retired, I guess, but he's gross. And when he isn't being inappropriate with women, he's being an asshole to Mac and Alex. Especially Mac."

"Why?"

"I'm not sure exactly. There's a lot of history there I don't know." She pauses, winding a lock of brown hair around one finger and giving me a thoughtful look.

I know what she's thinking, or at least what I would think if I were her. I'm from Mac's past, and maybe we both have separate pieces of the same puzzle. But I have nothing to offer her. I overheard Mac arguing with his dad on the phone once, but my memories of that time are hazy and even if I knew more, it would feel like a betrayal to gossip about it. Although my ethics around gossip are obviously squishy, because I don't stop Cece when she starts talking again.

"I think maybe Mac and his dad are just oil and water. And on the business side of things, Senior doesn't approve of how either of the boys run the business. Did you know one of Kim's opponents offered the firm more money to work for him? Mac told him to fuck off, because he's a slimy asshole. I mean, he actually said the slimy-asshole part out loud to the guy trying to hire him. And one of those #metoo assholes tried to hire Alex to rehabilitate his image, but Alex refused. Tara—she's Alex's PA—she said Alex hung up on him. Their dad would have taken both of them on. It's all about the money for him, you know? There were some tense days around the office when he found out the boys didn't."

Cece is a wealth of knowledge, and some of the information she's sharing isn't what I would have expected. Warming to her subject, Cece crosses her legs, bouncing her foot as she talks.

"Mac and Alex are nothing like their dad. They care about outcomes, not just paychecks. And, huge plus, neither of them is a lech. Well…"

"What?" I prod when she doesn't go on.

She hesitates and it almost seems like she's silently asking if I'm sure I want to hear this. When I don't respond, she says, "Mac's a slut, but he's not like his dad. He's never messed around with anyone at work or anything. I've never even seen him so much as give a coworker or client an inappropriate look. Except you. You should have seen his face when you walked into his office for that interview…" She trails off, her long hair brushing her shoulders as she shakes her head and grins at me.

"I did and I'm pretty sure he wanted to murder me." After he got over his initial shock, there was no question Mac was angry. None.

"Fuck you, murder you, it's a fine line," Cece teases, and I laugh because yeah, that's true. Or at least it used to be. We spent a lot of time fucking and fighting back in the day, sometimes at the same time.

At least now I can be fairly sure Mac didn't hire me as step one in a plot to get in my pants again. If that's what he wanted, and he's that scrupulous about work relationships, he never would have offered me the job. Which is good, because I don't want that either. "How come you know so much about it if he's so discreet?"

"Discreet? That's your word. He doesn't get involved with women he works with, but Mac is who he is, and he doesn't hide that. For one thing, he brings a different date to every social function he attends. For another, who do you think makes his dinner reservations? Or drops off his suits at the dry cleaner with lipstick smeared on the collar? Or schedules his quarterly STI check?"

I'm nodding along, because of course, that all makes sense, until I take in her last point and then I choke on my own saliva.

Quarterly? Jesus.

Either Mac really gets around or he's careful to the point of paranoia. Given what I know about how careful he is—or rather, isn't—my money is on the former. Not that I'm judging, since I was just as careless with him.

"Well, that seems really inappropriate for an employee," I wheeze, but Cece is unfazed by my reaction.

"Yeah? Who do you think will be folding your unmentionables at some random laundromat in Sioux City? You don't understand how crazy your life is about to get, and it's my job to manage the details. For Mac, sometimes that means picking up his lunch and a box of condoms." She shrugs like this is completely normal.

Maybe it is. What the hell do I know about life on the campaign trail? Or life as a spoiled bachelor with more money than common sense? If he and Cece are both happy with the situation, it's none of my business. "What do you think Mac would say if he knew you were telling me all this?"

"I don't know. Let's tell him when we land and find out." Cece laughs and nudges my shoulder before adding, "I get it. You think I'm a gossip, but I'm not telling you anything about him that isn't common knowledge. Everyone knows at work he's a professional and out of work he's a womanizer. I promise it wouldn't take you long to figure it out on your own."

"Yeah? Quarterly STI tests are common knowledge? Just one of those things everyone knows?" I give her a skeptical look, because I can't help but feel she's betraying Mac's confidence and, strangely, I feel protective of him.

"Okay, that isn't common knowledge, but I figured you should know since you're going to hook up."

"Cece," I scold, deploying my best mom voice, accompanied by what I hope is an intimidating glare. It doesn't seem to be any more effective on her than it is on Tristan though.

"Well, you are."

"I am not interested in hooking up with him. And you just said he doesn't sleep with women he works with and we are, in case you haven't noticed, coworkers." I count off the reasons on my fingers and then jab them at her chest. "It's not happening."

"Okay," Cece says, but it isn't agreement.

"What about Alex?" I ask, a little terse. Not that I really care about him, but I need a change of subject. Anything but Mac and how irritatingly certain Cece is that we'll fuck.

"It's kind of funny how different they are." Her tone doesn't sound amused at all. If anything, she almost seems sad when she continues, "Mac is kind of rowdy and full of bluster, but underneath it all he's a giant marshmallow. Work hard, play hard and all that. Alex is all work, no play. He's more uptight, more reserved. A nice guy, just... kind of aloof. For living in the same city and working together, they aren't particularly close."

All roads lead to Mac, it seems. But this particular detail strikes a chord with me because I'm tight with my sisters, and it makes me sad for both MacKenzie brothers that they don't have that kind of relationship. "That's too bad."

Cece nods and opens a bag of pretzels. "It is, especially since their dad is such a jerk. It seems like that should have made them closer."

Carefully steering the conversation away from the MacKenzie's, I chat with Cece a little more about the campaign and then, discovering we are both avid readers, books. The change of subject is helpful and by the time we land in L.A., I've put Cece's gossip out of my mind. Mostly.

Since Mac and Alex were in first class, they're already waiting for us when Cece and I step off the jetway. Alex asks if we enjoyed the flight, but otherwise few words are spoken as Mac leads us on a race through the airport. I don't think he's trying to make it difficult for me to keep up; after all, Cece is hustling along after him without complaint so this is probably a regular occurrence, but really, would it be so difficult for him to consider maybe everyone isn't 6'2 with a stride that eats the ground?

LAX isn't a small airport and by the time we've reached the car Kim sent for us, I'm panting, so I stand back, taking a second to catch my breath while Mac holds the rear door of the SUV open and Cece crawls in. Seconds later, when I follow her into the backseat, I realize my mistake. She slid all the way across, leaving me in the center, while Mac—yes, fucking Mac—gets in on my other side.

Stupidly, I expected him to take the front seat, since he's the older brother. It would be a cold day in hell when I took the backseat so one of my younger sisters could ride shotgun. But I failed to take into account that Alex, despite being the younger brother, is a good three, maybe four inches taller than Mac. As uncomfortable as the backseat must be for Mac, it might literally be impossible for Alex to fold his tall, lanky frame into it. Well, maybe not literally, but Mac isn't going to make his brother suffer through the experience.

Lesson learned. I need to pay more attention and make sure Cece gets the middle in the future. That might be hard though, because as I'm leaning into her space, contorting myself in a variety of ways to try and avoid even the briefest contact with Mac, she gives me a sly smile that says she did this on purpose.

The driver pulls away from the curb and Mac puts on his seatbelt, his fingers brushing my hip when he fastens it. My body tenses and it's as if that brief touch had been something very different, because my skin is burning and all I can think about is the way he used to touch me. My breathing quickens, and a familiar weight settles in my center. He used to be so—

"Stop thinking about it," Mac says under his breath, interrupting my thoughts. It's annoying he could so easily guess what I was think-ing, except…that means he was thinking about it too. There's no way I'll give him the satisfaction of knowing he's right though.

"I was thinking about the traffic," I say, staring straight ahead between Alex and the driver at the long line of brake lights in front of us. "I wonder if L.A. is worse than D.C.?"

"Sure you were," Mac mutters and shakes his head, turning away to look out the window.

"Actually, Boston, New York, D.C., and Chicago are all regularly ranked as worse than L.A. It's just people from L.A. whine about it more than the rest of us," Alex says, having heard my comment. The driver laughs and shrugs and Alex, Cece, and the driver continue to talk about traffic. Only Mac and I are silent, both trying to pretend the other isn't there.

Fortunately, it isn't a long ride to the hotel. As we pile out of the backseat, I give Cece a threatening glare, but she shrugs like she has no idea what's bothering me. This could be annoying. She can play little sister to Mac all she wants if that makes her happy, but I already have two of my own, and I'm not in the market for another.

Alex retrieves our bags from the rear of the SUV and hands them off to the bellhop while Mac turns to Cece.

"Get us checked in then come on up to Kim's suite, okay?"

"Sure thing, boss." Cece gives him a jaunty salute, he rolls his eyes, and she heads for the front desk. Which leaves me alone with the MacKenzie brothers, trailing after them like a lost puppy on the way to the elevator.

Once we reach Kim's penthouse suite, I'm surprised by the number of people and the flurry of activity in the room. It's a lot to take in—all three cable news networks are playing on various laptops and televisions, and aides are talking over one another, some on their phones and others with each other. I expected a presidential candidate's immediate surroundings to be hectic, but this is pandemonium.

And then out of the chaos, Kimberly Dunn herself appears. The fine lines around her mouth and the crow's feet at the corners of her eyes are more prominent than on TV, making her seem a little older. But the warm expression on her face and the light in her hazel eyes as she makes a beeline for Mac give her a joyfulness that is also rarely seen in news clippings. She wraps him in an affectionate hug, and he returns the gesture, kissing her cheek and sharing a few soft words with her before releasing her and turning her toward Alex, who receives a similar welcome.

Mac takes a step back and raises one hand, fingers bent, beckoning me forward. "Kim, this is Gwendolyn Pierce. Gwen's a new hire to manage your social media accounts."

"Ms. Dunn, it's an honor to meet you," I say as she shakes my hand. Even I can hear the reverence in my voice, but I don't care. It *is* an honor to meet her.

"Please, call me Kim, and I'm thrilled to have you. I know Mac would only bring me the best." Tucking her blond hair behind her ears, she smiles before asking, "Where's Cece?"

"Getting us checked in. She'll be here shortly."

"Oh, good. Shall we get started then? I've got an updated draft of my speech for tonight and I'd like you to give it a look..." The sound of her voice trails off as she and Mac wander deeper into the suite, toward the dining room.

Alex and I have been forgotten. He's standing next to me, his hands in his pockets, a faint smile curving his full lips.

I give him a sidelong glance and ask, "So, what are we supposed to do now?"

"They'll let us know when they need us. In the meantime, you can tell me how you know my brother." Alex ushers me toward the balcony. After the stuffy flight and the dreary weather in D.C., a little sunshine is appealing. Leaving the French doors open, Alex leans on the stone railing and reminds me of the question he asked, and I have yet to answer. "Well?"

"I don't know him, and if I did, don't you think he'd tell you about it?"

"I think I'm going to like you, Gwen," Alex says, his smile widening. The MacKenzie genes are painfully strong, and the playful, teasing quality of Alex's smile reminds me of Tristan.

"Thanks, Mr. MacKenzie. I hope we have a productive working relationship too." I force the words out, but I'm feeling disoriented and I rub my arms, turning away from him to look out over the sprawl of Los Angeles.

Ever since my interview, I've been struggling with my guilt and worry, and I expected working with Mac to be awkward and uncomfortable until I'm able to come clean. But I didn't anticipate that Alex would rouse those same feelings.

This man is Tristan's uncle.

"I know you're trying to drive Mac nuts with all that 'Mr. MacKenzie' nonsense—and, hint, it's working—but you needn't bother with me. Everyone calls me Alex." He's deeply amused by this entire conversation, which seems like a normal little-brother reaction. It's a relief too, because he apparently hasn't noticed my sudden discomfort.

Standing around with nothing to do isn't helping either. What I need is to keep busy so I won't have time to dwell on the secrets I'm keeping from Mac. "Okay, Alex. But isn't there something I should do right now? I'm feeling a little useless, and I want to make a good impression."

"Really. Your busy time will be when she's out in public. Taking pictures and videos and making note of any good bits of conversation with voters, anything you can use for the social media accounts. And of course, you'll have to spend some time curating her accounts, but for now, until they get you set up, enjoy the downtime." He leans closer, lowering his voice as he says, "I'm the one who is a useless waste of space on this team."

"What do you mean?" I ask, unable to hide my surprise. From everything I've learned so far, I'd assumed Mac and Alex were equals in the company and on the campaign.

Alex studies the L.A. skyline with a thoughtful expression. When he turns back to me, he's smiling, but it doesn't quite reach his eyes. "Never mind. Mac tells me you've only recently moved to D.C. How are you liking it?"

CHAPTER 9

MAC

I DIDN'T REALIZE Gwen and Alex were out on the balcony together until they came back in, their heads bent close as they laughed. A sharp pang of irritation makes me clench my fists under the table. I'm fucking jealous of my own brother. Over a woman who won't even acknowledge she spent the better part of a summer riding my cock. It's irrational and fucked up, and I need to get a damn hold of this situation before I do something stupid.

"Gwen?" My irritation seeps into my voice, and Gwen jumps a little, Alex steadying her as she turns to face me.

"I'm sorry, Mr. MacKenzie. How can I help you?" Her voice is calm, which only makes me more irritable, and I'm struck by the impulse to do whatever it takes to get a reaction from her. Any reaction. This is not good, because yeah, I've always been impulsive, maybe even a little rash, but Gwen brings it out in me like no one else. And she fucking works for me now.

"Here." I slide an iPhone across the table. "That's for you. All the social media apps have been installed and Kim's accounts logged in.

Change the passwords at least once a week so you don't get hacked, and keep the list updated with Dan in IT. Use that phone for nothing —nothing—but creating and posting content for her. The last thing we need is for you to accidentally share your freakiest fantasies from her accounts."

"I know how to do my job, Mr. MacKenzie." She narrows her eyes, glaring at me, and I'll be honest, it feels good. Not exactly the dramatic reaction I was hoping for, but it's better than the plastic smile and blank stare she's been giving me since she reappeared in my life.

Alex is standing behind her, glaring at me over her shoulder, and that feels pretty good to.

"Good, then we shouldn't have any problems. There will be a rope line tonight before the event. Stick close to Kim. There should be some good opportunities for content. Otherwise, just retweet some flattering pundits and—"

"Actually," she interrupts, not at all tentative, and it's fucking hot, "I've been thinking a lot about this. Social media is most effective at reaching out to younger voters, but a few memes and inspiring quotes isn't going to cut it. For that demographic, it's about engagement. They want to feel like they have actual access to the candidate. She—we—shouldn't just be posting content. We should be responding to other people, having conversations. Really participating in the platforms. Instead of talking *at* people, we should talk *with* them."

Looking down at the table, I rub my thumb across my lip, considering what she said. It isn't a bad idea. Actually, it's a really great one. But Kim doesn't have the time or, frankly, the familiarity with social media necessary to pull that off. Other politicians could and have, but they've been younger, digital natives. They intuitively understand social media in a way Kim never will.

I'm about to say as much when Alex joins the conversation. "Some of our celebrity clients do something similar. Put a note in the bio for each account. Something about the account being run by staff, and tweets directly from Kim are initialed. That way it's honest...they know they aren't talking directly to her when Gwen comments, but it still creates a sense of engagement and interest."

"See? Not so useless," Gwen murmurs, smiling over her shoulder at Alex.

What in the hell is that about?

"I like it." Kim is nodding her approval, but she's watching me, waiting for my buy-in.

"Yeah, okay, that's good." I pin Gwen with a hard stare. "But no shit-posting with trolls. No responding to critics or arguing with reporters. Keep it to friendly chit chat with supporters and call it a day. You got that?"

"Got it," Gwen says through gritted teeth.

"Good." I glance at my watch then back to Gwen and Alex. "We've got a couple of hours before we have to leave for the rally. Why don't you two go find Cece and get settled."

Gwen and Alex leave, and Kim sends her own staff after them. Once we're alone she leans back in her seat, arms crossed over her chest, and beats back a smile. "So what's the story?"

"About what?" I know damn well what.

"If you don't trust Gwen to handle my social media, why did you hire her?"

"She can handle it."

"Then why were you such a dick?"

"I know you're biased, Kim, but surely it hasn't escaped your notice I am, in fact, a dick."

She laughs and slaps one hand on the table in agreement. "True enough, but that was over the top even for you. You have a history with her. Or have you hired your booty call, and that was fallout from a lover's quarrel?"

"I'm not sleeping with her." I roll my eyes, not loving this conversation and not afraid to let her know it. As one of my closest friends, no subject is off limits with Kim. But there's a maternal component to our relationship too. That combination can make some conversations with her uniquely uncomfortable.

"Now."

"Right."

"If that changes, it better not effect either of your jobs."

"Of course not."

"How are your mom and dad?"

I was hoping she'd change the subject, but this one isn't really an improvement. "Mom is good. She started volunteering at our old school, helping in the classroom for the younger grades. Apparently, parent participation isn't what it used to be, so the school is happy to have her and it keeps her busy."

"I'm glad to hear it. She was always so good with little ones. She should have been a teacher. Or had a dozen kids instead of just you two brats." She smiles fondly before applying the pressure again. "And your dad?"

"The same as always. You should ask Alex. He'd know better than I would."

"Oh, Mac. I wish you could work things out with him." She sighs and rubs both hands over her face, looking tired all of a sudden. She knows my relationship with him is fraught and it bothers her, as it does my mother. But we'd never gotten along, and there's no hope of that changing now. A fact she and my mother refuse to accept.

"You and Mom and Alex and…well, everyone but him and me." I shrug, unwilling to get dragged into a conversation about repairing a relationship that's been broken my whole life.

She shakes her head and frowns at me but lets it go. "You've had a long day with the flight, and it'll be a busy night tonight. Why don't you go and get some rest before we have to go too?"

"Yes, Mom," I quip. I don't feel my age often. Thirty-four is still pretty damn young in the grand scheme of things. But today, yeah, I'm not too proud to admit I'm feeling a little beat down. Maybe it's Gwen, or the travel, or the campaign, or the shit with my family, I don't know, and it doesn't really matter. All I know is that a little sleep can only help.

After finding Cece—naturally, in the hotel bar—and collecting my keycard, I head for my room. Cece has already hung my suits and put my toiletries in the bathroom. She even left a protein bar on the bedside table, because she knows we probably won't have dinner until after Kim's event tonight. Cece may be a pain in my ass, but I'd be an ill-dressed, unorganized, victim of starvation if it weren't for her.

Stripping down to my boxer briefs, I toss my suit on the back of the chair before I slide between the cool sheets. But as soon as I close my eyes, I'm assaulted by the thought of Gwen sitting so close to me on the ride from the airport. It was torture. So close I could smell the light citrus bite of her perfume and yet unable to do a damn thing about it.

Then this afternoon, the determined look on her face and the steely tone of her voice when she explained her thoughts on social media strategy only made me want her more. I acted like an ass, and she gave exactly zero fucks about it, refusing to be derailed. It reminds me of the way we used to fight and fuck when we were younger and it's impossible not to imagine what it might be like now. Would she break as easily as she did back then? How long would I need to tease her with my mouth and fingers and cock before her expression softened and her voice grew husky and she begged me to fuck her?

Christ, the poor woman is just trying to do her job, and all I can think about is fucking her. I am a creep, no better than my goddamn dad. A really stupid creep, because I never should have allowed this to happen, and I definitely shouldn't be stroking my dick thinking about Gwen. I've gone years without fantasizing about her when I masturbate and now, she's walked back into my life, refusing to admit she even knows me, and I haven't had an orgasm without thinking of her since. It's fucking pathetic and I'm apparently incapable of stopping it, because I've already pushed my boxers down and taken my cock in hand.

My fantasies get tangled up between past and present, simultaneously remembering how it used to be and wondering if it would still be the same. Would she still gasp in that quiet, surprised way that was uniquely her when I thrust inside her? Even now, alone in a hotel room, the memory is enough to make my cock throb. Was her pussy really as slick and tight as I remember? Would she still claw at my chest and back like a wild animal, biting and nipping and kissing like she couldn't get enough of me?

Tightening my grip, I groan with frustration. She's too much temptation. No matter how hard I try, I can't forget how good it felt to come inside her while she chanted my name like a prayer, her body quivering around me. And that's what I'm thinking about when I come now, imagining I'm spilling inside her instead of all over my own stomach.

When I've finished, I collapse back against the pillow, staring at the ceiling as I will my heart to stop racing, because now that I've come, I can only think about one thing.

I am so completely and thoroughly fucked.

CHAPTER 10

GWEN

At the rally last night, I managed to avoid Mac, not that it required much effort on my part. He was so entirely focused on Kim I'm not sure he even remembered I was there.

Working the rope line with her before her speech was a blast, though. Kim's a natural one-on-one with voters, and it was exhilarating to witness the way they responded to her up close. I got some amazing pictures that really captured that and received an encouraging amount of attention on Instagram.

But the big speeches are harder for her. She comes off a little cold and aloof, I think because she's nervous. As a result, we were all a little anxious as we stood just off stage watching. Cece, Alex, and I exchanged occasional comments on how she was doing or how the crowd was reacting, but not Mac.

He might not have been aware of my presence, but I could hardly look away from him. Everything about him telegraphed his deep concentration. He stood a few paces away from the rest of us, one hand in his pants pocket while he absently brushed the thumb of his other hand across his lip or raked his fingers through his hair. He nodded when he thought she was doing well, smiled faintly when the crowd laughed or cheered, and stared at her with unblinking intensity when she stumbled over a turn of phrase. It almost seemed like he thought he could will her to loosen up and relax with the force of his own thoughts.

Mac's single-minded focus was a thing to behold. It should have given me a lot of hope. Working together should be a breeze if he's always that distracted. But at the same time, it reminded me what it was like to be the object of his unrelenting attention. It made me want to drag him away from the stage and find a quiet corner where I could fall to my knees in front of him and lick and suck and kiss his cock until all that terrifying, exciting focus was directed at me. I tossed and turned all night thinking about that and what it said about me that I was still so attracted to him. Especially given the enormous secret I'm keeping from him.

I've hardly seen Mac today. We drove from L.A. to San Diego, making several stops along the way at cafes and diners where Kim could stretch her legs and shake hands, prolonging what should have been a two-hour trip into a nearly day-long affair. Mac rode with her, which meant Cece and I had the backseat to ourselves while Alex rode up front with the driver. I was so busy stalking Kim and her interactions with the public that there wasn't time for anything else when we were stopped.

Kim is giving a big immigration speech tonight, hence the choice of San Diego for the venue. She's huddled with Mac and her campaign manager Brian near the edge of the stage, nodding along as they give her a last-minute pep talk. But I can already tell the mood tonight is more upbeat than it was last night, because all three of them are laughing and smiling.

"She's going to knock this out of the park," Cece says with a beaming smile when Kim bounds onto the stage and Mac comes to join our little group.

"Damn right she is," he agrees with a confident nod and a wink. He actually winked at her. Even Cece seems surprised.

"You're in a good mood," Alex says with narrowed eyes. It reminds me so much of my sisters that I can't contain a quiet laugh. Only a sibling would be suspicious of a good mood.

"It's been a good day," Mac says with a shrug before glancing down at me to ask, "What are you snickering about, shorty?"

"Hey, hey, I'm not short," I say, still laughing, because his good mood and the crowd's enthusiastic response to Kim are infectious.

"You are in this crowd," Alex points out with a grin, and he's not wrong. At 5'7", I'm taller than average, but that's not impressive compared to my current companions. Alex must be close to 6'5, Mac is 6'2, and even Cece is a couple of inches taller than I am.

"Well? What was so funny?" Mac asks, circling back to his original question.

"Oh, nothing, it's just that you two—" I gesture between the brothers, "—remind me a lot of my sisters sometimes."

"You have sisters?" There's a brief flash of surprise in Mac's expression, though I don't know whether it's because he's surprised to learn I have them or just surprised I shared the information.

"Two. Willie is twenty-two and Livie is seventeen. Livie wants to go to William and Mary in the fall, and she's been accepted, but out-of-state tuition is ulcer inducing, which is why we moved for her senior year. Not that in-state tuition is much better, but I'll take what I can get."

I can see the wheels turning in his head, the questions forming in his eyes, but it's Alex who asks, "You're paying for your sister's education?"

"Well, not all of it, but as much as I can." I give Alex a gentle elbow between the ribs and a teasing smile. "Unless you want to give me a raise already?"

"Would if I could, but I don't control the purse strings on your contract. Mac's a cold-hearted bastard, so good luck appealing to his sympathies." Alex gives me a consoling pat on the shoulder and everyone, even the cold-hearted bastard, laughs.

After that, we direct our attention back to Kim's speech, and she's radiating excitement by the time she comes off the stage. Cece was right—Kim did knock it out of the park, and everyone knows it. In the car on the way back to the hotel, we're all scrolling through our phones, scanning headlines on the major news websites. Consensus of the talking heads seems to be that was the best speech of her career.

In the hotel lobby, Cece suggests we get a drink before bed, and we're all too happy to agree. It was a good night, and no one is ready for it to be over. The hotel bar seems particularly crowded for so late on a weeknight until I realize many of the other patrons are campaign staff and reporters from the press pool assigned to Kim.

Fortunately, we're able to find an open table on the patio and fall into easy conversation, mostly rehashing the highlights of the day and especially Kim's speech, while we wait for our drinks. The waitress has just delivered our beer when I catch a whiff of what I'm pretty sure is marijuana. I don't see anyone on the patio smoking; the scent is drifting on the evening breeze from somewhere in the direction of the pool. I glance at Mac next to me, a small smile forming on my lips as I watch him sniff the air, a look of longing on his handsome face.

"Do you still smoke?" Too late, I realize what I've done.

"I told you they knew each other," Cece hisses at Alex, not nearly as quietly as she thinks.

"No, it wasn't as much fun once everyone started legalizing it." Mac grins at me, his knee bouncing off mine under the table. He's obviously pleased I've finally acknowledged our past, even if I didn't do it on purpose.

"Do you miss it?" If his expression a moment ago is any indication, he does.

"Not usually. Except…" He leans closer to me, so close I can feel his warm breath in my ear when he whispers, "I miss it after a good, hard fuck."

It's as if the wind has been knocked out of me. Cece's voice sounds miles away as she asks what he said, Alex's response—that he's fairly sure he doesn't want to know—is no less distant. All I can hear is my own heartbeat, and all I can think about is all the lazy hours Mac and I spent in his bed all those years ago. He's leaned away again, his elbow on the arm of his chair, chin in hand, as he watches me with a lopsided smile, and I can't look away.

"Hey, Mac! You got room at your table for one more?"

I'm jolted out of my trance by the new voice and look up to see a redhead standing next to our table. A quick glance around the patio tells me there aren't any available tables, but why did she have to interrupt us? More importantly, why do I care? I should be glad for the distraction, because my thoughts weren't headed anywhere good.

"Sure, Stef, pull up a chair."

She apparently already knows Alex and Cece, but once she takes a seat—on Mac's other side, of course—Mac introduces me. Her name is Stefanie Clark, and she's a reporter for the *Washington Observer*. I guess that explains why they all know each other. PR people and reporters often have symbiotic relationships.

"I didn't expect to see you in Kim's pool," Alex says to Stefanie with a darting glance in Mac's direction.

"I requested the Hennessey pool." When Cece hums her approval, Stefanie laughs and continues, "Right? But the bosses think they know better, and I figure Dunn's campaign has some perks too." She accompanies that comment with a flirty smile for Mac.

Whoa, whoa, whoa. What's going on here?

Is she coming on to him? Not that I blame her. He's a good-looking guy—he probably gets hit on all the time. But this feels different. It isn't just flirting. It's familiar, knowing, and I shift in my seat, uncomfortable with the realization. I'm not stupid enough to be jealous, but that doesn't mean I enjoy watching another woman make a pass at him.

"You might be surprised just how few perks there are," Mac says, pushing his chair back, and the startled look that passes between Alex and Cece confirms my suspicions. Mac looks between the three of us. "I'm off to bed. Don't stay up too late, kids. We have an early flight tomorrow."

As Mac passes behind Stefanie's chair, she presses a scrap of paper into his hand, not even bothering to be discreet about it. Mac stuffs it into his pocket but otherwise doesn't acknowledge her.

"What's his deal tonight?" Stefanie asks, staring at his broad back as he walks away.

Alex's gaze settles on me, his expression speculative. "I have no idea."

CHAPTER 11

MAC

AN HOUR after I left everyone else on the patio, I take the elevator down two floors and knock on Stef's door. She answers, throwing it wide, in nothing but a slinky blue nightgown that would have made my dick ache a week ago. Now it doesn't even merit a twitch of interest.

"I wasn't sure you'd come." She closes the door behind me.

Tossing the crumpled paper with her room number on it on the bed, I don't waste any time explaining exactly why I'm here. "I didn't want there to be any confusion. We're done."

"Can't say I'm not disappointed, but sure, that's fine." Stef shrugs and sits on the edge of the bed. "You found someone else?"

"I'm not sure," I answer, because it's the truth.

There are a thousand reasons I shouldn't get involved with Gwen, but I'm still as selfish as I always was, at least when it comes to her. I'm not stupid enough to read anything into her finally acknowledging our past though. That had been inevitable, and there's no

77

reason to think Gwen wants anything to do with me beyond our new professional relationship.

Still, I have to end things with Stef. We've been doing the friends-with-benefits thing for a while, and I'm certain she isn't harboring secret romantic feelings. Honestly, if Gwen hadn't shown up again, I could see carrying on with Stef for a lot longer than I did most women. Good sex, good conversation, zero expectations. It was an ideal situation. But it wouldn't be right to continue with her when someone else seems to be the only one who can get my dick hard. Even if that someone else wants nothing to do with me.

"What does that mean?" Stef laughs and leans back on her hands, her knees slightly parted.

I take a minute before answering, letting my gaze wander over her curves, lingering on her full tits and willing my body to respond to the provocative view she's giving me. Still nothing. *Fuck.* "Nothing good."

"Oh, see, that sounds like a story I want to hear," she teases as she gets up and walks with me back toward the door.

"Maybe some other time," I answer, opening the door.

"Well, you know where to find me."

"Thanks, Stef." I lean over, brushing a friendly kiss across her cheek before stepping into the hallway, only to be met with Gwen's accusing blue eyes.

She's standing in the center of the hall, ice bucket tucked under one arm, wearing a pair of flannel pajama pants and an old University of Michigan T-shirt. If looks could kill, I'd be nothing but a pile of smoldering ash. But my dick is straining against my zipper, demanding to be let out, because even Gwen's hostile glare is sexier than other women's come-hither glances.

"Thanks for dropping off that press packet, Mac. Have a good night." Stef waves before closing the door, though I'm sure she's pressing her ear to the other side.

She obviously read the situation and was trying to help. I appreciate the effort, but I doubt it will do me much good.

"The ice machine on our floor is broken." Gwen clips out the words and starts marching down the hall again without sparing me another glance.

Like a leashed dog, I follow.

The room with the vending machines is little more than a closet, and I crowd in next to Gwen, silently watching as she slams her bucket on the shelf and presses the button. Her temper is so hot it's a wonder the ice isn't melting as fast as it tumbles out of the machine.

Neither of us says anything and when her bucket is full, she snatches it up, holding it in front of her like a shield as she turns toward me and the entryway I'm blocking. We stare at each other while I consider what to say and she considers the best way to dispose of my body. At least, I assume that's what she's thinking, based on her expression.

I briefly consider telling her the truth, though that isn't apt to go over very well. *Stef and I used to fuck, but I ended it tonight because I'd rather fuck you. So how about it?*

Yeah, that would get me justifiably slapped. But instead of trying to find a way to explain myself that doesn't end in violence, I do the one thing I really want to do anyway. I goad her. "Jealous?" I ask with a smirk. I'm well aware this approach is just as likely to end with me getting smacked.

"No. You can put your dick wherever you want," she snaps.

Sweet, innocent Gwen. Will you ever learn not to give me an opening like that? "Can I?" Taking a step closer, I crowd her against the wall opposite the vending machines. With my hands on either side of her shoulders and her bucket of ice pressed between us, I dip my head and skim my lips over her throat. "Can I really? Because there's only one place I want to put it right now, baby."

Tell me to stop. Slap me. Do something, I silently plead with her, even as I press closer, because I know this is wrong, but I can't stop myself.

"Don't call me that. I know why you do it." Her voice is sharp but a little ragged with vulnerability too. She's angry, all right, but not because her boss is being holy-fucking-hell-I'm-going-to-sue-you-and-own-your-company-when-this-is-over inappropriate but because I called her "baby." A pet name she used to love to hate.

"I don't think you do, Gwen," I murmur, teasing my fingers under the hem of her shirt to stroke her hip, contemplating the wisdom of taking the bucket away from her.

"Mac…" It's a strangled squeak of sound, barely recognizable as my name, and the bucket slips from her grasp and clatters to the floor, scattering ice around our feet.

Not wasting a second, I press forward, crushing her against the wall as our mouths come together. Just as it always did, our kiss seems to speak a language known only to us, unique and intimate and full of all the things neither of us has the courage to express with words. When she sucks on my lower lip, she's saying *I've missed you,* and when I nibble at the corner of her mouth, I'm asking *why did you go?* She bites me. *It doesn't matter, I'm here now.* I lick the seam of her lips. *I want you.* She opens for me, inviting me to deepen the kiss. *Then take me.*

Gwen's hands are around my neck, her fingers flexing in my hair, digging into my scalp. With a growl, I slide one hand under her shirt and over her stomach to palm her breast. She isn't wearing a bra and although her body has changed some over the years, the feel of her in my hands is still achingly familiar. She arches into me with a needy moan and I grind against her, showing her exactly how hard I am for her.

"Mac, oh God, Mac…" She shifts against the wall, parting her legs as I shove my other hand inside her pants and drag my fingers through her slit. Touching her is even better than I remembered. She's hot and wet and swollen, and my cock throbs so hard I feel lightheaded.

"I know, baby. I know." Yanking her shirt up on one side, I dip my head, tugging her nipple between my teeth. Her skin tastes like everything I've ever wanted, and a hot spark of possessive demand ignites, burning in my chest like a wildfire. I don't want to fuck her this time. I want to own her, so she can't leave me again. It's fucked up and wrong, I know that, and I hate the insecurity it exposes in me, but the worry she'll vanish again is so fierce I can't help but hold her tighter to remind myself she's here now. "Will you still beg for it, Gwen?" I ask, ghosting the pad of my thumb across her clit, there and gone before she can react.

She doesn't answer. Instead, her hands find my belt, deftly unbuckling it before she pops the button on my trousers and drags my zipper down. Moments later, she's tugged my boxers lower, tucking the elastic band under my balls, and my cock springs out between us. She looks down, licking her lips as she wraps her fingers around my shaft and rubs her thumb over the swollen head, spreading around the bead of pre-come she finds there. It takes every ounce of willpower I possess not to push her to her knees and thrust between her plump lips.

"Maybe I'm not the one who'll do the begging this time," Gwen says, her voice husky as she raises her gaze to mine.

With a grin, I gently press a finger inside her to the first knuckle, rubbing wide circles around her clit with my thumb, giving her more but not quite what she wants. She lets out a garbled moan and her knees buckle; the only thing holding her upright my hands on her body and my weight pressing her to the wall.

"More, Mac, please, more," she moans, and my smile widens.

"See, baby? You're always the one who begs. That's just how it is." But even as I taunt her, I reward her. My thumb settles on her clit and I thrust two fingers fully inside her, pumping in and out as she bucks against my hand.

In response, her grip tightens around my shaft, finding the perfect rhythm, sliding up and down my length, and I grind my teeth, resisting the urge to pull her pants down and bury myself in her welcoming pussy. I need her to come first.

"That's it. Ride my hand and come for me," I coax with quiet words and demanding caresses until her breathing hitches and her grip on my cock falters, her body spasming around my fingers. Using my other hand, I tug her pants over her hips, eager to turn her around and replace my fingers with my cock as soon as the last tremors of her orgasm have subsided.

I'm getting ready to do just that when the compressor in one of the vending machines behind me kicks on, the rattling hum of noise dragging me out of the moment so abruptly I shake my head with bewildered confusion.

What the fuck are we doing?

"Gwen, wait." I grit out the words, my voice a hoarse rasp, because she's jacking my dick again with renewed purpose.

She doesn't listen though, and she still knows my body as well as I know hers. Knows exactly what I like, the perfect tempo with just the right amount of pressure, to bring me to a blistering release before I even really know what's happening.

"Fuck," I groan and shove her shirt up again, the fabric bunched under my palm as I plant my hand between her breasts and rock my hips, driving into her grip. Grabbing my other wrist with her free hand, she drags it to her mouth and sucks eagerly at the fingers that moments ago were inside her. And that's it, I'm done for. My cock jerks, and I come with a loud groan, painting her stomach with semen.

We're both panting for breath and the silence might be awkward, but I'm too transfixed by the sight of my come dripping down her belly to notice. If I stare too long, that view alone will be enough to make my softening dick come alive again.

"We shouldn't have done that," she finally says, pulling up her pants and scooting around me to put as much space between us as the small room will allow. Her back is pressed so tight against the snack machine she'll probably have an impression of the keypad between her shoulders tomorrow. The sudden wariness in her expression is like a knife twisting in my gut.

Christ, I'm such an asshole.

"Let's get what you came down here for and get you back to bed." I bend over and swipe her ice bucket off the floor. There isn't really anything else to say, because as much as I might dislike admitting it, she's right.

Gwen waits while I refill her bucket and then follows me back to the elevators. Neither of us speaks on the way to her room, but once we've stopped outside her door, she takes the bucket of ice from me and looks up, her eyes clouded with uncertainty. "So, what happens now?"

"I don't know. What do you want to happen?"

"What we just did…it was great, like old times, you know? But…" She ducks her head, averting her eyes and letting the sentence hang.

"I'm your boss, and we have a complicated history," I acknowledge.

"I think maybe…" Her voice hitches and she turns away from me, wiping her eyes. When she starts again, her voice is steadier. "I think maybe it would be best if I turn in my notice and we can just go on as if we'd never found each other again."

"No, that's not what's best." Grabbing her by the shoulders, I turn her toward me. She is not quitting her job because her asshole boss makes her uncomfortable. I am not my father.

"Mac, you can't really believe—"

"What, Gwen? That we're both adults who can act like it? I do, actually. If you like the job, if you want the job—hell, even if you just need the job until you can find something better—keep the job. This," I say, waving one finger between us, "has nothing to do with that."

"That's sweet of you to say, it really is, and I appreciate it, but it isn't realistic," she insists with a sad smile.

"Maybe, but I don't think either of us is thinking real straight right now. Give it a little time, and we'll figure out the best way forward." I pause, considering it for a second, then add with a wide gesture, "And which way actually is forward."

Gwen's laugh is weak, but her smile is genuine when she nods her agreement.

Later, back in my room and halfway through the bottle of mediocre scotch I ordered from room service, I'm drunker than I've been in a long time and no closer to understanding what I should do about Gwen.

The most pressing issue is convincing her she doesn't need to quit her job. Not that she can't quit if that's what she really wants, but we're reasonable—okay, sort of reasonable—adults and we can handle this. Yes, fingering her and coming on her stomach in a hotel hallway was reprehensible, and I wouldn't blame her if she never wants to see my face again. But if she wants the job, if she likes it but for her creepy boss, she should be able to keep it. If that means promising something like that will never happen again, so be it, because it shouldn't happen again anyway. It can't happen again.

Unless she wants it to happen again.

I pour another glass of scotch, an apparently futile attempt to drown that obnoxious voice in my head. Gwen's the most potent drug I've ever encountered, and part of me—the reckless, greedy part— wants to pick right up where we left off. But it's not that simple.

Her disappearing act was bad enough the first time; I can't set myself up for that again. Maybe I could get past it if she'd tell me what happened but so far, she hasn't seemed interested in volunteering that information, and that's the only way I want it, the only way it would mean anything. Or maybe I'm just too stubborn to ask.

Closing my eyes and sinking lower in my chair, I consider our contradictory recollections of our history. I loved her. I maybe didn't realize it until she left, but it smacked me hard once she was gone. The memory of that heartache is still sharper than I'd have guessed after all this time, and when I think back on our months together it seems so obvious. But she doesn't believe me now and wouldn't have believed me then. How can there be anything in front of us when we don't even agree on what we've left behind?

Besides, I wasn't then—and I'm still not—looking to get married and have a family, and Gwen was the kind of girl who wanted those things. That was the reason I held back with her, denying my own feelings and occasionally stomping all over hers when I worried she was getting too attached. I didn't want to get in the way of her finding that someday with some other guy, even if I was too selfish to end things myself so she could get on with her life. And the thing is, all of that is still true. I'm never going to marry her or have kids with her, and I would bet my last dollar she still wants those things.

Maybe we're both dragging around too much baggage and there

really isn't any way to make things work between us. It's a bitter thought, but the inescapable fact is it might be true. And if it is, if I can just accept that, then there's no reason we can't figure out how to work together without any more drama.

It's the accepting-it part that will be difficult.

CHAPTER 12

GWEN

THE RIDE to the airport is a quiet one. We all stayed up too late last night, some of us later than others, and Mac looks hung over.

When we get to our gate, he flops into a chair. Slouching low, knees spread, his sunglasses still perched on his nose despite the fact we're indoors, he's radiating a *leave me the fuck alone* vibe. It seems everyone else is happy to oblige him, because Cece wanders off to a nearby newsstand and Alex heads back toward the Starbucks we passed on our trek through the terminal with the vague promise that he might return with coffee for everyone.

"Hung over?" I ask, sinking into the chair next to Mac.

He grunts in answer and tips his head against the back of his seat.

So that's a yes, then.

It isn't very encouraging that he got drunk after leaving me at my door last night. I'm tempted to ask whether he reached a conclusion or the bottom of his bottle first, but I don't dare. Not in a busy airport with his brother and PA hovering nearby. Not when he's clearly not feeling his best. Definitely not when I'm so unprepared to hear his answer.

I did a lot of thinking last night too, and I'm glad Mac talked me out of quitting because I like this job. But Mac is a temptation I'm not sure I can resist and after last night, it seems inevitable. If I keep working for him, I will eventually end up in his bed. Unless he doesn't want me there once he finds out about everything I've been keeping from him.

I nearly blurted out the truth right there in the hotel hallway last night, my skin still sticky with his come. If he hadn't talked me out of quitting, I would have.

So now that I don't technically work for you anymore, you should know, you have a kid.

Thankfully, he interrupted that impulse because it definitely wasn't the right time, but I can't go on like this. Especially now that I can't hide behind pretending not to know him. The guilt and remorse just keep piling up like the sand dunes back home on Lake Michigan, and it will bury me alive if this goes on much longer. So, with a deep breath for courage, I start at the beginning.

"I was fifteen when my dad died. Willie—Willa—she's named for him. She was seven at the time. Olivia was only two. She doesn't even really remember him." I stop and give him a sidelong glance because he hasn't made a sound. He hasn't moved either. In fact, he's sitting perfectly still, his body tense with focus. He's listening.

Relieved, I turn straight ahead again before continuing. "My mom and I didn't ever really get along, but it got worse after Dad died. She had all these strict rules and crazy expectations. Like, she was mad when I graduated high school because I was salutatorian. She never congratulated me, just demanded to know why I didn't make valedictorian and then answered her own question. It was because I was stupid, obviously. So, the day after graduation, I packed up my shit and moved to Ann Arbor, where I'd be starting school in the fall anyway. My friend Lindsey, she's one of the smartest people I've ever met and—"

I'm interrupted by a quiet snort that seems to indicate Mac doesn't agree with my assessment of Lindsey, but he doesn't say anything, so I keep going. "Well, I don't know. She was valedictorian, and she graduated high school a year early, so she was about to be a sophomore and had an apartment off campus. I moved in with her and got a job at a donut shop and I tried to forget all the ways I was a failure, how much I'd let my mom down. Because that's what it felt like. No matter how hard I tried, I was never good enough. She was always disappointed in me, which meant I was a terrible daughter and maybe a terrible person, right?"

"No."

"It was a rhetorical question."

Mac huffs and waves one hand. *Carry on.*

"Getting away from her helped a little, but she called every day. If I didn't answer, she'd leave long, rambling messages on Lindsey's answering machine. Always with the diatribes about how disappointing and ungrateful I was, how I was setting such a poor example for my sisters and it would be my fault if they were failures like me. It was unrelenting, and Lindsey could see what it did to me, so the first weekend I was there she convinced me to go out to a club with her. I'd never done that before, but she said it would make me feel better. I didn't really believe her, but I figured it couldn't hurt, so I went."

I risk another peek at Mac. Anyone passing by on the concourse would probably feel sorry for him, the poor, exhausted businessman who just wants to catch a nap before his flight but instead got stuck sitting next to a crazy lady who won't shut up. But it's just an illusion; despite his casual appearance, his attention is razor sharp as he turns over my every word, weighing and analyzing them.

Satisfied that he's still with me I swallow hard and look away again. "It turned out, though, she was right about the club. Well, not the club exactly, but I met this guy there. We ended up having sex in his car, and it was the strangest thing because it didn't mean anything, I didn't even know his name, but at the same time it meant everything. You're going to think this is silly but he—"

"Silly that you're talking about me, to me, in the third person? Yes,

I think that's silly," Mac drawls lazily, as if he hasn't a care in the world. As if he isn't hanging on my every word.

"Shut up, the third-person thing is making this easier."

Another rolling hand wave telling me to go on, but this time when he lowers his hand he reaches for mine, turning it over and rubbing his thumb across my palm. His skin slides against mine and my heart beats a little faster, his gentle, reassuring touch encouraging me to go on.

"Anyway, it's silly, but he was just what I needed. For the first time in my life, I did something I'd been taught was really, really wrong, and I did it intentionally and that was…I don't know. I'd broken the rules and nothing bad happened. I'd liked it and there were no consequences and, you know, that made me think maybe Mom didn't know what she was talking about with all that other garbage either."

I stop to collect my thoughts, but Mac is apparently impatient, because he asks, "Did you ever see him again?"

It's my turn to huff with amusement. "It turns out we had some mutual friends and ran into each other at a party. From there, we… well, I don't know what you'd call it. It wasn't a relationship, and it wasn't just sex. It was this weird in-between. We never talked about school or our families or anything real. We didn't go on dates, at least not together. I went on a few with other guys, trying to bait him into taking me out, but it never worked. We'd fight about it and he'd say he didn't care who I dated as long as he was the only one I fucked, which was stupid because anyone could see it made him angry when I went out with another guy. But he'd never give in and just take me on a damn date."

"He sounds like an asshole." Mac pulls my hand into his lap, entwining our fingers. I appreciate the gesture, but the last thing I want is for Alex or Cece to catch us holding hands, so I try to tug my fingers free. He tightens his grip.

"He was," I reply, staring at our still-joined hands.

Was and is.

Mac lets go of me, the corners of his mouth twitching with the beginnings of a smile but his expression sobers, his features softening, when he asks, "So was it all bad then? Just meaningless sex with this douchebag who wouldn't even take you on a proper date?"

"No, God, no," I gasp, dragging in a deep breath that burns my lungs. "We had this crazy summer together and yeah, he could be an ass, but I wasn't always easy either and he was…he was my safe place. Sure, it bothered me he wouldn't take me out, but the rest of it? The part where he didn't ask questions or try to tell me what to do? That was amazing. He had no expectations of me. He's the only—"

"He had no expectations, and that was amazing?" He sounds skeptical and one brow is arching over top of his sunglasses, expressing his doubt.

"I'm not explaining it right." I pause to center my thoughts, trying to organize them in a way that will make sense to him. "My mom's expectations were so high and so impossible to meet. I felt like a failure all the time. It was liberating to know someone who didn't constantly push me to be something I wasn't. Like, he drank and smoked a lot of pot but he never pressured me to do it or judged me when I didn't. Even Lindsey did that, but he just liked me for me, and no one had ever really done that before. I mean, I'm not stupid. I know what he liked about me, but I didn't care. What was important was that he didn't try to force me into being someone I wasn't, and I felt like that's what everyone else was doing back then."

Mac scrunches up his face and lifts his chin, his voice tight. "What, specifically, is it you think he liked about you?"

"I was a reliable lay. Isn't that what most guys that age want?"

"I'd bet my left nut he'd have a different answer if you asked him."

The implication is clear, and he wants me to ask, but I'm not prepared for him to talk about love again. It's hard enough facing the truth of our past without his false memories clouding the issue further. And if they aren't false? That's even worse, because it means all my assumptions were wrong. It means maybe things would have been different if I'd told him when my Mom left. If I'd told him about Tristan. I'm too much of a coward to face those possibilities. "Maybe, but I'm probably boring you with all this. I should leave you alone so you can get some rest before the flight," I answer, my voice little more than a whisper. I wasn't sure how far I'd get in telling my version of our story, but I'm emotionally wrung out already and have been since our encounter last night. This seems like as good a place as any to take a break.

"You've come this far. You might as well finish it." He shrugs with an air of indifference that is a lie.

There's no way I can actually finish the story. Not today, not yet. I just don't have the emotional strength to do it all in one go, and I can't tell him about Tristan in the middle of an airport. We'll need privacy for that discussion. But I can buckle down and get through what he thinks is the finish to our story. "Well, like I said, we had this great summer together and then the first day of school, I was supposed to go to his apartment after my last class. I stopped at Lindsey's to shower and change my clothes and while I was there, Mom called. She'd gotten a new boyfriend, and he didn't like the little girls. Having kids around who aren't old enough to be left home alone really cramps a guy's style, I guess, and I think it bothered him even more because they weren't his kids, you know? So, Mom gives me this big lecture about what a disappointment I am and she ends it by telling me since I'm not going to live up to my potential anyway, she's leaving. She said I needed to come home and take care of my sisters because she and—shit, I don't even remember his name…whatever— she and her boyfriend were leaving in the morning and if I wasn't there, she'd turn Willie and Liv over to the state." Despite my inability to remember her boyfriend's name, I remember that night as if it were yesterday. Just talking about it makes my stomach roil and my vision get fuzzy around the edges, and I hope Mac doesn't notice the way my breathing has grown shallow and irregular.

"Jesus Christ." Mac sounds as gutted as I feel.

"Lindsey took me home. Mom and I argued all night. I tried everything to convince her to stay, but it was no use. She left the next morning, and in the blink of an eye I was eighteen years old and solely responsible for my eleven- and six-year-old sisters." I sigh, relieved to be finished.

"How did you…What did you do?" He sounds bewildered, like he can't imagine how I managed, and I get it. I lived it and it still feels unreal to me.

"The only thing I could, I guess. I got up the next morning and got a job. Eventually I went back to school part time, and I kept working full time and…honestly, it was really fucking hard. I don't know how I made it all work, but somehow I did."

"But you never went back and told that guy what happened? Didn't even let Lindsey tell him?"

I search his voice and his expression for any sign of bitterness, but all I find is confusion and hurt. That's maybe worse, because it feeds the guilt already gnawing at me. "No. I just… I was so overwhelmed and scared and, Christ, I was so fucking depressed. I mean, my life had just imploded, nothing would ever be the same, and we'd just had this casual, carefree fling. I know it was a jerky thing to do, disappearing like that, but it was for the best. I can't imagine how he'd have reacted if I'd dropped all that on him."

"Maybe he would have surprised you. Love makes people do funny things sometimes," Mac suggests.

"What do you know about it? You weren't there." Maybe I'm taking this third-person thing a little far. I know exactly how ridiculous I sound, but I'm too prickly in my vulnerability to care.

But Mac isn't intimidated by my sour response. Instead, he laughs, a loud, barking sound that startles me and makes him wince. Clearly, he isn't over that hangover yet. "You're unbelievable, Gwen."

"I'm glad I could entertain you." I yank my hand free of his and stand up, hastily adding, "I need to go to the bathroom and get a drink before we board."

"Hold up." Mac leans forward, elbows on his knees, and catches my fingers with his. Looking at me over the top of his sunglasses he says, "I'm sure you've figured this out already, but Stef and I used to fuck."

"Yeah, I got that, Mac," I say woodenly. My whole body is stiff, the anger I felt the night before simmering just beneath my skin again.

"I went to her room last night to tell her that was over. I haven't been with her, or anyone else, since you walked into my office all sass and delusion."

It's been a week. When he hasn't had sex in more than a year, I might consider being something close to impressed. But still, I'd be lying if I didn't admit I'm pleased by his admission. More evidence I'm still a fool. It shouldn't—*doesn't*—matter who he fucks. He's free to put his dick wherever he damn well pleases. Except in me, because I'm not going there again.

I don't know what it is about Mac, though, because I can't resist the opportunity to poke at him. Giving him a cool look, I ask, "Am I supposed to care?"

"I swear to God, Gwen, don't make me fuck you right here in this airport, because you know I'll do it." He grins and tugs on my fingers, urging me closer to him, but I resist, pulling my hand free instead.

"I'll take a rain check on that, Mr. MacKenzie."

As I walk away, I could swear I hear him growl. Yeah, he probably didn't like that "Mr. MacKenzie" business much. But when I peek over my shoulder, he's watching me, his full mouth tipped up in a lopsided smile that makes my pulse thrum and, as hard as it was, I'm glad I told him as much as I had today.

It may only be a start, but it's a good one.

CHAPTER 13

MAC

AFTER NEARLY A WEEK AT HOME, it's good to be back on the road. I've been avoiding Gwen as much as possible and, despite the closer physical proximity, that's easier to do when we're traveling. We're all so busy, utterly focused on Kim and her campaign, that there isn't time to worry about Gwen and the doe-eyed looks she keeps giving me. I don't know why she's doing it, or what it means, but it's a hell of a lot easier to ignore when I don't have the time to explore those questions.

Except now I'm standing outside her hotel room, psyching myself up to knock on the door. This shouldn't be a big deal. She forgot to pack her phone cord, so I volunteered my spare until she or Cece has a chance to stop off somewhere and get one. But it isn't as simple as handing over the cord and beating feet back to my own room. I mean, it should be that easy, but this is Gwen and it's been a long day and I'm exhausted and lonely and horny and I can't stop thinking about kissing her.

This is fucking ridiculous.

With an irritable grumble, I bang on her door. I'll give her the cord and then I'll leave. End of story. In fact, I won't even go back to my room. I never found time for dinner tonight and now that I think about it, I'm starving. I'll walk over to the diner across the street and get something to eat. I won't even step foot inside our hotel again until I'm so tired I—

My foolproof plan is interrupted when Gwen swings the door wide and greets me with a muffled hello. Muffled, because she has a mouthful of the apple she's holding in front of her face. On closer inspection, her mascara is smeared, giving her raccoon eyes, and her face—what I can see of it around the apple, anyway—is splotchy.

Frowning at her, I blurt, "Are you crying?"

"No. Shit, sorry. I was washing my face, but the mascara... You know, the waterproof stuff, it's..." She trails off with a flustered arm wave.

"Waterproof?" I suggest. She rolls her eyes, but the corners of her mouth are trying to kick up in a smile. Turning my attention to her apple, I give it an envious look. "Where'd you get that?"

"Cece, but I'm going to order room service in a few minutes." She must sense my hunger, because her eyes are taunting me as she takes another bite. The crisp sound of her teeth sinking into the fruit makes my stomach rumble.

"I was planning on hitting up that little diner across the street if you want to come." Inviting her to join me is the polite thing to do. She'll probably decline anyway and if she doesn't, it will be fine, if a little awkward. We're both adults, right?

"You wouldn't mind?"

"Of course not."

"Okay, just let me finish washing my face. Maybe I should change too. I feel a little fancy for a diner." Stepping out of the doorway to let me in, she looks down at her gray pencil skirt and lavender blouse with suspicion.

"You can't change, because then I'll seem even more overdressed," I point out with a gesture to my suit. I'm careful to keep my distance, though, because I'm pretty sure it's not a great idea for us to be alone together in a hotel room. A few short steps from a bed.

Fuck.

The faster we get out of here, the better.

"Would you mind plugging my phone in for me? It's over there." She waves her hand in the general direction of the table in the corner of the room before disappearing back into the bathroom.

"Work or personal first?" I call to her. Though both phones are iPhones, it isn't difficult to identify them. Her work phone is the latest model, while her personal phone is several generations out of date and has an annoying crack across the middle of the screen.

"Work, please. The other one's fine," she answers over the sound of running water.

After plugging it in, I'm just setting the work phone down again when the older phone beeps with an incoming text. I don't mean to read it, but the text is just there, right in front of me on the lock screen, and I've read it before I even realize what I'm doing.

Willie: Hey, Mom, it's me. Aunt Willie says you might already be asleep, but Rob invited me to stay over Friday night and she said I have to ask you. So, can I? If you're already asleep, I'll talk to you tomorrow. Love you, Tristan.

Mom? Gwen has a kid? That possibility never even occurred to me. Had she been married? Jesus, is she still married? No, that can't be. There are a lot of things I don't know about Gwen, but if she were currently married, she'd have never let the shenanigans at the hotel last week happen. So, she's divorced. Or maybe she never got married at all. Had it been an accident? God, wouldn't that be a kick in the teeth after having to raise her sisters too.

The sound of the bathroom door refocuses my thoughts, and I look up in time to see Gwen step out.

"Just let me grab my shoes and I'll be ready," she says as she walks around to the other side of the bed.

"Who's Tristan?"

As soon as the words are out of my mouth, she freezes. I'm not even sure she's breathing.

"You got a text, and I didn't mean to look but it was right there on the lock screen," I rush to explain, lest she think I went snooping through her shit at the first opportunity.

"No, no, that's okay," she says, her voice weak as she slowly turns to face me. A moment ago, her cheeks were bright and pink from the recent scrubbing, but now she's pale, the corners of her eyes pinched with stress or worry.

I close the distance between us and take her by the shoulders. "Hey, are you okay? I'm sorry, I didn't mean to upset you."

She laughs, but there's no humor in it and she won't meet my eyes when she says, "I'm fine but you should probably sit down. We need to talk."

"Okay, but—"

"Just sit down, Mac. Please." She brushes past me and picks up her phone, quickly scanning the text and then setting it aside again. Apparently, Tristan will have to wait until later for an answer on his sleepover.

When I've sat down, Gwen takes the seat across from me, chewing her lip. Her obvious anxiety is putting me on edge too, and I wish she'd just spit it out, whatever it is, so we can get this over with and go to dinner.

"God, I don't know how to tell you this," she murmurs, staring at the knot of my tie.

"Just tell me, Gwen. It can't be that bad."

She finally lifts her eyes to meet mine, her voice so quiet I have to strain to hear her. "Tristan is your son."

The whole world—or at least my whole world—shifts on its axis, and I blink at her, not sure I heard her correctly. I couldn't have. Did she just say I have a son? No, that's... I must have misheard her. That can't be right. "Can you say that again?" I force the words out around the rock that's taken up residence in my throat.

"Tristan is your son." She takes a deep breath, wringing her hands in her lap. "When I went home to take care of my sisters, I didn't know I was pregnant. And then I missed my period and I felt terrible but, you know, stress can do that, and God knows I was under unbelievable stress, so I really didn't worry about it. When I missed my period again in October, I still wasn't really worried, but I went to the doctor because I thought maybe she would give me some Xanax or something. But it wasn't stress, or at least not just stress. I was pregnant."

"You...you're sure he's..." I leave the question incomplete, because my heart is pounding in my chest and I'm sweating. Is this what a heart attack feels like? I think it is. Jesus, I might throw up. Of all the things I thought she might say to me tonight, even after I saw that text message, I never imagined it would be this, and now her words are replaying on a never-ending loop in my head.

Tristan is your son.

"Am I sure he's yours? Yes, there's no one else's he could be, and he looks just like you, but if you want a paternity test, you can have one. I don't want anything from you, though, if that's what you're worried about. I just...You had the right to know."

"I had the right to know as soon as you knew." I'm surprised by the anger in my voice, because all I feel on the inside is numb.

"You did, and I'm sorry. My only excuse is that my life was really fucked up, and I was overwhelmed and scared, and the thought of having to go back and tell you was just... I'm sorry, I couldn't do it. About the time Tris started to ask about his dad, I'd finally gotten my shit together and I thought I better try to find you. But all I knew was your name was Mac, and that isn't even really your name, so you can imagine how that went. Lindsey didn't have Jake's contact information anymore by then, and I don't know if you know this, but there are over thirteen hundred Jacob Browns in the United States, so that was pretty much another dead end."

The more she talks, her voice grows stronger, as if finally getting this off her chest after all these years is a relief, even if she is scared and uncertain of my reaction. But the more I listen, the farther away I feel and the more confused I become, because I have no idea what I'm supposed to do or say now. How am I supposed to react to this? Not just the fact that I apparently have a kid but that he's... Shit, I don't even know when his birthday is or what his middle name is or if he likes mushrooms on his pizza. Do I even care about those things? I'm not sure. Maybe. No, I think I do. I must, because I keep thinking weird things like that instead of listening to what Gwen is actually saying.

Does he like planes like I did when I was a kid? Or is he more into race cars or trains? Does he skateboard or play soccer? What video games does he play with his friends? And speaking of friends, who is Rob, and how much does Gwen know about his family? Fuck, what am I thinking? None of that is important right now.

Gwen has stopped talking. She's just sitting there, hands folded in her lap, staring at me with a hesitant, mildly impatient expression, like maybe she's been waiting awhile.

"I don't know...I don't know what to say," I finally manage, although I'm not entirely convinced it's really me talking. I mean, it's my voice, but I don't know where the words are coming from or what I might say next. "I never wanted kids. Never even considered it. I don't..."

"You don't have to do or say anything. We can pretend this never happened, if that's what you want. Now that I know how to find you, I'll have to tell Tris when he's older, because he has a right to know too. I can't promise he won't come looking for you then but...I don't know, I guess that's between you and Tris when and if that day ever comes." She sighs and slumps down in her seat, hugging herself, and suddenly all my dull, muddled emotions sharpen into focus and I'm angry. Really fucking angry.

"Is that what you expect? I'm the one who is supposed to disappear this time? Just walk away and pretend we never had this conversation? Why the fuck tell me at all if that's what you want?" I don't remember getting up, but I must have, because by the time I finish, I'm pacing in front of the window and Gwen is watching me with wary eyes.

"I don't expect anything, I told you that. If you don't want to be involved in Tristan's life, that's fine. We'll be just fine. If you do, that's fine too." She stops, dragging in several loud breaths in an attempt to regain some semblance of calm, and then says, "Tristan is the only thing that matters to me. All the choices here are yours, and I'll respect whatever decision you make as long as you don't hurt my son."

"Your son?" The words are out of my mouth, hot and angry, before I can stop them, and her cheeks color with anger too.

"Biology doesn't make a father, Mac."

If only she knew how fucking well I know that. "Oh, fuck off, Gwen. Could you give me more than ten fucking minutes to figure out how I feel about this?"

"You can have all the time you need." She's so damn calm, and that only makes me angrier until she says, "And you can be as angry at me as you like. I know this is all my fault and—"

"Don't do that," I interrupt more harshly than I intended, and she looks up at me, startled. "It's not all your fault. We never talked about birth control, not that I remember anyway. I just assumed you were on the pill or something and that was… It was a stupid, reckless assumption, and I should have known better. I *did* know better. You're the only one I've ever been so careless with. So no, it's not all your fault. Your fault you didn't tell me until now? Yeah, you own that. But you getting pregnant in the first place? That's on both of us."

Except, even as I'm telling her this, I'm having second thoughts. Not about my own responsibility—I'm pretty clear on that—but about her not telling me. Yes, that decision was all hers, but there are mitigating circumstances, aren't there? What would I have done in her shoes? I can't imagine being so young and becoming unexpectedly responsible for two younger siblings. And then, as if that weren't enough, to find out she was pregnant too? It must have felt like the literal end of the world to her. What did I ever do to make her think I might be there for her in that kind of situation?

Christ, I wouldn't even take her on a date.

It wasn't unreasonable for her to assume I wouldn't want anything to do with her or the baby. The worst part is she was probably right. It's damn likely the guy I was back then would have bolted and maybe…big fucking maybe…thrown some money at her on my way out the door. No, that isn't actually the worst part. The worst part is now I'm almost thirty-five, I'm supposed to be older and wiser, more responsible, and I'm still not sure I'm not going to bolt.

"Thanks, Mac. I appreciate that. Really."

Wait, what's she thanking me for? Oh, right, for not being such an enormous bag of dicks I'd blame her because I didn't use a condom. Pretty low bar, to be honest. Any guy who'd blame her for… Fuck, I'm getting distracted again. This doesn't matter now. It's not like we can change any of it. I need to figure out what I'm going to do, and that feels like an impossible task. I'm overwhelmed and confused, and I don't even know where to start.

Do I want to meet him? I'm not sure but I think maybe. Would it be a one-time thing, just to satisfy my curiosity? Or would I want some kind of relationship with him? How would that even work? What would it look like? With the campaign, I'm going to be gone most of the…

"How are you managing this job? With all the travel?" I ask abruptly.

"Willie and Livie. Between the two of them, and with a little help from one of our neighbors, they're able to watch him while I'm gone without too much trouble."

I may be clueless when it comes to kids, but I know adults and I know Gwen. The way she's chewing her bottom lip and refusing to make eye contact are indication enough there's something more she isn't saying.

She must miss him, and she probably feels guilty for leaving him. She might even be worried I'll be a judgy asshole about it. As if. Everything I know about kids and how to raise them can be summed up in three sentences.

Don't get them wet. No bright lights. Don't feed them after midnight.

Okay, four sentences.

Kids are basically gremlins.

The point is, I'm in no position to judge Gwen's parenting, and I hate thinking she might be worried about that. "You know, when he gets out of school for the summer, he could come with us." *What the fuck did I just say?*

Gwen is staring at me, wide-eyed and open-mouthed, as if she's asking herself the same question.

"I don't know why I said that," I gasp because now I'm almost certain I am, in fact, having chest pains.

"It's all right. This is a lot for you to process. I won't hold you to anything you say tonight."

Why is she letting me off the hook like that? Not just for the stupid thing I said but for all of it. Why isn't she sticking up for herself? Demanding back child support and future support too? She's not just entitled to it, she deserves it. How hard was her life, still practically a kid herself with nothing but a high school diploma, working and putting herself through school and raising three kids? I can't even fucking imagine.

And what was I doing while Gwen and her sisters and my kid were struggling to get by? Living on my trust fund, smoking dope and drinking beer and going to grad school, because I had nothing better to do. And when I did finally nut up and get a job, it was a cushy gig in the family business. But here she sits, telling me she doesn't expect anything of me. As if the way it all happened was the way it was supposed to happen.

"I don't know what I'm going to do, Gwen. I don't know if I want to meet him or... I don't know. I need to think. But I'll call my attorney tomorrow about getting child support sorted so—"

"I don't want your money." She's stormed across the room to stand in front of me. Arms crossed over her chest, she glares at me, eyes hard and jaw set. She's daring me to argue. Like I've done something wrong by offering to do what anyone would agree is my obligation. Anyone but Gwen, apparently.

"Gwen, I... What's happening right now?" I ask, blinking at her in confusion. Shouldn't she be glad, or at least relieved, I'm willing to do this without a fight? How could that have possibly provoked her? Maybe I'm not having a heart attack. Maybe it's a stroke or some kind of mental break. That would explain how lost I am.

"What's happening," Gwen snaps, her eyes flashing dangerously, "is you aren't listening to me. I told you I don't want anything from you, and I meant it."

"And I appreciate that, I really do," I say, forcing my voice to remain even. But despite my best efforts, I can hear the strain in my tone as I continue, "This isn't really about what you want though. You're entitled to child support and whatever else happens, whatever else I decide, that's my responsibility."

"We are not your obligation, and we do not need your help. Where is this even coming from? You've never cared about what you were supposed to do a day in your damn life, and now all of a sudden you want to do the right thing?" She's still angry but there's honest perplexity in her question too, and that stings.

It's true that I've made a habit of flouting expectations, but I never wanted to hurt the innocent bystanders in my life. I never pushed the limits quite that far, at least not on purpose. I'd obviously failed Gwen. "I'll admit I'm a selfish asshole, but whatever else you might think of me, I'm not such a douchebag I'd let a kid who didn't ask for any of this pay for our mistakes." It isn't a great response, I know that, but it's the best I can manage under the circumstances.

"Jesus Christ, you are an enormous jackass," Gwen shouts, stepping closer to me, and the tenuous hold I have on my own temper gives way.

"Now I'm a jackass because I want to help? What the fuck is wrong with you?" We're nose to nose, and I figure it's fifty-fifty I'll get slapped within the next ninety seconds.

"You're a jackass because my son is not a mistake." She's shaking with rage. Even our legendary fights when we were younger don't compare to her reaction now.

"That's not what I meant, and you fucking know it."

"I don't care what you meant. We don't need you or your money."

It feels as if I'm having an out-of-body experience, because there are huge chunks of tonight I doubt I'll remember tomorrow. One of those missing pieces is probably going to be how Gwen ended up pinned against the window with my tongue in her mouth. Because right now, actually in the moment, I have no fucking clue how we got here. One minute we're arguing, and the next we're tearing at each other's clothes like wild animals.

"This is a mistake," Gwen gasps between frantic, hungry kisses while her nimble fingers unknot my tie.

"It is. A big one," I agree. "Tell me to stop."

"Don't stop, Mac. Please don't fucking stop." She's finished with my tie and started on the buttons of my shirt, but I push her hands away and turn her toward the window, too impatient to wait. After more than a decade of missing her, of needing her, I can't wait.

Holding her against the window with one hand between her shoulders, I wrestle my wallet from my pocket with the other, retrieving the condom stashed there before dropping my wallet. I grew out of random hook-ups with random women a long time ago, but I've never gotten out of the habit of keeping a condom on hand, just in case.

"Hurry," she whines, pressing her forehead against the cool glass and arching her back, pushing her ass toward me.

Groaning around the corner of the cellophane packet I've pinched between my teeth, I jerk her skirt up around her waist. She's wearing lavender panties that match her blouse, because this is Gwen and of course she is. Fumbling, first with unzipping my pants and pushing my boxers down, and then with opening the condom, I contemplate whether I should help her out of her panties or just shove them out of my way. But my dick, already so hard it hurts, throbs as I roll the latex over it, and my mind is made up. She can take her panties off later.

"You sure you want this?" I ask, my voice hoarse as I nudge her panties aside and slap my dick against her dripping pussy. Even that brief contact sends a jolt of electricity racing down my spine, and I squeeze my eyes closed in anticipation.

"Jesus, yes, fuck me," she demands, her hips swaying in blatant invitation.

But after all these years, after longing for this moment for so long, I need to see her face. Despite the urgency and despite what she's just told me—or maybe because of it—I need to be closer to her.

Catching her around the waist, I haul her over to the bed and press her down on her back. Gwen spreads her thighs, moaning softly as I settle over her, the tip of my cock prodding at her entrance. She's so hot and wet and slick—as perfect as I remember—but it's her eyes, locked on mine, that makes my heart slam in my chest.

With a snap of my hips, I bury myself in her depths, and Gwen cries out, bucking up to meet me. I set a frantic, punishing pace, and I'm vaguely aware that later I'll probably feel bad for being so rough with her. Except she just bit my pec so hard I'm seeing stars and I have to grab a fistful of her hair to pry her off me.

"Watch it, or I'll bite back," I growl.

Gwen snarls and claws at my back, demanding more, harder, and I'm happy to comply. To focus on the longing and the lust instead of the anger and hurt and confusion still sparking between us. Because I've always been able to lose myself in Gwen and, even though she's the cause of my current distress, that hasn't changed. I've wanted this moment for too long and whatever might happen after, I'm going to bask in it for as long as I can.

CHAPTER 14

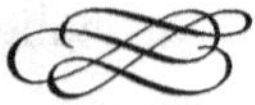

GWEN

My hotel room looks like the site of a frat party. Somewhere between round one and two we got our clothes off, leaving them scattered from one end of the room to the other. My bra is draped over the TV, all the blankets and most of the pillows are on the floor, and although I don't remember doing it, a lamp has been knocked off one of the nightstands. It was wild but now that it's over, we're both silently lying on the bed, carefully not touching, and it's…awkward.

Over the years, I've had a lot of time to think about how Mac might react when I finally told him about Tristan. I imagined dozens of scenarios, and yet not one of them ended with us in bed together. That was probably naïve of me and I'm not complaining, I'm really not. Mac has never disappointed in the sack. But it only makes this more complicated.

"Christ, I'm hungry."

"That's a good sign. It means you're probably not in shock." I lean over the edge of the bed and grab the sheet off the floor, pulling it back up to cover myself. I'm feeling too vulnerable and exposed to be lying around naked with him.

"Hold up," Mac orders, snaking an arm around me and pulling me back to him so we're more or less spooning. So awkward.

"I don't want to cuddle with—"

"What's this?" he interrupts, his fingers brushing over my ribcage.

"A tattoo," I answer, like I really think he's such an idiot he doesn't know that, despite the ink marking his own body—a snarling tiger on his left shoulder and a cobra winding its way around the opposite arm, from his forearm up over his bicep to his shoulder where its fangs are bared, midstrike. He already had them the first time I knew him and I want to crawl all over him, tracing every line and shadow with my tongue and fingers, relearning the tattoos and him. But now isn't the time for that. There probably won't ever be a time for that.

"On the left side of your ribcage. I feel like I remember telling you—"

"No. No, no," I insist, as much to him as to the creeping memories of a long-ago summer afternoon.

"Think you'd ever get a tattoo?"

"I can't imagine ever liking something so much I'd put it on my body forever."

"Never say never, baby."

"Okay, so if I get one, where should I put it?"

Mac hummed thoughtfully, his eyes sweeping over the length of my naked body. "Right here," he said, his fingertips dancing across my ribs on my left side.

"Why there?" I asked, nuzzling into his neck, enjoying the lazy intimacy of the moment.

"Because if something was ever important enough to you to wear it forever, it would be important enough you'd want it near your heart, and you aren't the kind of girl who gets a tit tattoo." I could hear the teasing smile in his voice.

"What kind of tattoo would it be then?" I whispered.

"Knowing you, your dog's paw print or some other equally sappy shit."

"I've never even had a dog." I laughed and raised up to look at him.

"You will. You'll have two-point-five kids and a white picket fence and a dog who shits in your husband's shoe. The poor bastard won't even care, because he loves you and you love the damn dog, and that'll be good enough for him." His voice was lighthearted, playful even, but there was an uneasy undercurrent lurking in it too.

"That's quite an imagination you have there. What about you? Will you someday have a dog that shits in your shoe?" As soon as the words were out of my mouth, I wished I hadn't asked and I held my breath waiting for his answer, trying to convince myself it didn't matter what he said.

"Nah, I hate dogs."

"What kind of monster hates dogs?" I gasped in mock outrage, trying to cover my disappointment. Disappointment I had no right to feel, because he'd always been clear with me about what this was.

"Gwen?"

"Hmm?"

"Shut up." Mac kissed me, softening what might otherwise have been a harsh command. And I shut up, because then he lifted me and adjusted our position until, when he brought me back down on top of him, his cock filled me and slow, lazy sex, the kind scorching summer days were made for, followed.

How much of that day does he remember? Can he still feel the sultry breeze that drifted through his open apartment windows, prickling our skin as we laid on his couch? Does he still hear the baseball game on TV and the squeals of the neighborhood children outside that provided the background noise for our languid teasing and talking? Has he thought about it at all between that day and this one? Or is he only thinking of it now because my tattoo prompted his memory?

With a hard swallow, I force myself to focus on the present and the still-smug smile curling Mac's lips.

"You don't get to say I told you so. I put it there because you gave me the idea. Who knows where I might have put it if you hadn't?" It's hard not to smile, because this feels so damn familiar, and his light caresses almost tickle as he bends closer, studying the cartoon tiger cub that's playfully rolling over my ribs.

"June 2, 2009." He reads the date under the tiger, his finger tracing over it, then glances up at me, one brow raised in question. "His birthday?"

All I can do is nod, because the moment suddenly feels charged with…something, I'm not sure what. Maybe just charged with uncertainty. Mac must feel it too, whatever it is, because he stares at me, holding my gaze and I want to look away, but I can't. My breath hitches and panic grips my heart because I can feel words forming in my throat, threatening to break free, words I can't ever say out loud. Stupid, foolish words like *please want us*.

Finally, Mac clears his throat and rolls away from me, throwing his legs over the edge of the bed. His voice is gruff when he says, "I'm going to order room service. That okay with you?"

"Sure," I say, forcing a smile.

He orders a pizza, and I'm surprised and touched that he remembers to order half with mushrooms for me. "Does Tristan like mushrooms on his pizza?" Mac asks as soon as he's hung up.

"No," I complain. "And he won't even go halvsies with me. He claims that even the tiniest speck of mushroom contaminates the whole pizza."

"It does," Mac says with a grin.

"But you've always split with me." No one would accuse Mac of being reasonable very often, but at least when compared to a ten-year-old he is.

"I did. And someday he will too. Well, maybe not with you. But give him a few years, and the right motivation and he'll change his tune," Mac explains as he wanders around the room picking up his things.

"I can't believe you just said that. I can't even think about that." And then, when he's lifting up the blankets and shaking them, I add, "Are you looking for something?"

"Found them," Mac exclaims, retrieving his black boxer briefs from a tangle of sheets. After putting them on, he comes back around the bed to sit again, leaning against the headboard.

"You're not going to put your pants on?"

He answers my question with a frown and a question of his own. "Do you want me to put my pants on?"

"Well, I mean, I don't care, but someone has to answer the door for room service and it's not going to be me. The whole boxer-brief thing is...uh..." I pause long enough to wave a hand in the general direction of his dick. "It's a flattering look for you, but I'm not sure room service will appreciate it."

He grins but doesn't argue and once he's found his pants and put them on, he sits down again. We wait in silence for the food, neither of us sure what to say. But he's antsy, fidgeting with his phone and generally looking restless. Maybe a little small talk would help.

"So, do you and Jake still keep in touch?"

Mac just nods. Apparently, he isn't going to make this easy for me.

"How is he?"

"Great. Married, lives in Seattle, running a venture capitalist firm. Three kids, two girls and a boy. They're good." It's as if he is giving me a professional baseball player's stats. Games played, 32. Earned Run Average, 6.14. Saves, zero. I'm about to give up on conversation when he asks, "Lindsey?"

"She's good. She's a best-selling author with nine published books."

"What kind of books?" He seems surprised and maybe a little interested, and I get excited in anticipation of his expression when I drop this bomb.

"Self-help books."

Mac does not disappoint. His expression morphs from surprise to disbelief then horror before he says, "You're fucking with me, right?"

"I am not fucking with you. I don't get it either, but she sleeps on an enormous pile of money every night, because an awful lot of people like her advice."

We spend the rest of our time waiting for room service catching up on mutual friends from our shared past. With the ice finally broken, the conversation is smooth, and it's easy to forget, for a few minutes anyway, everything else that's happened tonight. Once the pizza arrives, we eat our first piece in more or less comfortable silence.

"Will you tell me about him?" Mac asks when he's reaching for his second slice.

"Sure. Would you like to see pictures?" I offer as I reach for my phone.

"I...uh..." Mac is apparently rendered speechless, pizza halfway to his mouth, and he blinks at me like it never occurred to him I might have pictures. Or maybe like he doesn't even know what pictures are.

Dammit, I've spooked him. This feels a little like trying to tame a wild animal. Maybe I should read one of those books about the cowboys who catch and break mustangs. It could help. "It's okay, you don't have to," I rush to reassure him, but he's shaking his head.

"No, I want to... I just, I mean..." He stops and takes a deep breath before trying again. "Yeah, I'd like to see pictures."

Scooting closer to him so I can hold my phone in front of us both, I open my messages first, scrolling through Livie's until I come to the picture she sent me this afternoon. Tristan is looking straight at the camera, smiling wide, showing off his newly missing tooth. "He lost a tooth today," I explain, pointing to the gap as if Mac might miss it.

"Um." He swallows so hard I can hear it.

"You okay?" I ask softly. I want to look at him, to see his expression, but I don't dare. I'm a coward, too scared of what I might find if I do.

"Yeah, sorry, it's just... You said there was a resemblance, but I didn't expect..."

"It to be like looking in a mirror?"

He nods and I can't help it; I risk a little sideways peek at him. He's staring at the screen, unblinking and a little pale, as he rubs his thumb across his lip. The box of pizza is forgotten on the bed next to him.

"Do you want to see some others?"

Another nod.

With as overwhelmed as I'm feeling, it's hard to imagine how much worse it must be for Mac. Or at least that's what I tell myself, because his shell-shock is both understandable and driving my own anxiety through the stratosphere. Swiping through to my cloud storage, I open the folder labeled Tristan. Pressing the phone into Mac's palm with my shaking hand, I say, "Pretty much his whole life is in this folder. Why don't you look around a little while I tell you about him?"

"Sure, thanks."

"I'm not sure where to start. Is there anything specific you want to know, or should I just start rambling?"

Mac pauses in swiping through photos to study a picture of Tris over Christmas break at the Air and Space Museum. "He likes planes?"

"He does. He's never been on one, and he's constantly harassing me to take him. He wants to fly around the country and go to all the baseball stadiums."

A small smile teases at the corners of Mac's mouth, and he glances up long enough to ask, "Who's his favorite team?"

"The Detroit Tigers, of course."

That's an acceptable answer, because Mac nods and turns back to my phone. "What's his full name?"

"Oh, funny you should ask that, William." Using Mac's actual first name was not apparently as clever as I thought it was, because he narrows his eyes at me. I sigh and shrug. "I think I told you Willa's named after my dad. He was a William too. And…so is Tris. William Tristan Pierce. But it was too confusing with Willa, so he's always been Tristan. Kind of cool coincidence, right?"

"No," Mac says flatly. "I'm glad he's named after your dad, that the name means something good to the two of you. It doesn't to me."

"Oh, I'm sorry, I didn't—"

"No, it's fine. You didn't know."

Since Mac doesn't say anything else, instead quietly swiping through photos, I fill the gap in conversation with whatever little facts about Tristan come to mind. "His favorite color is green, very specifically grass-green, because summer is naturally his favorite time of year. His favorite foods are tacos and pizza. He and Olivia play way too much Minecraft, and he likes to hide Willa's things just to be a pain in her ass. He's been begging for his own phone for ages now but I'm not ready for that yet, so I keep telling him no. Not sure how much longer I'm going to be able to hold out on that."

When I pause to take a breath, I notice Mac is staring intently at my phone, so I lean over to peek at the screen. "Oh, that's his first picture."

I have such a mix of emotions looking at it, same as I did when it was taken. I'm in the hospital bed holding an hours-old Tristan in my arms. Olivia is lying on the bed next to me, utterly enamored with the baby, and Willa is standing next to us, beaming with her own excitement. But the expression on my face...such a mix of love and sheer terror and happiness. It was the most confusing moment of my life and it's almost like being right back there again every time I see it.

"You seem..."

"What?" Most people who've seen the picture comment on how happy I look with my new baby. Maybe that is how it appears to them, or maybe they only see what they want to see. Some of them probably recognize the truth, but they're too polite to mention it. Whatever the case, I want to know what Mac sees.

"I've never seen someone so..."

"Happified?" I suggest when he seems to struggle for the right word.

"What?" Mac's head jerks up and he stares at me in confusion.

"Olivia says that's my happified look. Half happy, half petrified," I explain.

"Oh, yeah, that's a pretty good word for it." Mac chuckles and turns back to the phone. His tone is painfully casual when he goes on. "Who was with you when you had him?"

"I was alone." Closing my eyes, I take a deep breath to steady myself before I go on, because I hate that word. Alone. For years, I felt so alone. Sometimes I still do. When I open my eyes, he's watching me, and I have to resist the urge to shut them again, to hide. "I was at work, waiting tables at a little Coney Island, when I went into labor. My boss gave me a ride to the hospital. That was about ten on Monday night and Tris wasn't born until four thirty Tuesday afternoon. Fortunately, Willa and Olivia's sitter was kind of a friend, I guess, and she kept them until I got out of the hospital. And she was nice enough to bring them up to visit a few hours after he was born."

"You shouldn't have had to go through that alone." His expression is so soft and earnest I want to hug him, but I hug myself instead.

"Thanks, but...I've had to do a lot of things alone, and as hard and scary as it was sometimes, I did it and now I have a happy and healthy son and two happy and healthy sisters and...and, you know, I'm proud of that. It was worth every happifying moment, because the three of them are my world. And I guess..." I have to take a second to swallow the lump forming in my throat before I can finish. "I want you to know, I meant what I said before. Tristan wasn't a mistake. No matter how much harder having a baby made things, I've never regretted having him. I guess maybe I should—none of this has been fair to you —but I don't. He's the best thing that's ever happened to me, and I'll always be thankful to you for giving me that."

There's another charged moment where we just stare at each other. I wish he'd take me in his arms and hold me and tell me everything will be okay. Partly because I've always wanted someone to share my burdens with, but mostly just because it's Mac and I've wanted him for as long as I can remember. And for one brief second I think he might actually reach for me, but he doesn't. Eventually he swallows hard and turns back to my phone, the moment broken as he swipes to the next picture of our son.

CHAPTER 15

MAC

I MEET Jake at a little hole in the wall bar down the street from the resort where Kim's fundraiser is being held tonight. I've been looking forward to seeing him ever since Cece told me he'd be in Napa on business at the same time we'd be passing through with the campaign. Now, with my whole life imploding, it feels like fate.

Jake is attending the fundraiser in a few hours, but I figured it would be best to brief him on my latest news ahead of time, so I asked him to meet me here first. It's a working-class bar and we're drawing a little attention in our tuxes, but we aren't apt to run into anyone else we know, and that's the important thing.

I've just finished giving Jake the rundown on the night before and he's sitting across from me, his expression nothing short of dumb-struck. It wouldn't be that unusual. Jake often thinks I've done some-thing stupid, but the long stretch of silence is getting uncomfortable.

"So?" I prod.

"She told you that you have a kid. Then you had sex. Then you had pizza and looked at pictures of the kid. And then you snuck out while she was sleeping and have avoided her all day." Jake has boiled the situation down to its most basic elements. I shouldn't have told him about the sex, though. He'd probably be less incredulous if I'd left that detail out.

"Yes, but I left a note, and I admit the sex was stupid but in my defense—"

"It was stupid, but I would expect nothing less from the two of you." Jake laughs and takes a sip of his whisky before asking, "So, how are you feeling about all this?"

"Which part?"

"Start with the kid." Jake gives me a get-on-with-it hand wave, as if I'm intentionally dragging my feet. Maybe I am.

"How am I supposed to feel about it? I've never wanted kids, and then all of a sudden I find out I've already got one and he's almost eleven years old? I don't know how to process that."

Jake opens his mouth, hesitates, then closes it again. Finally, with a sigh and a reluctant expression, he asks, "Are you sure he's yours?"

"She offered me a paternity test, but yeah, I'm sure." I grab my phone off the bar and navigate to the pictures I texted myself from Gwen's phone last night. Enlarging the gap-toothed picture of Tristan that her sister took yesterday, I tilt the phone toward Jake.

"Oh, that's uncanny." He glances up at me and then back to the picture. "He's a cute kid. What did you say his name is?"

"Tristan." I swipe through to the next picture.

Before either of us can say anything else, my phone buzzes with an incoming text from Gwen. There's no message, just a video, Tristan's smiling face staring out at me from the screen, and I have to close my eyes for a second to steady myself. It's the strangest thing, the way my heart does all kinds of weird flip-floppy things every time I look at his picture, something I've spent an unfathomable amount of time doing today.

When I open my eyes again, I press play and tilt the phone so Jake can watch too. He leans closer as the video starts.

"Hi, Mom! I hope you're having fun on your trip. I tripped and fell during gym class today, and Mr. Montgomery had to call Aunt Willie to

come get me. But I'm okay. Dr. Neuhaus was with her, and she said I'm fine and it's just a scraped knee. Did you know Dr. Neuhaus is Aunt Willie's girlfriend?"

There's another voice in the background, presumably Willa's, insisting Dr. Neuhaus is definitely not her girlfriend. Tristan ignores her, giving the camera a devilish grin.

"She for sure is, Mom! I saw them kiss. Anyway, thanks for letting me go to Rob's this weekend. His mom is going to make peanut butter cookies and let us play Minecraft, and I'm so excited. Her cookies are even better than yours. Anyway, Aunt Willie says you have a work thing tonight, so you won't be able to call at bedtime, but that's okay, I promise I'll brush my teeth just as good as I do when you're watching. I'll talk to you tomorrow." There's a slight pause, Tristan's eyes darting side to side before he leans closer to the camera, ending with a whispered, *"I love you, Mom."*

It's the first time I've heard his voice and I immediately play it through twice more, chuckling at his sing-song tone when he asks if Gwen knew Dr. Neuhaus was Willa's girlfriend. Before I can stop myself, I've texted Gwen.

Mac: *Thx. Did he really see them kiss?*

Gwen: *Yup, but Willie is stridently insisting they are only friends.*

Mac: *What's the story with this Rob kid? And what the fuck is his mom putting in those cookies?*

"Pretty sure she isn't giving ten-year-olds edibles, man," Jake offers, laughing as he reads over my shoulder.

"You never know." Tapping my phone against the bar, I wait for Gwen's response.

"So," Jake draws the word out and gestures to my phone, "you're not sure what you want to do, huh?"

"There's a big difference between being concerned about some-one's general welfare and being willing and able to commit to being a parent for the rest of your damn life," I point out, because it's a very clear distinction to me. I can't deny I care about the kid and I haven't even met him. But that doesn't mean I'm capable of being the dad he deserves.

"I know, I just think maybe you're overthinking this. I get it—it's a huge, life altering decision, but it's still simpler than you're making it." Jake slaps me on the back before adding, "But you've got to watch that shit. She's been raising him alone for ten years and he seems like a happy, well-adjusted kid. If she thinks you're second-guessing her all the time she's going to get pissed off, and I don't really think she'd be out of line."

Just then, my phone vibrates with Gwen's answering text.

Gwen: *They're in the same class. Both parents are teachers. Only child. They live a few blocks from us so the kids can get together pretty often. Nice family, I like them. But her cookies are better than mine and the bitch won't share the recipe.*

"Definitely not pissed," I say after I've read the text.

"She's humoring you. She doesn't want to scare you off. Just...be careful."

"Yeah, sure."

"So, I have a question."

"Lay it on me."

"Are you angry with her?"

"No. It's as much my fault she got pregnant as it is hers," I answer, even though I know that's not what he's asking.

"I mean for not telling you before," Jake clarifies, refusing to let me dodge the conversation. It's clear from the bite in his tone that he's angry on my behalf, even if I'm not.

"Not really," I admit with a shrug. It's hard to own up to my own failings, but Jake's always seen me clearly, so there's no point in obfuscating. "If she'd told me back then, I probably...well, I don't know what I would have done, but whatever it was probably would have only made the situation worse. Honestly, I'm kind of pissed she told me now."

"You'd have rather never known you had a kid?" He gapes at me in disbelief.

"Sure. I never wanted one, and she was pretty damn clear they don't need me, so what's the point? It's not like she and I can pick up where we left off back in college." It's selfish of me to even think it, let alone say it, but it's the truth. Ever since her interview, I've been dithering about what to do, but I've never stopped wanting her.

"Because you have a kid together?"

I nod. Isn't that what I just said?

"When you first saw that text last night, what did you think?" Jake looks as if this is a very important question and I don't see how that's the case, but I try to remember those moments before Gwen came out of the bathroom.

"I thought a lot of things, but I guess I assumed she'd probably been married and divorced and had a kid in the process."

"And that didn't bother you?"

"No, why would it?" I scoff. "It's been a dozen years. It's not like I thought she was celibate all that time. I sure as hell wasn't."

"So, you'd have still pursued her?" Jake is on the edge of his seat, as if he's barely restraining himself from grabbing me and shaking me.

"Yeah." What the hell is he getting at?

"Jesus, you are so damn dense." Jake takes a deep breath and pins me to my barstool with a stare so serious it's out of character for him. "You were willing to be with her when you thought she had someone else's kid, but the minute you knew it's your kid, you're not sure? That's fucked up. Like, I've heard a lot of assholes say they don't want to be involved with a woman who has some other dude's kids, but not you. No, you have to find a new, even stupider way to be an asshole."

"You know as well as I do, I'm not dad material. If it was some other guy's kid, it wouldn't really impact me. I wasn't thinking about a relationship, just, you know, like it used to be with me and her. But since it is my kid, Gwen's not going to fuck me in secret and keep lying to Tristan about not knowing where his dad is, you know?" I shrug as if that explains everything and I sort of feel like it does.

"Like it used to be with you and her." He picks that phrase out and gives me an incredulous look. "That was a relationship. I know you two are both so allergic to that word it would probably take decades of therapy to unravel, but it was still a relationship."

"Whatever." I wave a hand dismissively because even if he's right, and he isn't, it doesn't really matter. "If the kid was someone else's he'd already have a dad, so even if I were in a relationship with his mother, it wouldn't be the same. Her ex would do all the dad stuff, and I'd just be the cool guy who bought him ice cream sometimes or whatever."

"Maybe. Or maybe the ex would have been a deadbeat dad and the kid would have been wanting a lot more than ice cream from you. And newsflash, Mac, you'll be the deadbeat if you walk away from Tristan. The kid deserves his dad. If that's not you, all you'll ever be to him is the man who didn't want him. Maybe you can live with that, I don't know, but if you can, you're not the man I thought you were."

My tumbler of whisky hits the wooden bar top hard, spilling the sticky liquid all over my hand. Jake is glaring at me, so angry he'd be taking a swing at me if we were ten years younger. We've known each other a long time, and the fundamental problem of our friendship has never changed. He's always thought I'm a better man than I really am. "Maybe it's not that I won't do what I ought to do. Maybe it's that I can't," I mumble, my shoulders slumped.

"At one time or another, we've all thought we couldn't do it, but then you just...you just do it." Jake signals for the bartender to refill our drinks. When he speaks again, the fight has gone out of his voice. He sounds tired. "I was fucking terrified when Heidi told me she was pregnant with Meredith. We planned her, we'd been trying, and I was really excited about it. But as soon as I saw that plus sign, I was pants-shittingly terrified. And I was no less terrified with Autumn and Levi. And now that they're all here, I live in a constant state of fear because these tiny little people Heidi and I made, and I love more than anything else, are out there in a world I can't control. Anything could happen. Every single day of being a parent is scary, man. But the longer you do it, you get better at ignoring it." He pauses and chuckles before saying, "Or you get so used to living in a constant state of panic you forget what it was like before."

"Sounds lovely." I take another sip of my drink before asking, "So why do you keep having more if it's so fucking awful?"

"Because those three kids are the best thing I've ever done. Because if I hadn't done it, Meredith wouldn't have kissed me on the nose and told me to hurry home when I left on this trip. And when I threw my back out last year, Autumn wouldn't have been there with her blankies and her stuffies, sleeping next to me on the floor every damn night for a week. And Levi…well, okay, let's be honest, Levi mostly just shits himself and cries a lot right now, but on the bright side, you get to skip that part." He's quiet for a moment before adding, "All I'm trying to say is as bad as the bad parts are, the good parts are so much better, it is unquestionably worth it. And none of us know what we're doing, but we muddle through and figure it out. Think about it, man. Do you think Gwen knew what she was doing when she had him? Don't you think she was scared? Christ, she was just a baby herself, and she had two sisters to take care of too. But she buckled down and she did it, and I'd bet my last dollar she wouldn't change it for anything now."

This pep talk, if that's what it's meant to be, isn't making me feel better. If anything, it's making me feel worse, because Jake's right. Gwen had done it, and she'd said herself she didn't regret it. But I just don't know if I can, and my stomach turns at the realization.

I'm a goddamn coward.

"I'll grant you, you've gotten thrown in at the deep end. We planned our kids, and we had months to read all the books and scour the internet and get used to the idea. You don't get any of that. But you've missed the sleepless nights and diapers and godforsaken toddler years so…" Jake trails off with a shrug and it seems like he thinks that might be an even trade. "Take a little time to mull it over. No one can begrudge you that with as sudden as this is. But you'll get there. I'm sure of it."

All I can do is nod and wish I shared his certainty.

CHAPTER 16

GWEN

"I SAW a brochure for hot air balloon rides over Napa Valley. That could be fun," Cece suggests, winding a russet curl of hair around one manicured finger. She's always so perfectly put together and I have no idea where she finds the time, since she's usually running around taking care of the rest of us.

We're sitting at our table discussing what we should do with our free afternoon tomorrow while Alex schmoozes with donors nearby. So far, there's been no sign of Mac or Jake. They aren't late yet, but it's getting close.

Other than our brief text exchange, I haven't spoken to Mac since last night. After I accidentally fell asleep, I wasn't at all surprised to find him gone when I woke up. Honestly, I was sort of relieved. It's hard to guess how he might be feeling in the light of day, and I want to give him the space he needs to sort himself out.

"Hard pass, unless you want to hold my hair while I puke over the side." I'm not generally afraid of heights, but a hot air balloon seems ill-advised. It would be far too easy to tumble out of the basket and plummet to my death.

"What about a wine tour? Maybe we can find a reasonably priced limo to cart us around, so we don't have to worry about driving." Cece is tapping her lip thoughtfully when her expression brightens and she says, "There's the second- and third best-looking men in the room. Don't ask me which is which—I'll never tell."

I follow her gaze to find Mac and Jake standing behind me, hands in their pockets and smiles on their faces. They've been drinking already. Maybe not to the point of being drunk, but their cheeks are flushed and their eyes are gleaming. No one else would notice, but I spent far too much time with them in varying states of intoxication when we are all younger not to recognize it now.

"That means I'm second. She just won't say it because she's afraid you'll fire her." Jake smirks at Mac before turning to me. "Gwen, it's good to see you again. You look well."

"Thanks, Jake. So do you." To be honest, he hasn't changed much over the years. He still wears his black hair slicked back, and his smile is as full and boyish as it ever was, overtaking his whole face and accentuating his dimples. Only his green eyes seem to have aged, his gaze tired despite his cheer.

Standing and extending one hand to shake, I'm surprised when he pulls me into a hug. Jake and I didn't dislike each other, exactly, but it was no secret he thought Mac and I were bad together. I would have described him back then as friendly but wary. After I disappeared? Well, it seemed safe to assume my stock was at an all-time low with Jake Brown, so I never would have expected this kind of warm welcome. And now, when I can only assume Mac has told him about Tris? I can't imagine why he's being so nice to me.

"You know Jake too?" Cece asks as Jake and I separate, and Mac gives me an aloof nod in greeting.

"Wait a second," I say, holding up one hand. "Before we get to that, if they are the second and third hottest men in the room, who is first?"

"Alex," Mac and Jake say in unison and Cece's cheeks bloom such a deep shade of crimson they nearly match the Malbec in her glass.

"What? How did I not know this?" I ask, giving Cece an accusatory glare and I resuming my seat.

"There's nothing to know." Cece frantically scans the room. I assume she wants to make sure Alex isn't near enough to overhear this conversation, because she relaxes when she spots him by the bar.

Jake ignores her and rocks back on his heels, laughing. "She's had a crush on Alex for years. You'd have figured it out on your own eventually, Gwen. Cece doesn't do subtle. Although, Alex seems to be entirely unaware of the situation."

"How about instead of talking about that, someone finally tells me how you all know each other?" Cece's trying to change the subject, and Mac helps her.

"Jake dated Gwen's best friend the summer before Jake and I started grad school." It's not untrue, but it's not even close to the whole truth either. Especially with what he now knows, but I can't blame him for not being ready to share that just yet.

"So, tell me everything that's going on in D.C. How's your mother?" Jake says to Cece, smoothly guiding the conversation in a new direction.

As Jake and Cece fall into easy conversation, Mac wanders away without excusing himself. He's easy enough to find though. He didn't get far before he was swept into a conversation with a group of wealthy donors. If nothing else, Mac is good at his job, charming them with easy smiles and friendly banter.

How does he do that? He was so tense and distant just moments ago, but you'd never guess it now. He wasn't like that when we were younger. Back then, if we were fighting, everyone knew it, which only makes his smooth transition to charming campaign aide all the more unsettling. Has he matured and gotten better at managing his emotions? Or is it that easy for him to put Tristan and I out of his mind?

When it's time for dinner, Mac returns to the table. Throughout the meal and the speeches that follow, he is mostly quiet, and as soon as the organized events are over and the string quartet has begun to play, Mac leaves again, resuming his circuit of the room, shaking hands and kissing billionaire ass in furtherance of Kim's campaign.

I'm still sitting at the table, listening to Alex and Jake reminisce about their youth, when Kim approaches with a man in tow. I recognize him immediately—almost anyone would. Brandon Bennett is the American Dream come to life. When he was fourteen, he created his first app on the family computer in his parent's basement in Pittsburgh. By the time he was seventeen, he was a millionaire. Now at thirty-two, he's a billionaire and owns one of the largest tech and media corporations in the world.

"There you are, Gwen. I have someone I'd like to introduce you to," Kim says with a cheerful smile. She has every right to be cheerful tonight; from what I can tell, this fundraiser is going very, very well but I don't know why she wants to introduce me to anyone, let alone Brandon Bennett. "Gwen, this is Brandon Bennett. Brandon, Gwen is responsible for the changes to my social media presence you've been admiring." Then with an apologetic smile, she sighs and adds, "I'm sure you two can manage without me. I still have a lot of hands to shake before the night is through."

"Mr. Bennett," I murmur, a little star struck, as Kim departs and we shake hands.

"Please, call me Brandon." He squeezes my hand before releasing it. "The shift in the direction of Kim's social media was immediately recognizable when you joined her team. You're doing impressive work."

"It's nothing anyone else wouldn't have done." I hope he doesn't notice the blush beginning to warm my cheeks.

Kim and Mac have told me I'm doing a great job, but that isn't the same. Kim is the candidate, and Mac is my boss. They have a vested interest in the quality of my work. This is different, both because Brandon has no reason to notice my work at all and because he's Brandon. Fucking. Bennett.

"It is, or someone would have already been doing it. I told her if I weren't so committed to her success, I'd steal you away."

"Are you planning to run for office then?" I ask, desperately trying to maintain a calm appearance. It's not that he's attractive, although he is, with his sandy hair and hazel eyes. But Kim is the closest I've ever come to meeting a celebrity, and his level of fame makes her look like a nobody. It's intimidating as hell, and I have to discreetly wipe my sweaty palms on my skirt. Well, I hope it was discreet anyway.

"No, but you may have noticed, there's very much an eat-the-rich sentiment out there these days." He gestures as if indicating the world outside the hotel ballroom. "Not wanting to be eaten, I'll take all the help I can get."

"And yet you support a candidate who would like to make you considerably less rich," I point out with a wry smile, because while Kim isn't promising to resurrect the guillotine, she's very upfront about her desire to aggressively tax people like Brandon.

"That I don't mind. I have more than I can spend in a hundred lifetimes anyway. But I would prefer to keep my head when the revolution comes." He grins and I can't help it, I giggle. I fucking giggle.

What is happening right now?

"I doubt you need to worry about that. You aren't like most of these people," I say, glancing around the room at all the other wealthy guests. Most of them are old money and while Brandon Bennett is definitely one of the elite now, he didn't start out that way.

"Come dance with me then, and you can tell me what I am like," he says, offering me his hand.

"Oh, you're one of those then? You like to listen to other people tell you how great you are?" I tease and he leads me onto the dance floor.

"I admit it, my ego is insufferable. I even irritate myself sometimes."

He's a good dancer and a fun, witty companion, but even as he twirls me around the floor, making me laugh so hard my eyes water, I can't help scanning the crowd for Mac and, when I don't find him, wondering where he went.

The band breaks for a few minutes and Brandon reluctantly excuses himself, saying there are others he needs to speak with and promising we'll meet again. I'm still watching him stride away when Mac startles me, his voice low and close to my ear.

"Have a good time dancing with Bennett?"

"I did." I don't look over my shoulder at him.

"Give me your spare room key," Mac demands without acknowledging my response.

"Why?" As if I don't know. As if my heart isn't already beating wildly in my chest at the mere possibility. Brandon Bennett might be charming and funny and kind, but he doesn't make me feel like this. No one ever has, except Mac.

"You know why."

"You're drunk," I insist, although I'm not certain it's true.

"Not as drunk as I'd like to be." Mac lowers his voice before adding, "I'm sorry I've been avoiding you today, but I'm not sure I can be who you want me to be."

Unsteady, I sway a little on my feet, a knot forming in my throat. I always knew that this was the most likely outcome of telling him about Tristan, but hearing it out loud—the worry and doubt and anxiety in his voice—it's too much. Nothing could have prepared me for the grief I feel in this moment. "I already told you, I don't want anything." It was a lie the first time I said it, and it's still a lie. I don't want his money, that's true. But I do want him, and I'm disappointed in myself for my inability to leave our past where it belongs. Behind us.

"I want you," Mac says, and it's such a close echo of my thoughts I shiver.

"I know," I say, turning to face him before adding, "but the stakes are higher for me now. I have other priorities and I can't..."

"I know, I get it," Mac says, apparently having understood even though I couldn't find the right words to voice my thoughts. It's always felt like that between us, understanding and acceptance without words. When we were young, the way he seemed to get me without my having to explain made me feel closer to him. Now, it just makes the gulf growing between us seem wider.

"So, that's it then? You've made up your mind?" I know this isn't the time or place to ask that kind of question, but there was a finality to his tone I can't ignore.

Mac dips his head and rubs his lip, seeming to consider that for a long moment. When he lifts his head, he shrugs, his eyes dark as he says, "I don't know. I'm sorry."

And then he walks away as if he hasn't just shattered my heart into a million pieces, because that "I don't know" feels an awful lot like a "yes."

<h1 style="text-align:center">CHAPTER 17</h1>

MAC

"Don't be afraid to go hard on that point, Kim. It's one of your strongest," Brian interrupts when she has given another anemic response.

The mock debate, with various campaign staff, party operatives, and friends playing the parts of her competitors, has been going on for more than two hours. Progress is slow, and Kim's growing frustration is obvious.

My role in today's activities—faux debate moderator—is the perfect distraction for me. Or it should be, but for the first time in years, work isn't enough. It isn't every day you find out you have a half-grown kid.

"Can we take a break?" Kim asks with a pinched frown.

"Sure thing," Brian answers, his voice soothing. "Just relax. We have all day."

"And all night," someone else calls more grimly from the back of the room. I don't turn around to see who it was; Brian is already glaring in that direction as he shepherds the crowd out of the room. He'll handle it.

"What the hell is wrong with me?" Kim mutters, collapsing into the chair next to me.

"Nothing. This shit is hard. If it wasn't, everyone would do it."

She nods but says nothing. She's staring at her hands folded in her lap, her brow creased. It's tempting to give her a pep talk or otherwise fill the silence that's fallen between us. Not just because supporting her is my job but because I'm desperate for distraction too. But her life is in such a constant state of chaos and upheaval these days—there's always something to do, some speech to give or donor to schmooze, and a few quiet moments to center herself is probably more useful than anything I might say.

"Oh," Kim gasps, her eyes lighting up with mischief when she finally speaks. "I almost forgot to tell you. Brandon Bennett is really impressed with Gwen's work for the campaign."

"She's doing a great job," I agree in a tone that's admittedly terser than I'd like. Work-related or not, Gwen is the last thing I want to talk about right now. And especially not in relation to Brandon Bennett. When she danced with him, I had to step outside under the pretense of having a cigar with one of the guests. I don't even like cigars, but that was better than watching her blush like a schoolgirl with her first crush when Bennett smiled at her.

"My point is he will try to poach her when the campaign is over. If you want her to stay at The MacKenzie Agency, keep that in mind."

Avoiding Kim's gaze, I shift in my chair, uncomfortable with the direction of my own thoughts. Shuffling Gwen off to work for Bennett would solve a whole lot of my problems. Well, maybe not solve, exactly, but Bennett is based on the west coast and by all accounts, he's a generous employer. It would be a good gig for Gwen, and having her three thousand miles away, on the other side of the country, might be for the best. Especially if I decide I can't be Tristan's dad.

"Why are you scowling?"

"Forget it. We should be talking about the debate tomorrow," I deflect, attempting to refocus the conversation on work. Kim has enough to worry about right now without me dumping my shit in her lap too.

She grimaces, shaking her head. "I need to get out of my head a little and think about something else for a few minutes, and you've been an edgy mess the last couple of days. So do us both a favor. Tell me what's got you so tied up, and please, for the love of God, distract me. Talk to me about something that isn't the election."

I can understand where she's coming from. Most conversations, even with those close to her, tend to center on the campaign these days. Policy, strategy, the other candidates, the next rally or speech or debate. It's all vital to her success, and it's all anyone seems to talk about anymore. It's easy to see how exhausting that might be. And, at least in some ways, counterproductive. Sometimes a little distance and a fresh eye are more helpful than analyzing something into the ground.

If only I could apply that to my own life.

Leaning forward, elbows on my knees, I put my face in my hands, avoiding her gaze. "Gwen and I knew each other in college. We had a...thing."

"I bet you did." She chuckles with understanding.

"Right, well, we also apparently had a kid."

"Oh." Several beats of silence follow and then, more to herself than to me, she says, "I wasn't expecting that."

"Yeah, me neither." Straightening in my chair again, I give her a confused look. "I had a kid all this time and I never even knew it. It's strange, you know?"

Kim considers that for a moment, and I can see the questions in her eyes. Questions to which I don't have any answers. Talking with Jake yesterday, I was honest about the things I was thinking and feeling, but it's different with her. I can't lie to her, but she'll be disappointed in me if I tell her the truth. "I'm sure it was quite a shock."

"Yeah." I nod, and then the silence stretches out between us, palpable and yet not uncomfortable. It's always been that way with Kim, ever since I was little and she babysat Alex and me. She's always been there with a listening ear when I needed her, only offering advice if asked. Her low-pressure approach makes her easy to talk to and makes me less defensive than I was with Jake. Or Gwen, for that matter. "I don't know what to do," I admit.

"Yes, you do." The warmth in her brown eyes softens the firmness of her tone. "You're just scared. Anyone would be."

"I don't know how to be a dad. You know as well as I do, I didn't exactly have a good role model," I point out. As much as Kim urges me to reconcile with my dad, she knows some of the reasons for our rift. Some of them. Others, I can never tell her or anyone else.

"You didn't," she agrees with a brisk nod. "But sometimes we have to rise above our circumstances, and I know you're capable of doing that. Like with Amy. She adores you, and you're nothing like your father when you're with her."

At the mention of Kim's granddaughter—Jess' daughter—my already unsettled stomach knots. Amy. One of the few secrets I've kept from Kim, one of the few lies I've ever told her. Or rather, never told her. An enormous lie of omission, one I can't ever correct. "It isn't the same," I say through gritted teeth, because the truth is right there, on the tip of my tongue, begging to be told.

Before Kim can answer, the door at the back of the room swings open, and we both turn toward it expectantly. I don't know what she's thinking, but I welcome the interruption, ready to return to work. To focus my concentration on something other than Gwen and Tristan and my dad and Jess and Amy. Before I make a mistake and say something I can't.

"You ready to jump back in?" Brian asks from the open door. Someone behind him in the hall is laughing, a loud, braying sound that grates my raw nerves.

"Sure thing," Kim says, pushing out of her seat. And as everyone else files back into the room, she looks down at me, her voice quiet. "Being a father is a choice. Maybe it's time you stopped letting your father make yours for you."

~

GWEN

CECE and I have the day off, because there's a debate tomorrow and Kim's spending her day in intense preparation. I don't know what Alex is doing but when I suggested we invite him to join us, Cece shot me down before I even finished the sentence. No doubt, Mac is hovering over the debate prep like a nervous parent.

Blowing out my breath, I take another sip of my wine. It's hard not to feel bitter when Mac can muster more interest in a political candidate than he can his own son. He seemed genuinely curious when he looked through Tristan's pictures. It was encouraging. But after the fundraiser last night, I'm far less hopeful.

As if he's senses I'm thinking about him, my phone rings in my purse. I know it's Mac because last night after the party I got a little drunk in my room and gave him his own ringtone. CeeLo Green's "Fuck You."

"Um, you going to get that?" Cece asks, giving me a sidelong look.

"Nope." But as soon as the ringtone stops, my phone beeps with a text. Maybe I'd better at least check and see what he wants. Pulling my phone from my purse, I angle it away so Cece can't see the screen.

Mac: *How's Tristan today? Knee feeling better?*

"Ugh." I jam my phone back in my purse without responding. I can't deal with his hot-and-cold act right now. Cece and I are three stops into a four-winery tour, and I've had too much wine for his shit.

"You want to talk about it?" Cece asks tentatively.

I do. I had a very drunk, very weepy call with Willie last night, and as helpful as that was, it wasn't what I really needed. Because even though she's all grown up now, Willa will always be some kind of hybrid sister-daughter to me, and right now what I really need is a friend. "Hypothetically, do you think it's better for a kid to have an asshole for a father or no father at all?"

Cece's quiet for a moment, staring into her wine glass, before she finally says, "I'm not sure. Take Mac and Alex." Fortunately she doesn't notice my flinch at Mac's name, because she's still looking into her glass. "Their dad is definitely an asshole. Mac says he'd be better off without him, but Alex says their dad is imperfect but better than nothing. And then there's me. I don't have a dad and I would give... Well, I wish I did, that's all."

"So it sounds like you'd agree with Alex?"

"Yeah, I guess so." She glances up then, giving me a goofy smile. "And not just because I want to ride him like a rollercoaster." Then when our laughter has subsided, she gives me a serious look. "Why do you ask?"

"My son's dad is kind of... I don't know. I guess he's not sure how involved he wants to be." I choose my words carefully, so I don't give anything away.

"I didn't know you had any kids," Cece says, both brows raised and her eyes wide.

"Well, I try to keep my personal drama out of the office, you know?" Truth, but easier said than done when the baby daddy in question is our boss.

"Yeah, I get it." Cece nods and refills both our glasses. Thank God we have a driver carting our drunk asses around this afternoon. "Do you want him to be involved?"

"I... Yeah, I do. For Tristan's sake and, if I'm honest, for selfish reasons too. But I'm not objective. Maybe that really isn't the best thing. And in the end, it doesn't matter what I want. I can't force him to have a relationship with his son."

"Yeah, that really sucks. I'm sorry he's being an asshole and making things hard for you, but if it's any consolation, Tristan will be fine no matter what. I mean, look at me. I'm not going to lie, I have a boatload of daddy issues, but I'm mostly fine, as long as you don't count my habitual fixation on emotionally unavailable men."

"Is Alex emotionally unavailable?" I ask, seizing the opportunity to change the subject. As much as I need to talk to someone, it feels wrong talking to Cece about Mac like this, even if I haven't identified him. Besides, maybe talking about something lighter—or at least someone else's problems—is just what I need.

CHAPTER 18

MAC

CECE'S irritated grumbling from across the table draws my attention. We met for breakfast in the hotel restaurant, and she's been off the whole time. If I had to guess, she's hung over, but it seems like there's more to it than that. She's currently stabbing her scrambled eggs like she has a personal vendetta against all eggs, chickens, and possibly farm animals in general.

"Get up on the wrong side of the bed this morning?" I ask. I've seen little of her since the fundraiser the day before yesterday, what with my being tied up in debate prep yesterday.

"No. Did you know Gwen has a kid?"

I freeze, unable to answer, but Cece doesn't give me the chance anyway.

"Don't tell her I told you this, okay? She probably wouldn't like me blabbing about it but...ugh. Apparently, the asshole sperm donor is jerking her around, doesn't know if he wants to be involved in the kid's life or whatever. Why are guys like that, Mac? I don't get it.

Gwen is great, and I bet her kid is amazing, but this asshole can't even see—"

"I'm the asshole, Cece," I blurt, interrupting her.

"What?" She glances up, confused and distracted by her own anger, but when our eyes meet, her fork clatters against her plate and she gasps, "Oh, no."

"Yup," I say, sipping my coffee, because I can't stand the way she's looking at me.

"I don't… H-How can that be?"

"I told you, we knew each other in college. We…lost track of each other, and I never knew she was pregnant. Tristan's ten, almost eleven now, and I didn't know anything about him until she told me the other night." I've left a lot out, but that's more or less the gist of the situation.

"She never said how old he is. I just assumed he was a baby. A toddler maybe."

"I guess she needed someone to talk to but didn't want to cause problems between you and me." That's Gwen. Even when I'm being a gigantic asshole, she's being the bigger person and protecting me. She and Tristan both deserve better than being stuck with me.

I was aware Cece and Gwen were spending their day off together yesterday, but it hadn't occurred to me that Gwen might confide in my PA. Not that I could blame her for needing someone to talk to, especially when she'd been so careful not to point the finger in my direction.

Cece's quiet for a long moment. Her eyes are wet and her lower lip trembles when she finally says, "I never would have expected you to act like this, Mac."

"Act like what?" I ask and, yeah, I'm defensive. "I've known for less than seventy-two hours. I'm sorry if I'm not handling this the way you think I should, but I'm still trying to come to terms with the fact that he exists at all, let alone figure out what I'm going to do about it."

"I get that it's sudden and that it's hard, but you owe it to Tristan to get over yourself and step the fuck up," Cece hisses across the table. "Because whatever your issues are, he didn't ask for any of this, and let me tell you, knowing your father didn't want you? It makes you question your self-worth every damn day. It's taken me a hell of a lot of therapy to get to the point where I can say it's not my fault my father took off, but I still don't really believe it."

I knew Cece's dad hadn't been part of her life, but she never really talked about it. I always assumed it hadn't affected her much, and I'm sorry to learn otherwise but still, she's way out of line here. "Sometimes an absent father is better than a bad one."

"Bullshit. Are you a murderer? A rapist? Are you going to beat him?" She scoffs and rolls her eyes. "You're my friend, Mac, and I love you, but you know what you have to do here. This isn't what you wanted and you're imperfect, just like the rest of us, but you aren't a bad guy. Or at least, I didn't think you were."

Before I can respond, she throws her napkin on the table, gets up, and walks out. Apparently, she doesn't have anything else to say to me. But that's okay, she's said enough.

All this time I've been thinking about myself, but what about Tristan? Right now, he thinks I don't even know about him and I'm sure that's hard, but what would he think if Gwen had to tell him I knew but wasn't interested in meeting him? How would that make him feel?

Rejected.

The back of my neck prickles, my face hot, because I know what that feels like. It's the root of my problems with my dad. Even when I was little, long before I was old enough to realize what an all-around terrible person he is, I knew he didn't want and love me the way he did Alex. I knew, and no matter how much love and affection Mom and Aunt Vicky and Ruth and Kim heaped on me, it was never enough to replace what was missing. I can't do that to Tristan.

With a shaking hand, I pull my phone out of my pocket and text Gwen.

Mac: *Where are you?*

Gwen: *In bed, hung over. Why?*

Mac: Last time I was hung over you ambushed me. Now it's my turn. On my way up.

Gwen doesn't reply to the text but when I knock on her door, she immediately flings it wide, expecting me to catch it as she turns back toward the bed. She's wearing one of the big fluffy hotel robes, her blond hair wild and her eyes lined with dark shadows. Without a word, she crawls back into bed and pulls the covers over her head.

"You going to be okay for the debate tonight?" I ask, standing at the end of her bed.

"Yes. I just need to die first. I'll be fine later. What do you want?"

"I want to meet Tristan," I tell the lump in the middle of the mattress before my creeping self-doubts can take hold again.

She gasps, throwing the comforter off and bolting upright. "You do?"

"I do."

"You're sure? Because—"

"I'm sure, Gwen." I swallow hard, thinking about how I want to say the next part. "The thing is, I didn't ask for this, but neither did he. Maybe we can make the best of it together."

"Oh, God, I'm so relieved." She sniffles and collapses back against the pillows, jamming the heels of her hands against her eyes.

"Are you going to cry?" I ask warily, because I'm not sure my own shaky nerves can handle a crying Gwen right now.

"No." She hiccups, because she's definitely crying.

Shit.

Floundering and unsure of what to do or say, I move around the bed to sit on the edge and pull her into my arms. "Just tell me one thing," I say into her hair. "Are these happy tears or upset tears or…?"

"Happy tears. Relieved tears too. But mostly happy tears." She sobs, knotting her fists in my shirt and burying her face in my chest.

I hate that she's crying but at the same time, knowing I made her this happy feels…kind of good. Strange, but good. So I do the only thing I can—I hold her and rub her back until she's worked through it, relaxing against me as her tears subside. "Better?" I ask when her breathing has evened and she's no longer shaking.

"Yes, thank you."

"Anytime." And I actually mean it. Stroking her hair, I ask, "So how do you envision this working?"

"I don't know. It's up to you, really. I'm not going to force you into some rigid visitation schedule or anything. The only thing I care about is that you keep your word. If you tell him you will be there, be there. Beyond that, it's up to you, and maybe him, I guess." She shrugs and…Jesus, she just wiped her nose on my shirt, and I'm not even mad. What the hell is happening to me?

"Okay." I kiss the top of her head before suggesting, "How about when we get home from this trip, I meet him, and we can just see where it goes from there?"

"That sounds good." She looks up at me with watery eyes and a soft smile.

I nod and swallow the urge to kiss her, because God do I want to kiss her but that won't help anything.

"I kind of want you to kiss me, Mac," she says, her eyes dropping to my mouth.

"I'm not sure—"

"If it's a good idea? Me neither." She's stretching toward me, tipping her head back even more, and it's impossible to resist.

Brushing my lips over hers, I murmur, "I didn't come here for this."

"I know." She tugs my lower lip between her teeth before adding, "If you had, I wouldn't be offering it."

Loosening her robe, I push it off her shoulders. She shrugs out of it, and I bite my lip because she isn't wearing anything else underneath. As she scoots away from me, toward the center of the bed, her glorious body on full display, I say, "You are the most beautiful thing I've ever seen."

"Don't be silly." Her blush spreads from her cheeks, over her neck, to her collar bone. "Get your clothes off, Mac."

I rarely take orders from anyone. What can I say? I've always had problems with authority. But an order like that, coming from her?

You'd think I'm in boot camp and she's the meanest, scariest drill sergeant the Army ever produced for as quickly as I strip.

Once I'm in bed with her, I press her down on her back and lavish every inch of her body with kisses and tender caresses, starting at the top of her head and slowly working my way down. I kiss her forehead, her eyes, her cheeks. And then I linger on her mouth, our tongues twining together until she's gasping and squirming under me. Her eager response is almost more than I can take, but I'm determined to take my time, to savor every touch and sigh no matter how difficult it might be.

"Mac…"

"Not yet, baby." I kiss my way down the column of her throat and across her collarbone before turning my attention to her breasts. Closing my lips around her nipple, she cries out and arches under me, her hands on the back of my head as I suck and lick first one hard little nub and then the other. When I move away again, she whimpers, but I ignore her to leave a trail of kisses over her belly.

"Please, Mac, touch me."

"I am touching you," I tease, smiling against the expanse of skin just beneath her navel. Her belly isn't quite as flat as it was a dozen years ago, maybe because she had a baby or maybe simply because she's older, but that's the thing about Gwen. She's never been the otherworldly catwalk version of beautiful. She's more girl-next-door than impossibly gorgeous. And yet, she's always been my ideal. The woman against whom I've judged all others.

"You know what I mean." Fisting my hair, she tries to push my head lower.

"Do I?" I resist her eager hands to lick the point of her hip.

She groans my name and the sound is laced with so much impatience and frustration I can feel it in my bones.

"Like this?" I move lower, draping one of her legs over my shoulder and kissing the inside of her thigh. I take a deep breath to steady my own overeager lust because I want to savor this, but it doesn't help. The sweet scent of her arousal floods my senses, and I can't contain a groan of appreciation.

"Nooo…" Gwen raises her hips off the bed and pulls my hair.

"Like this, then?" I drop a kiss on her mound, and she digs her heel into my back.

"I swear to God, Mac, I'll—"

She stops abruptly with a choked cry when I close my lips around her clit, sucking and licking it greedily. Gwen bucks against me, so I press one forearm across her hips to hold her still while I worship her with my mouth. Her taste is all at once both familiar and new, and I can't get enough. I thrust against the mattress, unable to ignore my aching cock even if I want to focus all my attention on her.

"Oh, God, I'm going to come."

Her whole body is quivering and when I slide my first finger inside of her, she lets out a strangled wail and falls apart, writhing and sobbing with pleasure. I want to lick and kiss her through it and then do it again and maybe one more time after that, because that's how much I love the way she tastes and the way she moans my name and shudders when she comes. But I can't do it; I need to be inside her.

It's a compulsion, an addiction I can't deny.

CHAPTER 19

GWEN

WE WERE GONE ALMOST a week and I'm chomping at the bit to see Tristan, not just because I miss him but because today's the day. Tristan and Mac are going to meet.

Our plane landed at Reagan National Airport an hour ago. I metro'd home to drop off my bags and wait for Tris to get home from school, but once there I couldn't relax, my nervous energy making me fidgety and uneasy. Fortunately, except for work, my whole life is all within a few blocks, so I made the short walk to Tristan's school and I'm waiting on the sidewalk when the kids stream out the door. I wave when Tristan spots me and starts running toward me.

"Mom!" He throws himself into my arms, giving me an exuberant hug.

"Well, hello to you too." I laugh, hugging him back and holding on until he pulls away. "I guess you missed me after all."

Of all the days Tristan might have decided public displays of affection are okay, I'm glad he chose this one, because I'm a wreck. In his short life so far, today feels like one of the most momentous. Bringing

Mac and Tris together is the right thing. I know it is. But it also changes everything—for all of us—forever, and it's impossible not to be nervous about that.

"Yeah, maybe a little." Tristan shrugs and steps back, his gaze darting around to see if any of his friends witnessed our embrace.

"So, I have the rest of the day off and it's pretty nice out. I thought maybe we could take a walk and then go to the park for a bit. What do you think?" It is unseasonably warm for late January and we still have a half an hour before we're supposed to meet Mac at the park. Not that I'll tell Tris that. Mac's given me no reason to doubt him. Once he decided, he's been committed. But I'm a mom first; I have to protect Tristan, and I won't tell him what's about to happen until Mac is standing right in front of us. I won't take any chances with Tristan's heart.

"Sure, Mom, that sounds great." He skips ahead of me, and I let him until we get to the corner. When I reach for his hand, he tries to duck away.

"Uh-uh, young man. You're holding my hand when we cross the street." I make another grab for him, this time successfully. The feel of his soft hand in mine settles my nerves, so I tighten my grip just a little.

"Oh, come on, Mom." He rolls his eyes but doesn't fight me.

I get it. He's afraid one of his friends might see and that would embarrass him. And he's probably confused, because I don't always make him hold my hand anymore. But the thing is, I'm feeling a little melancholy. As much as I want him to meet Mac, as much as I want him to have his dad in his life, for them to know and love each other, it's a little bittersweet too. These are the last moments where Tristan will be mine and mine alone, and I'm going to horde them like a dragon with a precious treasure.

Once we've crossed the street, I release his hand, and Tristan walks backward in front of me, arms flailing wildly. Laughing and smiling, he tells me about the last week while I was gone. He's in an especially jovial mood today, and I hope it's a good sign for what's to come.

If nothing else, his happy chatter smooths over the rough edges of my anxiety. Taking a deep breath, I remind myself this is all going to be okay. No matter what happens, Tristan and I will be okay. But no matter how many times I tell myself that, no matter how bright and happy he is today, I can't entirely banish the scary whisper in the back of my head.

What if it all goes wrong?

When Tristan tells me that Rob's parents got him an aquarium for his birthday, which naturally leads to begging for an aquarium for his birthday too, I check my watch, my vision blurring a little around the edges as I stare at the digital numbers. It's time.

"Come on, the park's right here. Let's go in for a few minutes, okay?" I put my hand on his shoulder and pull him in close to my side, trying to ignore the uneven jittering of my heart.

"Sure, Mom. So anyway, the fish are all different colors and..."

I'm a terrible mother because I'm not listening. While Tris rambles on about the fish, I scan the park for Mac, heaving a huge sigh of relief when my gaze settles on him. He's sitting on a bench, hands clasped in his lap, waiting for us, and when our eyes meet, he smiles.

MAC

WHEN I SPOT Gwen and Tristan walking toward me, I stand, shoving my hands in my pockets to hide the persistent shake I seem to have recently acquired. Tristan is chattering enthusiastically, and Gwen is giving him soft smiles and encouraging nods, keeping him talking. But he's a smart kid, and it doesn't take him long to figure out something is up.

His steps slow, and she gives his shoulder a soft nudge. They're close enough I hear her say, "Come on, Tris, there's someone I want you to meet."

"Who?" Tristan asks suspiciously, but he's followed Gwen's gaze and he's looking right at me, eyes narrowed and lips set in a firm line.

I give him what I hope is a warm smile, but it feels strange on my face, like my skin is stretched too tight over my bones.

They've stopped in front of me, and Gwen turns Tristan toward her and ruffles his hair as she squats in front of him. Taking hold of his chin with her thumb and forefinger, she says, "So, today's going to be a really big day for you, tiger, and it might feel kind of confusing and overwhelming. But I need you to know that whatever you feel, it's okay, and I'm going to be right here the whole time, all right?"

Holy shit, Gwen is an amazing mom. How does she know what to say? How to do this? Because, not that I know anything about raising kids, but that seems like the reassurance he might need, and it never would have even occurred to me.

"Is he your boyfriend?" Tristan asks, giving me that same distrustful look. Apparently, I'm more impressed with Gwen's speech than he is.

A surprised burst of laughter escapes me, but Gwen taps her forefinger on his chin. "Hey, look at me." When he does, she says, "This is my friend Mac, and I'm really excited for you to meet him, because he's your dad."

As soon as the words are out of her mouth, the rest of the world falls away. I can't hear the cars passing by, or the other people laughing and talking in the park. I can't even hear the roar of the train as it pulls into the nearby Metro station. There's only Tristan and Gwen and the sound of my own heartbeat thumping in my chest as I hold my breath and wait for his response.

He gives me a sidelong look, his skepticism replaced by curious interest that soon develops into outright gawking as he turns toward me. "You're my dad?" he asks, his voice stronger than I would have expected.

"Yes, and I'm really excited to meet you." I squat too, my forearms on my knees, so we're at the same level.

"You are?" He sounds bewildered, like he's surprised by that, and my heart stutters and squeezes when I realize how close I came to never having this moment with him.

"Of course. You're my son. And besides that, your mom says you're a pretty great kid."

"Mom says you're pretty great too. Did you know she calls me tiger because you have a tiger tattoo?"

"I didn't know that." A happy grin splits my face, and I glance over at Gwen to find her blushing and shaking her head.

"Do you think I could see it sometime?" And then before I can respond, he rushes ahead with, "I mean, if you want to see me again."

His naked vulnerability is crushing, even more so because I can easily imagine myself letting him down. He deserves a better dad than the one he got. One who would know the right things to say to bolster his confidence and make him feel secure. One who didn't worry his kid might be better off without him.

"I'll tell you what, Tristan," I start, reaching for his hand. When he puts his soft hand in mine, there's a zing of energy, like supercharged static electricity, and I have to take a deep breath before I can finish my thought. "We'll do whatever you want. I want to see you again, but the most important thing is that you're comfortable, so we only have to do that if it's what you want, okay?"

Last night Gwen and I laid in bed in a hotel room in Reno and spent most of the night talking about how we thought this conversation might go and the kinds of things we wanted to say to him. She's nodding along with my words, so I guess I'm doing okay, but Christ, this feels terrible; all I want is for him to say he wants to see me again and waiting, even a few seconds while he thinks it over, is fucking torture. Is this how Gwen felt when she told me all the choices were mine and then I acted like a prick and left her hanging for days? I owe her the mother of all apologies.

"Yeah, I want to see you again." He pauses for a beat and then asks, "Can I have an aquarium?"

"Sorry, tiger. Your mom's still in charge of all that stuff," I answer with an apologetic smile.

Tristan shrugs as if to say, *well, it was worth a shot.* "Where do you live?"

"Arlington. I know you haven't lived here that long, do you know where that is?"

"Yeah, the hospital Aunt Willie works at is in Arlington. It's close." He points in a vaguely north-ish direction.

"It is close," Gwen agrees. "But you know how I travel for work? Well, Mac travels for work too. In fact, we work together. That's how I found him again. So, you can't see him any time you want, because he'll be gone sometimes just like I am."

"Right, but when I'm in town, you can see me as much as you want, okay?"

Gwen and I did seriously talk about letting him travel with us some over spring break or during the summer, but we decided it was better to wait and see how things go before we raise the possibility with him. For all I know, by the time summer gets here, I'll be old news, and he'd rather stay home and play with his friends.

"Yeah, that's cool."

"I don't know about you guys," Gwen says as she straightens, "but my knees are starting to hurt. Why don't you two go sit on the bench, and I'll just stay here and check my email."

"Okay," Tristan says, marching over to the bench. His easy acceptance of this small distance from his mother, even if she is still well within sight and earshot, seems encouraging.

"Is this going okay?" I ask softly before going to join him.

"You're doing great. He likes you."

"Are you coming?" Tristan shouts from his place on the bench. Her smile widens and she gives me a gentle push in his direction. When I've sat down next to him, he asks, "What am I supposed to call you?"

"Whatever you want. You can call me Mac, like your mom does. Or my mom calls me Will. That would be okay too. Or—"

"Why does your mom call you Will? I thought your name was Mac?"

"My whole name is William Zachary MacKenzie. Most everybody calls me Mac because of my last name. But you know how moms are, and mine insists on calling me Will."

"Your name is William too? That's so cool."

"I know, right?" And as I say it, I catch Gwen smirking at me over the top of her phone.

Oh, you think it's cool now, do you?

All I can do is shrug and smile before turning my attention back to Tristan as he exclaims, "Mac is way cooler than Will though."

"Yeah, I think so too."

Tristan is staring across the street at the Metro station when he quietly says, "What about Dad? Am I allowed to call you that?"

Panic creeps up my spine, my skin prickling. I don't know how to answer his question. Do I want him to call me dad? Unclear and, given his age, I hadn't really considered he might want to, which just goes to show what little I thought I knew about kids is wrong. But as with many of my problems, this one goes back to my dad, and I can't allow his shadow to impact my relationship with Tris. If I do, I'm no better than he is. "You're allowed to call me whatever you want, and you don't have to decide now. Why don't you take some time and think it over? I'm okay with 'hey you' until you figure out what feels right, okay?" I finally say, my voice not as steady as I'd hoped.

"Okay," Tristan agrees with a goofy smile and he leans closer, bumping his shoulder against my arm. Then he tips his head back until our eyes meet, his expression more somber. "There's a lot of stuff I've always wanted to know about you, but I feel kind of mixed up and I don't know what to ask now that you're here."

Oh, kiddo, I'm sorry because I think you get that from me and boy, do I ever know how you feel right now. "That's all right, I get kind of mixed up when I'm overwhelmed too, but if you want, I can tell you a little about myself and you can just listen, or if you think of something you want to ask you can. Sound good?" I turn toward him, my arm across the back of the bench behind him, and my own brain gets even fuzzier when he smiles up at me and nods. "Okay, well, I grew up right across the river in Washington, D.C. I have a younger brother, Alex, and we had a babysitter who had a daughter who was the same age as Alex, so we grew up together and she's kind of like a sister. Her name is Jess."

"I've always wanted a brother," Tristan says with a sigh. Then, screwing up his face, he says, "But no sisters. Aunt Willie and Aunt Liv are annoying enough."

"Uh…" I give Gwen a panicked look, because I did not anticipate that.

Just ignore it. I do, Gwen silently mouths with a shrug.

Good enough for me. "Anyway." I tap my hand on the back of the bench, trying to clear my head. "When I was in school—"

"Were you good at school?" he interrupts.

That's a tougher question than it seems, because my lack of respect for authority goes back as far as I can remember. I did okay in school, and college too. Mostly a B and C student with enough Ds thrown in to give my mom and dad the occasional mini stroke. But I never tried. My underachieving ass coasted by on my parents' money and connections. Who knows how well I might have done if I put in even a minimal effort? It seems safe to assume Gwen wouldn't appreciate me giving him a completely honest answer. "I did okay." He seems satisfied with that answer, and I'm all too happy to move on. "I got my bachelor's degree and then my masters at the University of Michigan. That's where I met your mom."

"Was she pretty?"

Another unexpected question, but this one I can answer honestly. "The prettiest girl I'd ever seen."

He screws up his face at that then asks, "Did you love her?"

Okay, maybe honesty wasn't such a great idea. *Fuck it. In for a penny, in for a pound.* "Yeah, you know what? I did." I ignore the way Gwen rolls her eyes and shakes her head.

"Do you still love her?

What in the ever-loving fuck have I gotten myself into? I look to Gwen, but she holds her hands up and takes a step back, unwilling to help me out of the hole I've dug. "Uh, things with your mom and I are kind of complicated. What's important for you to know is that I like her a lot, and now that I've found you guys again, I'm not going anywhere." That's apparently an okay answer, because Gwen gives me a thumbs up.

"What do you like on your pizza?" Tristan asks out of the blue.

Yup, definitely my kid. "My favorite is just pepperoni and cheese, but I'll eat most anything as long as there are no mushrooms or anchovies." I scrunch up my nose to show exactly how gross I think mushrooms and anchovies are.

"I hate mushrooms too!" Tristan fist bumps me and even does the exploding-fist thing at the end, and I burst out in laughter.

"You know what, Tris?" Gwen asks, taking a step closer to us.

"What?" He sounds suspicious and I don't blame him. She has that twinkle in her eye, the one that says she's up to something.

"When Mac and I get pizza together, he always orders mushrooms on half for me."

"You do?" Tristan gives me a wide-eyed look that says he thinks that's akin to giving her my only remaining kidney. When I nod, he asks, "But what if the pizza guy gets mushrooms on your part?"

"Then I pick them off."

"We should go get pizza. I'm getting hungry." Tristan glances between us with an expression so hopeful I could never say no. But Gwen does.

"How about we do that next time? Because this is a school night, and I bet you have homework you still need to do tonight."

"I guess." Tristan's shoulders slump and he says, "But could we still have pizza tonight, Mom?"

"I don't know…all I eat on the road is junk. I think I might like something home-cooked tonight." Gwen is biting her lower lip, and I recognize her faux resistance even if Tristan doesn't.

"I'll let you get mushrooms on half," Tristan says in a sing-song voice.

"Oh, well, in that case, pizza it is." Gwen laughs and then says, "We should probably get going, Tris."

"Do we have to?" It's a full-on whine, and he kicks his feet in the dirt, frowning at his mom, but I can't help but give her what feels like a dopey grin.

He likes me. He doesn't want to go.

"Yeah, we do." Her voice is sympathetic but not to be argued with and seems to be meant for both of us. When he nods, she turns to me. "Did you Metro?"

"I did. Walk to the station with me?" I'm not ready for this to be over either.

They both agree, and Tristan skips ahead of us as we start on our way.

"Well played on the mushrooms, Mom," I tease, keeping my voice low so he won't hear.

"He wants to impress you, and I'm not above using that to my advantage," she says with a grin.

"He wants to impress me? That sounds like a terrifying amount of responsibility."

"It is. But once in a while, you can use it for things like mushrooms, so it's not all bad."

We're both laughing when we reach the crosswalk, and Tristan turns around to whisper-hiss at his mom, "Please don't make me hold your hand right now."

I turn away, partly to play along so he'll think I'm not listening, but also so he won't see how close I am to losing my shit laughing.

"Okay but walk. No running," Gwen answers firmly.

When we cross the street, Tristan ahead of us again. I'm still struggling not to laugh. "How the hell do you keep a straight face, Gwen?"

"I don't always." She admits with a shrug and a smile.

"Hey, you!" Tristan is giving us a big toothy grin and standing next to the turnstiles, waiting for us to catch up.

"What's up?" I ask when we draw even with him.

"Do you think…" He scuffs one shoe against the pavement and looks up at me with uncertain brown eyes. "Do you think I could have a hug before you go?"

Even Gwen is surprised, so I don't feel too bad about stuttering a little before I answer him. "Oh, uh, sure, yeah, of course."

As soon as the words are out of my mouth, Tristan's thrown his arms around my waist, his head pressed to my stomach, and I'm staring at Gwen, wondering how the hell I never knew this could be so cool. After the hug, we say our goodbyes, promising to have pizza together soon, and they wave me through the turnstiles.

There's a train waiting when I get to the platform, but I don't board. Instead, I stand at the railing and watch as Gwen and Tristan walk away. I'll catch the next train. What's fifteen minutes of waiting when I can still see them right now?

CHAPTER 20

GWEN

THE DARK, rumbling sky and pouring rain are bad omens. Or they would be, if I believed in that sort of thing, which I don't. I'm uneasy enough without superstition to amplify the sour feeling in my stomach.

"So, are we going to go in or…?" I ask, dragging my gaze away from the fat raindrops tracking down the passenger side window of Mac's car.

He's still in the driver's seat, staring at his parents' front door, his expression blank. We've been sitting in their driveway in silence for at least ten minutes. Mac's reluctance to go inside and the white-knuckled grip he still has on the steering wheel are the only clues to whatever he's feeling, because he sure isn't talking about it. "I wish you wouldn't have come," he says without looking at me.

When he mentioned he was planning to tell his parents and Alex about Tristan today, I invited myself along. He was quite clear that he did not want me here, but I insisted. As much as I wronged Mac by keeping Tristan from him all these years, I wronged his family too.

They have a grandson and nephew they don't know about because of me. The least I can do is face the consequences of my choices head on.

Besides, I was enough of a coward when it came to telling Mac, and I know how difficult this is for him. I'm not going to make him do it alone. "Why? So you could sit in the driveway all afternoon without anyone nagging you to go in?" I tease, trying to lighten the mood, but Mac isn't having it.

"I'd already be inside if I'd come alone."

Oh. "I'm sorry, Mac. I only meant to help. I can wait here if you want," I offer, twisting the strap of my purse around one hand. I don't know how he can be so still when he's clearly under so much strain. My anxiety makes me restless.

"Let's go," Mac grumbles, throwing open his door without acknowledging my offer.

By the time I've gotten out of the car and pulled my jacket over my head in a vain attempt to shield my hair from the rain, he's already halfway to the door, and I jog up the slate walkway behind him. Without knocking, he throws open the door and ushers me inside.

"Is this where you grew up?" I ask, shrugging out of my jacket. We've only made it as far as the foyer, and I'm already intimidated by the ostentatious display of wealth.

Crystal teardrops drip from the enormous chandelier that graces the center of the space, a wide-curved staircase flanking one side the room. The gleaming wood floors are covered by plush rugs, the walls dotted with gilt-framed mirrors and pictures. Not family photos though. On closer inspection, they're paintings. Probably one-of-a-kind by famous artists I've never heard of before.

It's more like a museum or the elaborate set of a period drama than a home, and it's hard to imagine a young Mac and Alex running through these halls. Except that staircase. It's not at all difficult to imagine them coasting down the wide bannister.

"The stairs were fun," Mac murmurs, reading my mind. Carelessly tossing his keys on a marble-topped console table against one wall, he takes my coat, hanging it with his in the closet. When he turns back to me, he plants one hand on the small of my back and gives me a tight smile. "Let's get this over with, shall we?"

"It'll be fine." I'm not sure who I'm trying to reassure more. Hopefully myself, because my bravado clearly isn't working on him.

"Right," he says with a clipped voice, his brow furrowed as he leads me deeper into the house.

We draw closer to the living room, the hum of voices drifting toward us. Alex's familiar tone, mixed with those of two older women and an older man. Mac's parents, obviously, but who is the other woman? I guess I'll find out soon enough, because Mac is turning me to the side, through a wide archway.

My gaze immediately finds Alex, sprawled on one end of the couch, and his eyes widen in surprise when our gazes meet. Mac obviously didn't tell them I was coming today.

"Will, you came!" the older woman perched at the opposite end of the couch from Alex coos, and I realize it isn't just me they weren't expecting. Her clear gaze flits to me, her warm smile widening even further. "And you brought a date."

Mac sighs next to me, and I barely resist the urge to elbow him between the ribs. Isn't he going to introduce me? Or say something? Anything?

Could this be any more awkward?

Yes. Yes, it could be more awkward, because then Mac's father, lounging in an armchair dwarfed by his big frame, turns a smug smile on his eldest son. Something I can't identify passes between them, but whatever it is, Senior's mood seems triumphant while Mac stares back at him, stone-faced and defiant.

Alex shifts against the cushions and gives Mac a disapproving frown before saying, "I'll make the introductions, then. This is Gwen Pierce. She's working with us on Kim's campaign. Gwen, I believe you've met our dad, but this is our mom, Joan." He gestures toward the woman who greeted us then turns to the other woman in the room, who has thus far remained silent, and adds, "And this is our Aunt Vicky."

"She works with you?" Vicky's eyebrows rise and she gives Joan a sidelong look, shaking her head. "Not a date, then."

Joan sighs and waves one hand at what is obviously her younger sister before saying, "I should go tell Ruth to set two more places for dinner."

"We aren't staying," Mac blurts before his mom can get up, and I finally give in, nudging his arm with mine. I know he's nervous, but he's acting like an asshole, and that won't make this any easier.

"Oh, well, then." Joan is struggling to hide her disappointment, but the pep has returned to her voice when she adds, with a chiding note for Mac, "I raised you with better manners than this, Will. Come sit down and make yourselves comfortable so we can visit until you have to go."

Their family dynamic is depressing. Senior sitting off to one side, pompous and self-righteous. Alex, seeking approval like an eager puppy. Joan, desperate for Mac's attention but accepting of his refusal to give it. Mac aloof and defiant. Even Vicky appears resigned to the tension in the room. They aren't a family at all, at least not like any I've known. They're separate islands, connected by unreliable ferries and ramshackle bridges.

I don't know any of their history, why they are so distant and disconnected, and it doesn't really matter. Not right this minute, anyway. What matters is that Mac is miserable, his brow pinched and his lips pressed in a firm line. And that makes me miserable. So when he stays standing near the massive fireplace, shoulders square and expression implacable, I remain by his side. Reaching for his hand, I lace my fingers with his, silently willing him to understand.

We're in this together.

～

MAC

WHEN GWEN SLIPS her hand into mine, I glance down, surprised and more than a little dismayed by the gesture. The urge to rip my hand away, lest mom and Aunt Vicky get the wrong idea, is nearly instinctual. But given what I—we—are about to tell them, that's probably inevitable anyway, so why bother? Besides, Gwen's soft grip is grounding, and I don't really want to give that up, even if I should.

"I'm not sure how to say this," I start, remembering that Gwen said very nearly the same thing the night she told me about Tristan. If she got through it, so can I. Staring over the top of Alex's head, my gaze fixed on the grandfather clock in the corner, I continue. "Gwen and I dated for a while in college, and we have a son. His name is Tristan. He'll be eleven in June."

Aunt Vicky gasps, raising one hand to cover her mouth. "Oh my God."

I can't bring myself to look at my mom.

"Why are we just finding out about this now?" Dad asks, his voice booming from the other end of the room. He isn't angry though. He's delighted, because I've just proven what he's always claimed. I'm just like him.

There are a dozen reasons I didn't want Gwen to come today. Because this will be awkward and likely ugly. Because I don't ever want her anywhere near my dad under any circumstances. Because I don't want the mistakes of our youth and the choices she made then to impact her budding friendship with my brother.

Mostly though, it's because I'm going to lie to my family. A bigger lie than simply claiming our relationship ever bore any resemblance to dating. And I don't feel even a hint of remorse about it, because they don't need to know the truth. Not about this. That's for Gwen and me and someday Tristan. Everyone else can fuck off, because she doesn't deserve their judgment.

"Because I just decided to tell you."

Alex arches one brow. He knows I'm lying. He had a front-row seat for my reunion with Gwen. He saw how we've both acted over the last few weeks. The way she pretended she didn't know me. It isn't much of a leap to guess that I didn't know. But it isn't Alex who betrays me this time.

It's Gwen.

"Mac didn't know either," she confesses, gently squeezing my fingers as if I'm the one who needs her protection.

"Can't say as I blame you for that. Junior's always been the unreliable sort." Dad's expression is stern, the lines of his face deep with censure, but his eyes are gleeful. "So what now, son? Are you going to play at being daddy?"

"William," Mom hisses, but Dad waves her off—no more bothered by her than he might be by a pesky, but harmless gnat—and stares at me expectantly.

"He isn't playing at anything," Gwen snaps. Her grip tightens on my hand and she glares at him, adding, "He will be a great dad, and he could use a little support from his family."

Dad gives her a thin smile and a short nod. It's meant to look like a silent apology, acquiescence even, but when his gaze meets mine, his eyes spark with contempt. *How's the view from behind her skirts, Junior?*

"Well, I don't know about the rest of you, but I think I am going to be a goddamn amazing uncle," Alex quips, cutting the thick tension in the room. For once, it actually feels like he is on my side, and I give him a thankful look.

"Pfft. Not if you keep cussing like that." Aunt Vicky chortles, all too eager to help Alex shepherd the conversation in a more pleasant direction.

"What are you talking about? You're the one who taught me the f-bomb," Alex teases, and Aunt Vicky nods ruefully. She taught us both a lot of four-letter words when we were young, so there isn't much point in her trying to deny it now.

"Can we meet him?" Mom asks, her voice so quiet I have to strain to hear her over Alex and Aunt Vicky's laughter.

"Eventually," I answer before Gwen can do something foolish, like offer to go home and get him now. "This is a lot for him, and we don't want to throw too many new people at him all at once." *Plus, I need to get the kid fitted for a suit of armor before he meets Dad.*

"Of course." Mom smiles.

She's disappointed. I can see it in the slight droop of her shoulders.

After all these years of nagging her sons about grandbabies, she finally has one, and she is no doubt excited to assume her new role as Grandma. I hate letting her down, if only temporarily, but we have to do what's right for Tristan, and deep down I know she understands that.

Gwen's soft tug on my fingers draws my attention. She subtly lifts her phone in her other hand, asking a silent question. *Pictures?*

Now she's asking permission? Not when she exposed my lie. Not when she told my dad off. But now. It's so ridiculous, I can't stop myself from smiling.

"What?" she whispers with a frown, either oblivious or indifferent to the fact that my whole family is staring at us.

"I'm glad you came," I admit, my voice low, and I'm as surprised as she is by my confession. I didn't mean to say it. Didn't even realize I felt it until the words came tumbling out of my mouth.

Gwen's blue eyes widen, the corners of her mouth tipping up in a smile that makes me feel a little lightheaded. Her happiness is like a force of nature, more powerful than the thunderstorm still blowing outside. My gaze drops to her lips and I contemplate the wisdom of kissing her right here in front of everyone.

"We make a pretty good team, yeah?" Gwen murmurs.

"Yeah," I agree, giving her hand one more squeeze before releasing it.

Gwen raises her voice, volunteering to show them pictures of Tristan. A moment later, she's sitting between Alex and Mom with Aunt Vicky hanging over the back of the couch so she can peer over their shoulders.

Dad is the only one who hasn't joined the gaggle around Gwen. All his attention is focused on me, his silent message coming across loud and clear.

You're no better than I am.

CHAPTER 21

GWEN

IT'S BEEN two and a half weeks since Mac and Tristan met and it's going...well. Great, actually. When we're not on the road, they're spending increasing amounts of time with each other. They haven't done anything alone yet and although I think they're both ready, I don't want to push either of them. It's coming though, and soon, because they're both growing more comfortable, acting more naturally instead of peppering each other with rapid-fire questions in some kind of weird getting-to-know-each-other on-steroids ritual.

When we are on the road, Mac and I are spending more time together too. He spends most nights in my hotel room and it's good. In some ways, it feels just like old times, and in a weird way it's familiar and comfortable yet still new and exciting. But we're keeping it on the down low, because no one needs to know we're screwing around again. It's not like we're dating, and this time I'm totally okay with that. I think we're working toward some kind of co-parents-with-benefits arrangement and honestly, that could work for me.

We're standing in the lobby of our hotel in Manchester, New

Hampshire, waiting while Cece checks us in and talking with Alex about the latest gaffes one of the other candidates made. He was caught on a hot mic calling his wife a bitch, and the media is in a frenzy. His campaign is sinking faster than the RMS Lusitania. Good riddance.

"Okay, we're all set," Cece chirps, rejoining us. "Alex, you're in 1412. I'm in 1414." She hands Alex an envelope of keys and tucks another in her own pocket. Then she opens a third and takes out the two keycards, handing one to Mac and one to me. "And you two are in 1410."

"What just happened?" Alex asks as Mac and I both stare blankly at the keys in our hands.

"Did you know he spends every night in her room?" Cece answers Alex's question with one of her own, ignoring us. Not that either of us is saying much. We both seem to be in some kind of stunned stupor.

"Sure, but—" Alex starts but Cece cuts him off with a hand wave.

"I'm not paying for two rooms when they're only using one."

"You aren't paying for any rooms." Mac's finally found his voice and his irritated exasperation is coming through loud and clear.

"That's true, but you can use the savings to fund my raise this year. You're welcome." Cece crosses her arms over her chest and glares at all three of us. I'm not even sure why Alex got a glare—he's got nothing to do with this—but the team mom has made up her mind, and she's not going to change it.

Mac tries again, this time more calmly but with no more success. "Cece, you can't—"

"I know, you two thought you were being so discreet, but everybody knows. Every. Body. We know, Kim knows, Brian and all the campaign staff knows. Hell, the entire press pool knows. It's getting weird, guys. You might as well just acknowledge it and move the hell on. I mean, you already have a kid together. Nobody is shocked by this development." Then she pauses, gives us both a stern frown, and waves one arm at the front desk. "I'll go get another room if you want, but it'll probably be on a different floor since I only reserved the three. And that means Mac's walk of shame every morning will be a lot longer and will include the elevator. Do you really want that?"

"Wait, wait, you might be on to something." Alex holds up one hand to silence her. "I had the room on the other side of Gwen last week in Des Moines, and that hotel had astonishingly thin walls. If we get another room and put her in that one, then at least neither of us has to listen to them." Alex turns on Cece with widening eyes, poking his finger at her chest. "I just realized the last couple of weeks, you keep assigning the rooms with Mac on one end, Gwen and I in the middle, and you on the other side of me. You're doing that on purpose, aren't you?"

"Possibly, and before you start yelling at me, there should be some perks for the person who has to do all the legwork. I didn't want to get stuck next to that freak show more than once." Cece shrugs.

"Oh, for fuck's sake." Mac throws up his hands in exasperation before grabbing his bags and stalking toward the elevator. Apparently, the decision has been made. We're sharing a room.

When we get to the room, Mac is still agitated, slamming the closet door after he's hung his suits.

"I can go get another room. It's not a big deal, and I don't mind."

He turns from his suitcase, his brows drawn together in confusion. "What? No. I want you here."

"You aren't acting like it," I point out tartly.

"I'm sorry." He sighs and runs one hand through his hair. "It's not that, really. I'm just irritated with Cece. She shouldn't do things like that without talking to me or, in this case us."

"You said she runs your life," I remind him.

"She does and usually she does a damn fine job of it, but every once in a while, she gets a wild hair up her ass and crosses the line."

"Like what else?" It isn't difficult to imagine Cece fucking with Mac's life in myriad harmless but hilarious ways.

"Two years ago, for my birthday, she got me a cat. She said I spend too much time alone and I wouldn't be so grumpy if I had a pet."

"And now the cat is…?" I chew my lip, trying not to laugh while I wait for his answer.

"Hers. She says she named it Mac's a Twat and calls it 'Mat' for short."

"That's…" I try not to laugh, I really do, but Mac is so pissed and it's so silly, and the laughter spills out before I can stop it. Through my giggles, I say, "I'm sorry, but that's hysterical."

Mac hums and glances at his watch. "We have twenty minutes before we have to meet up with Kim and Brian. You really want to waste it laughing?"

"I do," I insist. "I'm feeling a little self-conscious right now. She called us a freak show."

Mac is walking toward me, a wicked grin curving his full lips. "She doesn't know the half of it. Remember that time you—" He's interrupted by his ringing phone. "The Imperial March" from Star Wars, to be exact. He huffs and glares at it on the table.

"Don't you think you should answer that?" Whoever merits "The Imperial March" for a ringtone must be important.

"Not a chance. We were home for four days, four long miserable days where I couldn't fuck you. A ringing phone isn't going to stop me now." He's resumed advancing on me but I slowly back away.

We never talked about it, but we don't hook up at home. Outside of work, time at home is for Tristan, or our separate interests, so I understand Mac's enthusiasm. But the phone is already ringing again, and this time I'm so surprised by the ringtone I glance over at his phone on the table. My momentary distraction gives Mac the opening he needs to grab me and pull me against his chest.

"Wait, wait, wait." I'm pushing at his shoulders and laughing. "Are you for real? Alex's ringtone is 'Gangsta's Paradise?'"

"It's funny, right?" Mac grins and gropes my ass. "You got anything on under this skirt?" Exactly one time I let my laundry get away from me and I had to go commando, but Mac is ever hopeful for a repeat.

"Does he know?" A very unladylike snort accompanies my question.

"Of course not. Now about those panties…" He's fisted the fabric of my skirt and is tugging it up over my hips, but his phone is ringing again. Alex again.

"What if it's important?" The phone has stopped and started again, this time with "Take This Job and Shove It." "Who the hell is that?"

"Cece. I get confused about which of us is the boss sometimes. I'm sure you can see why." Despite the distracting phone and ridiculous conversation, he's winning me over. His lips on my neck and his hands inside the back of my panties, palming my ass, will do that. At least he was winning me over until he says, "I just need three minutes, baby."

"Three minutes? That's not how you impress a woman."

He scoffs, the hot rush of his breath against my skin making me shiver. "You like a good hard quickie as much as—"

Bang. Bang. Bang.

"Come on, Mac. There's breaking news. This is fucking urgent," Alex shouts through the door, still knocking.

For one split second, Mac and I stare at each other with stunned expressions and then we're both diving for our phones, tripping and stumbling over our own feet, and each other, in our mad scramble.

"Fuck," Mac growls, swiping his phone off the table before striding across the room toward the door. By the time he opens it to admit Alex and Cece, I'm scrolling through Twitter, trying to figure out what's going on. Kim's name is blowing up, but it's escalated so quickly and people's comments at this stage are nothing more than expressions of shock and surprise, so it's difficult to figure out what's actually going on.

"We need to get up to Kim's suite, like, yesterday," Cece is saying as I finally find a tweet that includes a link, but it doesn't matter now. Alex is already explaining.

"Apparently Kim had an abortion. Or at least, that's what the District Dispatch is saying." Alex is staring at Mac expectantly.

"No idea, but I guess we're about to find out." Mac grabs his coat off the back of the chair and heads for the door.

"Why does that even matter?" Cece complains as we trudge down the hall to the elevator.

"It shouldn't matter," Mac answers emphatically.

"But it will, if it's true." Alex frowns and stabs the button for the top floor with unnecessary force.

"You guys," I glance up from my phone with a wince. "The hashtag #Dunnisdone is trending, and it's brutal. Some are defending her, but there's a lot of criticism too. They're calling her immoral and selfish. Some of them are even calling her a murderer."

"That's..." Cece doesn't—or can't—finish her thought.

"The timing couldn't be worse with the New Hampshire primary tomorrow," Alex laments as we step off the elevator on Kim's floor.

"Oh, it definitely could be. We've got three weeks before Super Tuesday to clean this up." Stopping in front of the penthouse, Mac scrubs both hands over his face and frowns. "This is really going to suck. Ready?"

We all nod, and he knocks on the door. Brian answers immediately. "She's in the dining room with Tammy and Arnie," he says as he closes the door behind us. Tammy is one of Kim's closest friends, and Arnie is her husband. I'm relieved they're both here. The next few days will be rough, and she'll need the extra support.

No one says anything as we all file in and take seats around the table. Under the table, Mac's hand lands on my knee, but it doesn't feel sexual or playful or flirty. And as he talks, his fingers flex, holding on to me as if he's seeking comfort. Or maybe strength. I don't blame him; this conversation will be awful. If that helps, he can squeeze as tight as he likes.

"I'm sorry I have to ask, Kim, but I need to know so we can figure out how to handle this." Mac dips his head, avoiding eye contact. "Is it true?"

"It is. Jess was only three, and we were already struggling. I was working full time and going to school full time and babysitting you boys every minute I wasn't at work or school so I could justify accepting your mother's charity," Kim explains quietly with a gesture toward Mac and Alex. "I never regretted having Jess, but everything was so hard back then. Having another baby felt impossible, and I've never regretted that choice, either."

"That's understandable." Mac's soothing tone contradicts the tight hold he has on my leg. Slipping my hand under the table, I lay it atop his. He gives me a sidelong look, one corner of his mouth tilting up in a private smile meant just for me, and my heart flutters unexpectedly in my chest.

"Understandable to you," Tammy counters, a deep furrow creasing her brow. "A lot of people won't find it relatable at all."

"Those people can fuck off," Cece blurts before slapping one hand over her mouth and giving Mac a wide-eyed look, like she can't believe she said that.

"It's all right, Cece, and you aren't entirely wrong. Many of the people who will be bothered most by this would never vote for her anyway." With a sympathetic smile for Cece, who seems embarrassed by her outburst despite Mac's reassurance, he turns his attention back to the candidate. "You have three options, Kim, and it all depends on how much you're willing to share. We can stonewall them. Just flat refuse to address it at all. We put out a statement that doesn't confirm or deny. The downside to that strategy is a lot of people will assume that means it's true, but it will lack all context, which might be a turn-off for some voters in the middle."

"What else have you got?" Kim asks with a frown.

"Another option would be to acknowledge it's true but refuse to provide details because, again, it's a private medical issue, but most people will accept the story as presented by the *Dispatch*."

"That feels even worse than the first option," Brian says. "At least there, some people might doubt the story. I mean, the *Dispatch* is little more than a tabloid. And some people will agree it isn't anyone's business and probably respect her for refusing to cave. Admitting it without providing the details undermines that."

Mac nods his agreement before going on. "The best option—and by best, I mean best outcome, not easiest—is to tell the truth. All of it, or as much of it as you are comfortable with, but honestly, the more the better."

Kim nods. "Okay, the truth it is. Brian, can you get the communications team started on a press release? We need to respond quickly, but have Mac review it before you send anything out."

"Of course," Brian says, firing off a quick text message.

"We need to get Kim on one of the big-name shows tonight and surrogates on all the rest, women preferably." Mac is drumming his fingers on the inside of my leg, tapping out the tempo of his thoughts as he considers everything that needs to be done.

"We can do that." Brian nods, sending more texts.

"Morning shows too. Local media here in New Hampshire especially. We want to make sure people hear our side before they head to the polls tomorrow." Mac keeps talking, but I'm only half listening, too busy scrolling through social media watching the reaction unfold live. That is, until Kim says something that catches my attention.

"No, Mac. I understand what you're trying to do, but I told you, I won't exploit this. Stoking women's outrage for votes feels wrong."

I have no idea what he suggested to get this reaction from her, and maybe she's right about that specific thing, but she's wrong too and without thinking, I open my mouth and say so. "Shouldn't we be outraged, though? You're being held to a different standard. No one, not even the pro-lifers, would say a word about something like this if you were a man. I mean, look who they voted for the last time. How many people complain about the way you dress, or the way you sound, or that you're too aloof and cold? Nobody says those things about Richard Lesko, but it would be true if they did. It's a double standard, and we should be outraged because it is outrageous."

Mac's hand on my leg has stilled and everyone is staring at me. Cece is nodding and giving me a big smile, but everyone else appears to be stunned into silence.

"Yes, well, that's true," Kim finally says, clearing her throat before she goes on. "But I can't get angry. If I do, they'll just say I don't have the temperament to be President. It's a—"

The dining room doors burst open, admitting Kim's personal secretary, Holly. "You guys, you have to see this," Holly exclaims, flailing her arms with excitement.

"What is it?" Mac sounds irritated by the interruption.

"Just come... You wouldn't believe me if I told you... Sean

Hennessey..." Holly darts back into the living room without finishing a complete sentence, apparently expecting us to follow.

When we do, we find the TV tuned to one of the 24-hour news channels, the pundits breathlessly expressing their shock about something. And then they replay a clip, only a few moments old, of Sean Hennessey, one of the other democratic candidates, talking to a reporter.

"Senator, do you have any thoughts on the D.C. Dispatch's breaking allegations against Kimberly Dunn?" a fresh-faced young reporter asks him.

"Which allegations would those be?" Hennessey asks with a lazy drawl. It's a perfect affectation of disinterest, and yet there's a dangerous glint in his eye the reporter should have noticed, should have taken as a warning. But in his eagerness, he doesn't see it.

"That Representative Dunn had an abortion." The reporter is nodding and smiling, unaware of the trap closing around him.

"Oh, that." Hennessey's gaze brightens.

When he doesn't say anything else, the reporter prods, "Well, Senator? What are your thoughts on this issue?"

"Is it an issue?" Hennessey seems to give it some thought before saying, "I'm not sure it is, but you seem convinced, so in the interests of transparency I'll tell you this. When I was nineteen, I got an apadravya."

For a fraction of a second I can't breathe, and I wonder if Hennessey realized he was being filmed. But then, as if reading my mind, he glances toward the camera, his smile widening. He knows, and he's quite pleased with himself.

"Did he seriously just tell the world his dick is pierced?" Cece asks, one hand over her mouth.

"What's that?" The reporter on screen is frowning at Hennessey, trying to work out what's happening.

"Look it up. And when you're done doing that, I assume you'll be following up with all the other candidates to find out how many of them have paid for an abortion? Or if they take little blue pills? Or if they've ever cheated on their partners?" Hennessey seems exceptionally proud of himself, as if he knows with just a few sentences he's either knocked it out of the park or sunk his entire candidacy, and he's just reckless enough he doesn't care which.

Holly was right, though—none of us would have believed that without seeing it with our own eyes. Hell, I'm still not sure I believe it.

"Get Hennessey on the phone," Kim orders Brian.

Mac turns to her with a slow grin and jabs one finger at the TV. "If you make it out of the primaries, that is your Vice President."

"You're out of your mind," Alex say, staring at the TV with a stricken look. "His campaign is over."

"We'll see," Mac says before clapping his hands to drag the rest of us out of our stupor. "Let's get on it, people. We've got a lot to do."

CHAPTER 22

MAC

I'VE SPENT FAR TOO much of this day thinking about Sean Hennessey's dick and how it might impact the primary results tomorrow. I'd like to believe he stood up for Kim because it's the right thing to do, but the cynical part of me thinks Hennessey only did it for the votes. He has to know a lot of women won't like the way Kim was being attacked, so sticking up for her, even though she's the competition, might have some electoral benefit for him. But it was definitely a risky move, because talking about your dick isn't usually a winning political strategy.

Fortunately, I'm not running for office, because my dick is the only thing I'm thinking about by the time Gwen and I finally get back to our room. It's after three in the morning, our alarms will wake us in less than four hours, and I'm all but asleep on my feet already but...

"God, I'm so tired," Gwen announces with a yawn as she crawls into bed next to me. She's just come out of the bathroom, face freshly scrubbed and hair brushed into submission. I have to give it to her— no matter how tired she is, she doesn't deviate from her bedtime routine. But she's wearing a light blue cotton sleep shirt with "nope I'm going back to bed" emblazoned on the front in pink and black letters.

"What is that you have on?" I ask suspiciously. It never occurred to me that she doesn't sleep naked; she certainly had when we weren't officially roommates, but I suppose it makes sense. Tristan and her sisters have probably spent years barging into her room uninvited.

"My pajamas." She shrugs then adds with a devilish smile, "But I could take it off."

"Yeah? Not too tired then?" I ask, arching one brow and pulling her against me.

"I am pretty exhausted, but I'd probably sleep better after," Gwen says, reaching under the blanket to grip my hardening cock.

"That's what I was thinking," I murmur against her throat, electricity skating down my spine as I thrust into her hand and tug her nightgown over her hips. She isn't wearing panties and I groan with anticipation, gently nudging her legs apart so I can get my hand between her thighs. "But you first, baby."

"Mac." She laughs softly, her eyelashes fluttering, and I can't resist leaning in for a kiss. It's quick, soft, a tease of what's to come, and when we break apart, she breathlessly finishes her thought. "I will probably pass out after I come and you—"

"Will be fine. Wouldn't be the first time I've rubbed one out while thinking about you," I admit.

Gwen hums, the corners of her eyes wrinkling with a smile. But no matter how much she enjoys knowing I've thought about her when I masturbate, she isn't giving up yet. "Or," she purrs, drawing the word out with her husky, sexed-up voice until I shiver, "we could come together."

"So greedy. Let's see how it goes, okay?" I tease, pushing one finger inside her and slowly pumping my hand.

"No," she complains, her fingers tightening around my shaft. "I want your dick."

With a groan, I close my eyes. It's the only way I can concentrate. Gwen wasn't this bold when she was younger, at least not without a lot of coaxing, and I like this new, more brazen version of her. I'm nearly incapable of denying her, not when she's like this, and maybe not ever, but unfortunately, this once I have to disappoint her. "No condoms, remember?"

We ran out two days ago, and with as frantic as things have been with the campaign, neither of us has had the chance to get more. Really, she only has herself to blame, since she's the one who forbid me from having Cece pick some up.

"I'm on the pill," she whispers, her shoulders lifting in a subtle shrug.

Stilling, I look up at her, studying her face. She sounds so nonchalant, as if we're talking about the weather, and her expression only reinforces that. Her cheeks are flushed with arousal, her lips pink and kiss swollen, but her blue eyes are clear, without a hint of doubt or uncertainty.

"You'd be okay with that?" I ask, but she wouldn't have said it if she wasn't. Given our past, my confidence isn't quite as rock solid as hers seems to be though.

"Yes," she answers without hesitation, but her voice wavers when she adds, "Would you?"

"Not sure. Let me think about it later when every ounce of blood in my body isn't already in my dick, okay?"

Gwen nods and gives me a smile so sweet that I have to kiss her. And when our lips meet, it's soft and tender and full of emotions neither of us would admit out loud. Things I maybe don't even want to admit to myself. But when she moans into my mouth, her hips rocking urgently against my hand, it's like a fuse has been lit, and I can't wait.

Rolling onto my back, I take her with me, tugging her nightgown off as we go. Gwen leans forward, rubbing her soft breasts against my chest. There is nothing in the world that has ever felt so good as having her body pressed to mine, and I band one arm around her waist, holding her even tighter.

"Like this," I urge her, my other hand on her hip, guiding her. My cock is trapped between us, lying flat against my stomach, and the warm, wet folds of her pussy slide along my shaft with every roll of her hips.

I'm not going to last long like this, my balls already drawing tight. Even the smell of her hair, sweet and fresh like summer, makes my cock throb when she burrows her face into my neck. But Gwen is right there with me, on the edge and grinding her clit against my dick so hard I grit my teeth to keep from coming.

"That's it, baby. Get yourself off on my dick," I demand, both hands squeezing her ass, encouraging her to take what she needs.

And she does. Gwen comes on my dick and I come on my stomach and moments later, as she snuggles against me, sleepy and content, I hold her even tighter, warm feelings I don't want to examine too closely blooming in my chest.

CHAPTER 23

MAC

AFTER A CHAOTIC FEW weeks of campaigning, I'm relieved Super Tuesday has finally arrived. Kim badly needs a win today. Hennessey's beaten her in all three contests so far—the Iowa and Nevada caucuses and the New Hampshire primary. He won by fewer than a hundred votes in New Hampshire and caucuses are always unpredictable, so I'm trying not to worry. Besides, there is some good news. No one else is getting close to Kim or Hennessey's numbers, and the other candidates are starting to drop like flies. The problem is, if Kim can't rack up a few wins tonight, she'll be one of them.

Virginia is in the bag; I know that much. She moved to the state twenty years ago and worked her way up through local politics. Virginians love her, and it will be a landslide. But Virginia won't be enough if she doesn't score at least two or three other states too.

However it turns out, no one can fault us for lack of effort. We've been chasing our tails trying to make as many appearances as possible in the states voting today. Arnie and Jess took to the trail to stump for her, traveling separately from Kim so we could cover more ground, and that meant I was hopping between two and sometimes three different travel schedules to hold hands and calm nerves, while Gwen stayed glued to Kim. The result being I'm dog tired and haven't seen nearly enough of Gwen, but that's about to change.

Gwen got roped into meeting Willie and Dr. Neuhaus for coffee this afternoon, so I get to pick Tristan up from school and spend the afternoon with him, which is a first. I'm nervous about having him on my own, even for a few hours. Weirdly excited too, but mostly nervous. What if he doesn't like hanging out with me when his mom isn't around? Or worse, what if I lose him? Or he gets hurt somehow?

"Hey, what are you doing here?" Tristan smiles and lifts his chin in greeting when he finds me waiting outside the school office.

"Your mom sent me so she could grab a cup of coffee with your Aunt Willie. That all right with you?"

"Yeah, sure, but…" Tristan looks up at me, his brows drawn together in a scowl. "Why? She sees Aunt Willie all the time."

"Well…" I hesitate, because I'm not sure if I'm supposed to tell him the truth, but what the hell. "Your aunt wanted to introduce your mom to Dr. Neuhaus."

"I knew it!" Tristan shouts and performs an impressive end-zone dance, one fist pumping. "I knew they were a thing."

"Yeah, it looks that way." I chuckle as we walk out of the school together. I have to put my hand on his shoulder, steering him toward the parking lot when he starts for the crosswalk. He is surprised and seemingly impressed to discover I have a car.

"So, what are we going to do?" Tristan asks once he's fastened his seatbelt.

"Well, there's a place I want to show you. Then we're going to meet your mom and aunts for dinner." I haven't met Willa and Oliva before, so this is a big day in a lot of ways.

I'd be lying if I said I'm not nervous. After all, this is the first time since high school I've met a girlfriend's family, and back then I was too young and stupid to be nervous. But this is different. Gwen isn't my girlfriend, and there's no good reason for the case of low-key jitters I've had since we made these plans. But good reason or not, I can't shake it.

"Then what?" Tristan asks as I turn onto the George Washington Parkway. The kid is full of questions, but it's better than awkward silence.

"Then you'll go home with your aunts, and your mom and I have to go to work for a while." We'll be watching the primary results with the rest of the team from a hotel suite in Arlington.

"Where's this cool place we're going?"

"It's a surprise, but we're almost there. How was school today?" I change the subject, hoping to keep him distracted until the last minute.

"It sucked." Tristan peeks at me from the corner of his eye, checking for my reaction.

The little shit is testing me. A couple of weeks ago we were having lunch, and he complained that the onion rings sucked, which prompted a reminder from Gwen that he wasn't supposed to use that word. "Tristan, you know I know you aren't allowed to say that," I point out, mostly to buy myself a little time to figure out how I should handle this.

"Yeah, but you don't have to tell Mom. We need some guy secrets anyway. She doesn't have to know everything, right?" Tristan's giving me a hopeful look and I have to give the kid credit. He isn't wasting any time now that he's got me alone to see how he might turn this to his advantage.

"Well," I start, considering my words carefully. "Yeah, we can have some guy secrets. That's a good idea, actually. Maybe you'll like this place we're going and that can be our thing, something we do sometimes, just the two of us. But you still have to follow your mom's rules."

"But why? You're my dad so you should get to decide things too."

He should really consider becoming a lawyer when he grows up. That's airtight logic right there. "I can decide things. For instance, I've decided you still have to follow your mom's rules."

"All of them?" he whines, sounding much younger than his age.

"Yes, all of them."

"But I'm not allowed to eat pork rinds," Tristan complains, crossing his arms over his chest and throwing himself back in his seat.

I will not ask why. It doesn't matter. Gwen and I need to be a united front, even over something as stupid as pork rinds. She's the one who's been doing—is still doing—all the heavy lifting of being a parent. I will not undermine her, no matter what. I am not going to ask.

"Why not?" I ask, cringing.

"She says they're gross. Plus, one time I ate so many of them I threw up. After that she banned them."

It takes me a minute to answer, because I'm desperately trying not to laugh. Finally, I manage to say, "Okay, I might let you break that one once in a while on two conditions."

"What?" Tristan narrows his eyes. He already knows he won't like my conditions.

"First, no throwing up." When he nods solemnly, I add, "Second, that's the only one. You have to follow all the other rules. No trying to trick me or arguing about it."

He's gearing up for what is sure to be an epic attempt to convince me that more of Gwen's rules are unreasonable, but I'm not giving him the chance. "But—"

"All of them, Tris. I mean it. I don't care if she makes you stand on your head and count to one hundred every night before bed. You need to assume I always agree with her, because I guarantee you, besides this pork rinds bullshit, I do agree with her."

Fortunately, we've reached our destination and I've put the car in park, because Tristan is giving me a devilish grin. It reminds me so much of his mother, I have to force myself to listen when he says, "You said a swear word."

Fuck. I'm terrible at this. What the hell was Gwen thinking, letting me have him alone? "I did, but I shouldn't have and—"

I'm interrupted by the roar of approaching jet engines, and Tristan's eyes widen as he unclips his seatbelt and turns around to look out the back window.

Holding my breath, I wait for his reaction. Gravelly Point is less than an eighth of a mile from the runway at Reagan National Airport, and the planes are only a hundred or so feet in the air when they pass over the park on their way in for landing. It's a popular spot for plane enthusiasts, hopefully Tristan among them.

"Dad, I think that plane is going to crash on us," Tristan gasps, pointing out the back window at the approaching jet.

Dad? My heart comes to a screeching, shuddering stop for several long seconds while I stare at Tristan. When it resumes beating again, it's thundering in my chest so hard I'm sure he'd be able to hear it if it weren't for the rumble of the plane.

Tristan's never called me "dad" before. Most of the time, he's carefully avoided calling me anything at all. He's called me Mac a handful of times and "hey you" when he's feeling silly, but this is new and unexpected and…fucking amazing.

"It's not, I promise. We're perfectly safe here," I reassure him, tapping his shoulder so he'll turn around and look out the front window as the plane passes over us. "This is why I brought you here. I thought you might like watching the planes land at the airport."

"This is so cool." His momentary fear forgotten, Tristan presses his forehead to the windshield and cranes his neck, not wanting to miss a moment of the jets approach.

"Yeah? I'm glad you think so. Do you want to get out of the car?"

Tristan doesn't answer until the plane has landed. He's bouncing in his seat when he turns to me. "Can we?"

"Yeah, definitely."

We stay for almost two hours, sitting together on the hood of my car, watching the planes and talking. Most of the conversation is, not unexpectedly, about the planes and the airport, but we talk a little about school and his friends too. He doesn't call me dad again, but that's okay. Not that long ago, I was utterly certain I never wanted kids. Who would have guessed that a month and a half later, a towheaded little boy with my eyes and his mother's smile would turn a sunny March afternoon into the best day of my life when he called me dad? Not me, that's for sure, and even if he never says it again, I'll probably live the rest of my life high on the thrill of having heard it just that once.

CHAPTER 24

GWEN

"I'm still pissed I didn't get to meet Dr. Neuhaus," Olivia complains as we're walking to the restaurant to meet Mac and Tris.

"We can probably call her Diane now, don't you think? I mean, since Willie isn't pretending she's just a coworker anymore?" I tease.

"It's not my fault you had track practice." And attempting to get the heat off herself, Willie adds, "Besides, the day isn't a total loss. You get to meet Mac."

"You guys, it isn't like that," I insist for what feels like the hundredth time.

Mac has Tristan. Willie needs to end up with Tristan. Meeting for dinner seemed like the simplest way to transfer my kid between the two of them. Certainly much easier than me running around town picking him up and dropping him off. But it didn't matter how many times I explained my reasoning, my sisters were intent on giving me a hard time about this.

"It is exactly like that," Oliva trills, walking backward in front of Willie and me. "You have a kid together, you spend all your time together when you travel for work, and I know you're sleeping with him so—"

"Willa!" I glare at my middle sister, because she must have blabbed.

"I didn't say a word," Willie says, holding up both hands and shaking her head.

"She didn't. But, like, I've known for a few years now that you're actually a real human woman instead of some kind of weird nun-like mom-sister alien. And you know, it hurts my feelings a little bit that you talk about that stuff with Willie but not me."

"You're still in high school. It wouldn't be appropriate for me to talk about that sort of thing with you."

Olivia stops in front of us, forcing Willa and me to stop as well. Leaning in close, a mischievous smile curling her mouth, she says, "You know I'm not a virgin, right?"

I did *not* know that. I mean, if I really thought about—which I tried not to do—I assumed she probably wasn't. But confirmation is not needed or wanted. Of course, when I gave her the sex talk, I told her she could always come to me, but she never had, preferring Willie instead, presumably because they're closer in age and Willie was in nursing school by then. "That's irrelevant, and we are not talking about this. You're meeting Mac because he is Tristan's dad, that's it." I lean around Liv, gesturing down the block where Mac and Tris are already waiting for us outside the restaurant. "Come on, they're waiting. And I would suggest you do not embarrass me, either one of you, or I will kill you in your sleep. I'm getting sick of sleeping on the couch anyway." Not that our financial situation isn't improving now that I'm working, but with Liv going off to college in the fall, it just seems sensible to wait until then to make any drastic changes.

Mac and Tristan appear to be deep in conversation as we approach but they stop talking when we draw within earshot, and Tristan spins around to close the distance between us. "Mom, mom! It was so cool. We went to a park by the airport and there were so many planes and they were so close. At first, I thought they were going to crash on us, but they didn't." Tristan is bouncing on the balls of his feet with excitement.

"Wow, that sounds fun. Did you—"

Tristan is too wound up to let me finish. Reaching behind him he grabs Mac's hand, tugging on his arm and pulling him forward as he says to my sisters, "This is my dad, but you can call him Mac."

Mac laughs, ruffling Tristan's hair before shaking hands with both of my sisters. Tristan doesn't give them a chance for small talk though, launching into a painfully detailed accounting of all the planes they saw at the park. He could keep this up all day, so we herd him into the pizzeria while he continues to chatter. It isn't until we reach our table and Oliva pulls out the chair next to him that he stops talking about planes.

"I want to sit next to my dad," Tristan says with an indignant glare for Olivia.

"That's all right. I didn't want to sit next to a stinky boy anyway." Oliva moves around the table to sit next to Willa.

"I don't stink, you stink!" Tristan says, employing the classic *I'm rubber, you're glue* defense.

"That's enough, both of you. Nobody stinks. Now sit down and be quiet," I say, shutting them down before it can devolve into their usual sustained bickering.

"So, Mac, how is the campaign going?" Willa asks once we've all taken our seats.

Bless her heart, Willie isn't even a little interested in politics, but the change in subject is exactly what we need. Especially since Olivia is obsessed with the topic, a fascination that, given her age, continues to amaze me. It wasn't until I was in my midtwenties that I really took an interest in government and policy, but she's been captivated by it ever since her civics class in sixth grade.

The political conversation lasts until the waiter brings our food and once he's left the table, Olivia announces, "Well, I'm not eighteen yet so I didn't vote today but if I could have, I would have voted for Governor Carpenter."

I pause in plating Tristan's pizza to glance at Mac. Kim isn't just his candidate of choice, she's his friend, and I'm curious to see how he'll react to my sister's announcement.

"Why's that?" He asks, leaning forward as if he's really interested in her answer.

"She's the most progressive candidate. We need a Universal Basic Income, national healthcare, and a solution for college debt," Olivia explains.

"I agree," Willa pipes in, surprising me. I had no idea she cared about any of this, let alone had strong opinions about it. "The things I see at work, it's shocking. There are so many healthcare issues that could be prevented or mitigated if people could just afford to go to the doctor in the first place. And it's not right, everything Gwen had to go through to take care of all of us. We need a better social safety net."

"Yeah, I absolutely agree, and so does Kim, for what it's worth. But it doesn't matter who is in the White House if we don't have the votes, and right now, we don't. We're moving in the right direction, though, and that's part of my job. We don't just work for individual candidates or campaigns. Lobbyists and interest groups hire us to help make important but boring or unpopular policies seem sexy." Mac is looking over the top of Tristan's head at me as he talks. I can't quite read his expression, but it's making me uncomfortable. It almost feels like admiration or maybe pride, and I don't deserve either. I've only ever done what I had to do.

"That's bullshit," Olivia interjects, drawing his attention back to her. "Real people are suffering now. They can't wait for the privileged masses to catch up."

"Um, you swore!" Tristan points an accusing finger at Olivia.

"You're like the cursing police, aren't you, tiger?" Mac laughs and I can only assume he got at least one warning himself this afternoon.

"It's not fair. If I'm not allowed to say it nobody should," Tristan complains.

"You know what else isn't fair?" Mac asks then glances up at me, evidently checking in to see if I'm okay with him handling this.

He doesn't need to worry about that. He's been reluctant to take on any kind of real authority with Tristan, always deferring to me instead, and I can understand why. This is all new to him, and there's a steep learning curve. Besides that, he probably doesn't want to step on my toes. I hoped that spending some time with Tris without me around would help him feel more confident, and it appears it worked. It's a beginning, anyway. He'll have to figure it out eventually, or Tris will play him like a piano.

"Life," Tristan answers sullenly, because that's what I always tell him.

"Sure, I guess, but I was thinking about something else. You know how you get the summer off and you can sleep in and play video games, and not worry about school for three whole months?" When Tristan nods, Mac continues, "Well, grownups don't get that. Your mom and Willa and I all have to go to work all summer long. That's not fair, either. But maybe we could let you swear now and then if you went to work for all three of us this summer."

"Rob's parents are teachers. They get to swear and have the summer off," Tristan counters with a triumphant grin. My kid can find the loophole in any scenario, and I'm not sure if I should be more frustrated or proud about that.

With a bewildered frown, Mac shakes his head. "I did not think that through."

"Don't feel too bad, Mac," Willa says, giving me an impish smile. "When he was in first grade, he kept getting in trouble for whispering 'dammit' all the time. Turns out, he thought it was okay as long as he said it really quietly, because that's how Mommy said it."

"Oh, oh! Remember the time she decided we needed to start going to church?" Oliva's laughing so hard she can barely get the words out, and I'm contemplating crawling under the table. This has apparently gone from pleasant-family night to humiliate-Gwen night.

Willa nods and laughs helplessly while Tristan grins proudly. He knows what story is coming, even if he doesn't actually remember it.

"Mind you, Gwen never spanked any of us, but the one time she decided we should find religion, Tris kept talking during the service. He was, I don't know, maybe three." Olivia has to pause to giggle-snort before she can continue. "She threatened to take him out and spank him if he didn't quiet down. We were sitting near the front of the church, and he wriggled away from her and ran all the way down the aisle with his hands over his butt while shouting, 'please don't hit me, Mommy!'"

"Oh, Jesus," Mac wheezes through his laughter.

"We didn't have to go to church anymore after that," Tristan adds with a shrug, as if that was his plan all along.

"I could swear I remember telling you two not to embarrass me," I remind my sisters, adding a glare for good measure.

"We're not embarrassing you, Gwen. We're reassuring Mac so he doesn't get discouraged," Willa explains, and it's not even bullshit. Well, not totally bullshit, anyway.

They are definitely enjoying embarrassing me, but the part about reassuring Mac is true too, and it means a lot to me. We've been a tight-knit little family for a long time, and I wasn't sure how they'd feel about Tristan's dad intruding on that. Turns out I was wrong to worry. My sisters are amazing young women, and they're rolling out the welcome mat for Mac in whatever capacity he might join us. It makes my heart swell with pride and love.

After dinner, we're getting ready to leave, and Willie, Olivia, and I step a few feet away so Mac and Tristan can say goodbye. We're still close enough to hear their conversation, but my back is to them. Judging by the expressions on my sisters' faces, that's probably a good thing. Willa is smiling happily and Olivia—sweet, warmhearted Olivia—looks like she might be about to cry.

"Will I see you again before your next trip?" The hope in Tristan's voice is agonizing, and I hold my breath while I wait for Mac's answer, even though I'm almost certain what he'll say.

"We leave again day after tomorrow, but I'll work something out with your mom, okay?"

"Yeah." Tristan's quiet for a moment before adding, his voice barely a whisper, "I'm glad I know you now."

Willa makes a weird choking noise and turns away, Olivia is definitely crying now, and in the face of their emotional responses, there is no way I can hold it together either. Pushing past my sisters, I rush outside so Mac and Tristan won't see my tears.

MAC

IN THE CAR on the way to the hotel, Gwen is quiet, except for the occasional sound of sniffling. We had a good time at dinner with her sisters, or at least I thought so. One minute she was happy and laughing, and now, ever since we got up to leave, she's been on the verge of tears. And I didn't miss the way she rushed out of the restaurant while Tris and I were saying goodbye.

Did I do something wrong? If so, I don't know what it was. God, maybe I really am so bad at this whole parenting gig that I've fucked up in some colossal way and I'm too stupid to even realize what I did.

Since she hasn't said anything, Gwen clearly wants space. If she wanted to talk about it, she would. But between worrying about her and worrying that I've screwed up somehow, I have to ask.

"You okay?" We're idling at a stoplight, so I turn toward her, but she's looking out the window and I can't see her face.

"Y-yes." She hiccups and wipes her eyes on her sleeve. "I'm not sure what happened. I just got really emotional when you and Tris were saying goodnight. All those years when Tristan didn't have a dad or really any men in his life, I used to worry about him so much."

"You never had a boyfriend or anything?" We've never talked about it, probably because it isn't really any of my business, but I assume she must have dated.

"The light is green." Gwen nudges my arm as she shakes her head. When I turn my attention back to the road, she continues. "I dated, but I never wanted to introduce Tristan or the girls to anyone until I was reasonably sure the guy would be around for a while. My mom used to do that sometimes after Dad died, you know? Bring a new guy home every few weeks or months. It was confusing, and if we liked the guy, it was upsetting when he was mysteriously replaced by someone new. I didn't want to put them through that, and there never ended up being anyone long-term enough to bother."

"I don't think I ever would have thought of that," I admit, once again awed by how she's risen to the challenges of parenthood. It's intimidating and a little bit frightening, though, because while I wouldn't ever want to do something that might harm Tristan, there's so much I don't know. So many ways she protects and cares for him that wouldn't even cross my mind.

"Well, maybe someday there will be someone in your life you'll want Tristan to meet," Gwen says as I pull into a parking spot in the garage beneath the hotel. Her voice is casual, but she's holding her chin high, staring out her window at the BMW parked next to us.

"I wouldn't count on that. You know me." I throw the car into park and cut the engine. The likelihood of me meeting and settling down with someone is approximately nil, and she of all people ought to know that.

"I don't know. You seem like you've changed a lot since the first time I knew you." She shrugs and reaches for the door handle. When I put my hand on her arm, she stops, looking over her shoulder at me.

"I don't think I've changed that much. But that reminds me, I don't know what this is with you and me, but that shit last time, where you were sleeping with me and going out with other men? That's not happening this time."

"It's not?" She's chewing on her lower lip, her eyes sparkling.

"It's not." Leaning across the center console, I crowd her space, resisting the urge to touch her because if I do, I might not stop.

"Does that mean you'll take me on a date?"

"Sure, come home with me tonight, and I'll take you out to breakfast in the morning on our way to the office." I hadn't really planned to ask her back to my place, but it's been almost two weeks since we were last in the same city with the campaign. Our next joint trip is only two days away, but that feels like it might as well be a thousand years. Besides, now that the thought's occurred to me, the idea of having Gwen in my own bed instead of another random hotel is too good to ignore.

"You know I can't." Her expression sobers, and she waves one finger between us. "We're only a thing on the road. Here, at home, we're Tristan's parents and that's all."

"I don't remember agreeing to that." At best, it was an unspoken agreement, because we never actually discussed it. I assumed it just sort of worked out that way thus far, but apparently I was wrong about that.

"It would confuse Tristan. You said yourself you don't know what this is. I don't either. So how are we supposed to explain it to him? And how will he feel when whatever this thing is stops being a thing?" Gwen asks, her voice quivering with uncertainty.

"Maybe it won't stop," I say, tugging her arm and pulling her closer.

"What, you think we're just going to keep fucking forever?" She's leaning toward me now too and she licks her lips when her gaze drops to my mouth.

"I don't know. But I know all those years you were gone, I never stopped thinking about you, wanting you, and I really fucking tried. I've never wanted a woman the way I want you, Gwen, and I don't know what that means or how long it will last. You've always been uncharted territory for me. But I do know I respect the fuck out of you and, God knows why, but I trust you. If it all goes to shit, we'll figure out the best way to handle it for Tristan."

"You're a silver-tongued devil." She trembles when I stroke her arm but she's giving me a soft smile.

"Come home with me," I say before kissing her neck, just below her ear.

"I'll text Willa and ask her. I don't want her to feel like I'm taking advantage."

"Okay."

"And I have to be home before Tristan gets up in the morning."

"Sure, no problem."

"And we won't say anything to Tristan. If we're careful—"

"Whatever you say, but I don't think you're giving him enough credit. He'll figure it out. He figured out Willa and Dr. Neuhaus before anyone else." I'm a little surprised I need to point this out to her. Our kid is smart as a whip, and she knows that better than anyone.

Our kid. Huh. There's a phrase I never thought I'd use. It's been a month and a half, and it still gives me a jolt sometimes.

"You're right. Shit, you're right. What would we tell him?" she asks, dropping her forehead against my chest. She sighs, her voice ragged when she adds, "We can't do this, Mac."

"We can. And if he asks, we'll tell him the same thing I told him when he asked if I loved you. It's complicated, but he's the most important thing and he always will be." Palming the back of her head, my fingers tangled in her hair, I tip her head back so she's looking at me again, willing her to understand the things I don't know how to express.

The thing is, Tristan is important. But Gwen is too and becoming more so with each passing day. I don't know what that means, exactly, or how to explain it to her, but I do know I'm never more at ease than when I'm with her. Them. They're my family now, and whatever else happens, I'm certain we can figure it out.

"Do you mean that?" Her lips are a hairsbreadth away from mine, and the warm citrus scent of her perfume is clouding my brain.

"Which part?" I ask and, unable to resist any longer, I kiss the corner of her mouth.

"The part about Tris being the most important thing." She turns her face away so I can't kiss her again, but she rubs her cheek against mine, and the soft friction sets my heart pounding in my chest.

"Yes, or at least, I want to mean it. I've never thought much about anyone but myself, and sometimes that's still my first instinct. But I'm trying." It's an unflattering truth but one she must already know. If self-sacrificing parental instinct came as naturally to me as it did to her, she wouldn't have needed to walk me though this conversation.

"You'll get there. But…" She leans away, putting more distance between us before asking. "Do you want to know a secret?"

"I want to know all your secrets," I say with a grin that's probably verging on a leer.

"Seeing you with Tris, the way you are with him, it's sexy." In the warm yellow glow of the parking garage lights, her cheeks turn pink with her confession.

"What?" I'm so surprised by this revelation I can't help the bark of laughter that escapes with my question and her blush deepens.

"I'm sure it's just some weird evolutionary biology thing," Gwen backpedals.

"All this time, I thought women were making fun of men with the ridicule about dad jokes and dad jeans and dad bods, but really that's all just cover for the overwhelming dad lust, isn't it?" Of course, I'm kidding. In the last few years, Jake's become the master of lame-ass dad jokes and it's absolutely worth mocking. But I want to smooth over the rough edges of her embarrassment, and a little friendly teasing seems like the best way to accomplish that.

"You start wearing dad jeans, and this is over," Gwen says, attempting to maintain a straight face as she bites back laughter and reaches for the door handle again. "Come on, we've got to get upstairs. The first round of polls will close soon."

"No quickie in the car first?" I ask with an exaggerated frown, reaching for my own door.

"I think you can wait until we get back to your place," Gwen says and then, when we're both out of the car, she adds, "Besides, I'm not eighteen anymore. I'm not as flexible as I used to be."

"Hmm, I might have to test that for myself, but even if you're right, my car is a lot bigger these days." Draping one arm over her shoulders, I pull her into my side, both of us laughing as we walk together toward the elevator.

CHAPTER 26

GWEN

WHEN WE REACH THE PENTHOUSE, Cece greets us with two glasses of champagne, pressing them into our hands. Despite the generous size of the suite, it's crammed full of people, some I know and many I don't. Since Virginia is Kim's home base, and this is a big night with ten states holding their primaries and three more holding caucuses, there are more supporters on hand than usual.

Cece is all but vibrating with optimistic excitement, and I hope some of it rubs off on me. I voted first thing this morning after I dropped Tristan at school and then hardly thought about it again all day. Which probably isn't that surprising, given everything else I had going on, but now I'm all tied up with nervous energy. If Kim doesn't do well tonight, that probably spells the end of the campaign. How is everyone else so calm and relaxed? I'm so wound-up I have to hold my champagne flute with both hands to keep from spilling it.

"Are you nervous?" I whisper to Mac when Cece has moved on to spread her cheer elsewhere.

"About all this?" He gestures around the room, and when I nod, he shakes his head.

"How can you not be nervous? What if she loses them all?" I fret as quietly as I can. I'm sure I'm not the only one on edge tonight, and I don't want to feed anyone else's anxiety.

"She won't lose them all. She'll win Virginia for sure," Mac answers just as quietly.

"But Virginia isn't enough, and what if she does lose them all? Stranger things have happened. Do you not remember the last election?" I tug on the sleeve of his jacket, as if he doesn't understand how important tonight is and all the ways it could go wrong.

"I remember." The mere thought is apparently enough to make him scowl, but after a moment he gives me a reassuring look and bends closer so he can speak directly into my ear. "It's going to be okay. And if she loses them all, I'll console myself by taking you home and fucking your ass so hard you can't sit down for a week. Then tomorrow I'll call Hennessey and see if he wants to give us a job."

"Mac, be serious."

"She won't lose them all. It will be fine." He puts both hands on my shoulders, giving them a gentle squeeze. "Don't give yourself an ulcer over this."

"Willie says that's just a myth. Bacteria causes ulcers," I inform him smugly, much like Willie once informed me when she was in nursing school.

"Okay, but the point is—"

"Hey, it's seven o'clock! Georgia, Virginia, and Vermont are all closing." Arnie's booming voice interrupts Mac from across the room, quieting the bubbling chatter around us.

Everyone stares at the TV in silence, colorful graphics flashing across the screen. It's too soon to expect a result in Georgia or Vermont, but the anchor immediately declares Virginia for Kim, and the room erupts in clapping and cheers.

By the time the polls close in Alabama, Massachusetts, North Carolina, Oklahoma, and Texas at eight, I've found a seat with Cece and Kim on the couch in front of the TV while Mac mingles around the room, charming supporters and donors. As soon as the polls have closed, Massachusetts is called for Carpenter, which isn't a surprise, given it's her home state. Georgia, Vermont, and the other states that just closed are still too tight to call, and it seems to be getting to Kim.

"This is nerve-wracking," she grumbles, smoothing her skirt. "Why am I doing this again?"

"Because my mom will be the best President ever," Jess answers as she joins us, none too gracefully flopping down in her mother's lap. Since she's campaigned separately from Kim, trying to cover more ground, I've never actually met her, but I like her immediately.

Kim grunts under her daughter's weight and shakes her head. "Don't you think you're a little old for this?"

"You're the one who said I'd always be your little girl." Jess frowns at her mom with mock horror and gasps. "Was that a lie, Mother?"

"No, but I didn't think you'd still be sitting on my lap in your thirties." Kim laughs and pinches Jess's arm.

Smiling to myself, I try to imagine this scenario playing out with me and Tristan in another twenty years. As unlikely as that seems, it makes me laugh, and I'm still chuckling when Jess introduces herself.

"You must be Gwen." She smiles then looks past me at Cece, greeting her too.

"It's nice to finally meet you. I've heard a lot about you from your mom and Mac," I say, not just because it's polite but because it's true. Kim adores her daughter, and Mac is very fond of Jess. The way he talks, I sometimes think she's more of a sibling to him than Alex.

"Whatever Mac's told you, it's all lies." Jess tips her head toward Kim before adding with an impish smile, "At least, I'll claim it is as long as she can hear."

The lighthearted conversation seems to be a good distraction for Kim. When other guests try to draw her into conversation about the campaign she resists, instead remaining focused on our cheerful banter.

It's almost nine when they finally call Georgia and North Carolina for Kim. Lesko won Oklahoma, his home state and, if the polls are to be believed, it's likely the only one he'll win. Vermont was declared for

Carpenter. Hennessey hasn't won a thing yet, but Texas is locked in a three-way tie between him, Carpenter, and Kim. Who knows how that will turn out. Still, I'm starting to relax. We've won enough that the campaign will go on no matter what else happens tonight.

I'm still chatting with Jess and Cece, cheering each win and booing each loss as they are announced, when Mac joins us shortly before eleven.

"Don't look so stressed, Kim. You're doing well," Mac says with a pleased smile.

"Am I?" She gives him a dubious look, her nerves still unsettled.

"You know you are, so stop fishing for compliments," Mac teases before adding the reassurance she wanted anyway. "Even if you don't win anything else tonight, you've done what you needed to do."

"You're right." Kim nods emphatically as if trying to convince herself.

"Of course I am." Mac gestures for me. "Gwen and I are going to get going before it gets too late, though."

"What? It's still early. You didn't use to be such an old stick in the mud, Mac." Jess laughs, giving his arm a playful shove.

"I'm still not but…" The wicked gleam in Mac's eye is my cue to interrupt before he can finish that sentence because whatever it is, it would almost certainly be inappropriate and embarrassing.

"Okay, let's go." I stand abruptly, grabbing my purse and slinging it over my shoulder.

Mac grins, one brow arching sharply, but it's Jess who smirks and says, "Yeah, I didn't really want to hear whatever he was going to say either, so thanks."

"You kids are terrible," Kim says in that tone parents use when they're actually amused by the bad behavior.

"What? I'm innocent. The girls are the ones with their minds in the gutter." Mac straightens his shoulders and smooths one hand over his tie, the picture of a wrongly accused man. Everyone knows that for the lie it is and it gets the reaction he was hoping for, because we all laugh.

Mac is silent on the short walk to the elevator but as soon as the door slides closed behind us, he crowds me against the back wall. Bracketing my face in both hands, he's kissing me hard before I can so much as utter a startled gasp. His thumbs stroke my cheeks, and he nips and licks at my lower lip until I open for him, his tongue sliding against mine. It's a toe-curling kiss, the kind that makes my mind go blank and my skin tingle. The kind that makes me moan into his mouth and rub against him with an eagerness I've never felt with anyone else.

When the elevator dings, announcing our arrival in the parking garage, Mac doesn't break the kiss. Sliding his hands down my sides, then around to my ass, he lifts me, and I squeak against his mouth in surprise, clinging to him as he carries me out of the elevator. In real life, it's exactly as hot as it is in the movies—hotter even—and I'm eagerly rubbing against him, my skin warming with arousal. It isn't until we've reached his car and he's slammed my back against it that he breaks the kiss and sets me on my feet again.

Lifting his head, Mac scans the parking garage. But even as he scopes out our surroundings, presumably making sure no one else is in the vicinity, he's tugging up my skirt. Satisfied by whatever he sees —or doesn't see, I guess—he turns his attention back to me, using his knee to part my legs so he can stroke the swatch of cotton between my thighs.

"Mac," I start, intending to tell him we can't do this here. Not that I don't want to do it here, or just about anywhere with him, but we shouldn't.

My objections are forgotten, though, when he slips a finger inside my panties to tease my clit. With his other hand he's unbuckling his belt, slapping my hands away when I try to help him. The sound of his zipper is followed by his hand on my thigh, raising my leg until I hook it around his hip, and I can feel the pressure of his cock straining against my panties.

It took him nearly a week after I told I'm on the pill to decide he was comfortable going without a condom. I absolutely understand his caution around the subject, but I'm glad we're on the same page now. For one thing, it makes impulsive, reckless moments like this one a lot easier. For another, I like having him bare, with nothing between us, which means, at the moment, I'm irritated by the barrier of my underwear, separating my aching center and the broad head of his cock. I'm about to complain about that when Mac pushes the cotton aside and buries himself with a single driving thrust.

"Oh, fuck," I cry out, louder than I mean to, and the sound echoes in the cavernous parking garage. Mac makes a shushing sound and palms the back of my head, pressing my face to his chest as he rocks urgently against me. But as the coiling arousal in my center tightens, I can't control my keening whimpers of pleasure.

"You've got to be quiet, baby," Mac rasps close to my ear. "There's a security office about sixty feet across the way."

I don't know if it's the blinding orgasm that's on the cusp of detonation or the news that this location is even riskier than I realized, but it's just not possible to be quiet. In a last-ditch effort to prevent myself from making too much noise, I do the only thing I can. I bite Mac's chest, the fabric of his dress shirt bunching in my mouth.

"Fuck." Mac grunts in surprise, his fingers knotting in my hair, his pelvis slamming into me with more force.

In a moment of startling clarity, I worry the car alarm might go off, but the thought is gone as quickly as it came, replaced by a burst of sensation so intense it chokes out all other thoughts. It starts with the spasming muscles in my core, clenching and quivering around the hard length of Mac's erection, and spreads in a hot wash of bliss that leaves me weak-kneed and panting. With a ragged groan, he drops his head, his face in my hair, as he grinds against me, his cock pulsing as he comes.

When our breathing has returned to something resembling normal, Mac lets go of my leg and straightens, his fingers immediately finding the knot of his tie. He makes a mock choking sound before saying, "Next time, remind me to loosen this first."

"Here, let me," I offer, and he lets me work it loose around his neck.

"Thanks." He steps away from me and we both right our clothes before getting in the car.

"So how far do you live from here anyway?" I ask once we've both buckled in and he's backing out of the parking space.

"Eh, like, a half a mile. Maybe three quarters."

"Wait," I say, holding up one hand. "If you live that damn close to the hotel, what was that?" I flail one arm behind us in the general direction of the parking space we've recently vacated. I knew he lived in Arlington, but I naively assumed he lived on the other side of town, which might be a fifteen or twenty-minute drive. More if there were traffic, which is always a possibility, even at this time of night.

"It seemed like a good idea at the time." He gives me a wicked smile as he navigates through the maze of the parking garage.

"You're depraved." But I'm not really irritated with him. This is classic Mac. Risky public sex, in the parking garage of the very same hotel where our coworkers are still watching the primary results, because why not?

"Uh, I seem to recall having a lot of sex with you in a lot of places we shouldn't have. Some of it you even instigated, so you're not really in a position to get judgy." Mac grins at me and reaches over to rest one hand on my thigh before pulling into the street.

I don't have an answer for that, because he's absolutely right, so we ride in silence until he turns down a side street and then into an alley that runs between two rows of four-story federal-style townhomes.

When he pulls into the short drive in front of one and the garage door begins to rise, I gape at him. "You live here?"

"Yeah, it's too big, but I can't stand condos and I didn't want a long commute. Plus, I bought it as soon as I came back from Michigan and the housing market was still a mess, so I got a great deal." He shrugs, a rare blush spreading up his neck. For the first time I realize he's embarrassed by his money. It's both surprising and adorable, but that's not enough to dull the impact of something else I'm just figuring out.

Speechless, I stare at Mac until the motion-activated lights turn off. I knew his family had money, but I guess I didn't really understand how much. He'd bought what even at that time must have been a million-dollar home when he was twenty-five. It's incomprehensible, and I can't wrap my head around that kind of privilege. What must it have been like to never have to worry about money? While I was working two jobs and going to school and struggling to raise three kids—one of which was his—he was living a carefree life in a million-dollar bachelor pad.

It's always been obvious we had very different backgrounds, but it never seemed so stark as it does now.

CHAPTER 27

MAC

WHEN THE LIGHTS have gone off and she still hasn't said anything, I open my door, triggering them on again. She's wearing a stunned expression that doesn't quite fit her face, as if this is possibly the most surprising thing that's ever happened to her and her facial features just don't quite know the right way to express it. It seems like a bit of an overreaction, to be honest.

"So, did you just want to sit here, or do you want to go in?" I finally ask, because the lights will go out again soon.

That seems to snap her out of whatever trance she's been in, because she throws her door open, muttering something I don't catch as she gets out of the car.

Unlocking the door and turning on the lights, I hold it open for Gwen, letting her go in ahead of me. The first floor isn't much. The two-car garage takes up half of it, so there's just a small bedroom, a bathroom, and the front door.

"Nothing really to see down here. I don't use it. That's not even set up as a guest room or anything." I gesture to the bedroom, which is in fact empty except for a few random boxes in the closet, and then take her hand, tugging her toward the stairs.

On the second floor, the stairwell opens into the dining room in the center of the house. The kitchen is at the back, and the living room at the front.

"Can I get you a drink?" I ask as she follows me into the kitchen.

"Sure, whatever you're having is fine." Looking around, arms crossed over her middle, she's taking it all in, and I wonder what she sees.

Does she like my house, or does she think it's ostentatious? I made a conscious effort when I moved in to try to make it homey and comfortable rather than flashy and pretentious like my folks' house, but who knows if I succeeded? Given the way I grew up, my idea of casual might still be gaudy to her.

By the time I've retrieved two bottles of beer from the fridge, she's wandered into the living room and is running her hand along the back of the brown leather couch. I approach, offering her a bottle. Our fingers brush when she takes it from me, and I resist the urge to pull her into my arms and kiss her. We have all night.

When I take her hand, tugging her toward the stairs again, she says, "Don't you get tired of all these stairs?"

"Yeah, I sleep on the couch sometimes when I'm too lazy to drag my ass up here," I admit as we climb to the third floor. When we reach the landing and Gwen stops, I give her hand a gentle squeeze and shake my head. "We'll come back to this. There's something else I want to show you first."

She heaves a sigh, rolls her eyes, and follows me up to the fourth floor.

Sweeping one arm out to indicate the whole level, I say, "Three guest bedrooms. About the only time this floor gets used is when Jake and his family visit. Come on, one more set of stairs."

"Are you kidding me? I only counted four floors from outside." She balks, and I can tell she's considering telling me to go to hell.

"Trust me. You want to see this," I coax, rubbing my thumb across the back of her hand.

"Okay, let's get this over with."

It's hard not to laugh, because she sounds like she's on the way to the firing squad instead of getting the nickel tour of my place.

She pulls her hand free and starts up the stairs ahead of me. Pausing for a moment to admire the sway of her hips, I take a deep breath and adjust my hardening cock before following.

"What is this?" She asks over her shoulder once she's reached the door at the top of the stairwell.

"You'll see. Open it."

She does, taking three steps out onto the rooftop terrace before stopping so short I nearly run into her. "Oh my god, Mac," she murmurs and takes a few more steps then turns in a slow circle, soaking in the view. "This is gorgeous."

This terrace and its incredible view were the biggest reasons I bought the place. To the east, the Potomac shimmers in the moonlight, and beyond that, the lights of D.C. sparkle, all the landmarks of the capitol rising out of the darkness. The Washington Monument, the Lincoln Memorial, the Jefferson Memorial. Even the Capitol dome. I've lived here nearly a decade, and it still takes my breath away.

Leaning against the railing at the far end of the terrace, she's staring across the river, eyes wide and cheeks slightly flushed, and it seems she's unable to look away. I know the feeling.

"Well, is this worth all the stairs?" I ask lightly as I come up behind her and slip one arm around her waist.

"I never want to go back inside," she murmurs, leaning into me.

"We can stay out here as long as you like." I smile into her hair, inhaling her scent. "We can even fuck out here if you want."

"You would say that." Gwen glances to both sides, peering over the half walls that separate my rooftop from my neighbors, then looks over her shoulder at me with a teasing smile. "I bet this terrace has seen a lot of action."

"Maybe a little," I admit with a reluctant laugh. It's not like I have anything to be ashamed of, but still, I don't love the idea of talking about my former partners with her. It seems awkward.

Sensing my unease, she turns around and leans back, one palm flat on my chest as she cradles her beer in her other hand. There's a smile tugging at her lips when she asks, "Are you shy about your other women?"

"Not shy but…cautious," I admit.

"I'm a realist and I've always known exactly what you are."

"And what's that?" I ask, wrapping a lock of her honey-blond hair around my finger.

"A player."

"I don't know about that." It's hard to tell for sure, because I can't concentrate with her so close, but I think I might be offended.

"I do. I bet you've had way more partners than I have." Gwen's lips twitch and her eyes are sparkling. It's confusing, because she doesn't seem at all put off by this conversation.

"That doesn't bother you?" I ask cautiously. When we were younger, we both were jealous assholes, at least with each other, and I don't seem to have grown out of it, but maybe she has.

"I'm a little jealous, to be honest. You got to sow your wild oats and I feel like I missed out on a lot of that," she says, tipping her head up to look at the night sky. With a sigh, she adds, "But maybe it wouldn't have mattered. I'm probably too uptight to have ever sowed many oats to begin with."

Oh. She isn't jealous of the women I've been with. She's jealous of me and the freedom I had. It seems one of us has grown up, after all.

"Sowing oats isn't always all it's cracked up to be," I say, thinking about our earlier dinner with her sisters. Despite all the challenges they faced, the three sisters and Tristan are a tight, loving family. I may have had every other privilege, but I've never had that.

"If you say so."

"I do, and you aren't the only one who's jealous, you know," I confess. I'm not wild about rummaging around in my baggage and showing off my dirty laundry but for Gwen, if it might make her feel better, I'll do it.

"I know, I'm so sorry," she apologizes, her mood instantly dampening, and it takes me a minute to figure out the problem. Once I do, it's obvious.

Tristan. All the years she had with him that I missed. Yeah, I'm jealous of that too.

"Not what I meant, but we can talk about that in a minute if you want," I say, plucking her beer bottle out of her hands and setting it on a nearby table. Then, wrapping my arms around her and pulling her tight against my chest, I tuck her head under my chin and explain, "You and your sisters and Tristan. You guys are all so close. It's nothing like my family. I mean, you've met them, right? I'd give anything to have the kind of relationship you have with Willa and Olivia with Alex."

"I don't even have parents," she counters, mumbling into my shirt.

"True, but my mom is actually pretty awesome. Odds are once you and Tristan start spending some time with her, she'll adopt you too." No doubt she will. My mom is big-hearted and kind, hands down the best of all the MacKenzies.

"Well, that would only be fair." Her blue eyes are glittering in the moonlight, prettier than the view from my terrace, and my breath snags in my throat.

"Yeah, why's that?" I croak.

"Because my sisters are about three seconds from introducing you to people as their brother," she says with a grin. And then, her expression growing more thoughtful, she adds, "You know, between the two of us, we almost have all the working parts of a normal family."

"Eh, normal is overrated." Which is true, I think, if normal even exists. "And you're exaggerating about your sisters. They've met me once."

"Maybe a little," she admits with a shrug. "But not much. They like you, and they've been listening to me sing your praises for a decade. I think maybe in some ways you've always been a part of us."

"You talked about me?" Given that Tristan knew about my tattoo, among other things, I shouldn't be surprised, but I have a weird, fizzy sensation in my chest so I guess I am.

She's quiet a minute, studying my face, and when she finally speaks, her voice is thick. "I screwed up a lot with you, Mac. I know that, and I'm sorry. But from the beginning, I wanted you to be a part of Tristan's life, even if you weren't there. I wanted him to know you. So I told him what I could and I never, ever said a bad word about you in front of any of them."

Her voice is so emphatic, her expression so heartfelt, that I have to take several deep breaths to subdue the lump forming in my throat. When that doesn't work, I do the only thing I can. I make a joke. "That must have been difficult."

A small smile tugs at the corners of her mouth, but her eyes are serious when she asks, "Can we back up to that thing you said we could talk about in a few minutes?"

"Sure." And then, because I don't really want to talk about it, I warn her. "If you really want to."

I don't know what she sees in my expression, but she gasps, her eyes widening, and her voice is whisper soft when she says, "You are angry with me."

"You bet," I admit with a tight smile.

"Why haven't you said anything? Since that first night, you haven't brought it up at all." Gwen puts her hands on my chest and pushes, trying to put space between us, but I refuse to loosen my hold on her. To let her go. She wants to talk about this? Fine. But I am not going to allow it to drive a wedge between us.

"What good would it do to yell at you about it? Nothing we do now is going to change the choices you made then. And knowing you like I do, knowing what a good little rule-follower you've always been, I know you're beating yourself up about it just fine on your own. You don't need me to do it for you."

There's more I want to say, to try and make her understand, because Christ, this shit is complicated, but Gwen's eyes are welling with tears, her lower lip quivering, so I stop to wipe her cheeks. "You're comforting me right now?" She throws her hands up, blinking at me in disbelief. "I'm the asshole here!"

"Maybe that's why this works, because we're both assholes. Did you ever think of that?" I tease, giving her cheeks one more swipe and dropping a kiss on the end of her nose for good measure. When she shakes her head and gives me a watery laugh, I venture on. "Because that's the other thing, Gwen. I was—am, but worse back then, I think —an asshole, and we both know I would have walked if you told me. So yes, I am angry with you, but I'm twice as angry with myself, and I don't see what good could come of taking any of that out on you."

"That's… I mean, that makes sense as far as being co-parents or friends or whatever. But how can you still want me like this when I—"

"Don't," I say, pressing a finger to her lips. "Don't ask, because I don't have an answer. All I know is, since the first moment I saw you all those years ago, I've wanted you and I've never stopped. I'd super appreciate it if you don't test the limits of what might make me stop any further than you already have, but right now I'm exactly where I want to be. Are you?"

Waiting for Gwen's answer is torture, because my heart is slamming in my chest and the moment feels weighty with significance. But she doesn't keep me waiting long; pushing up on her tiptoes, her voice soft and her expression softer, she says the one word I wanted—maybe needed—to hear.

"Yes."

CHAPTER 28

MAC

FOR AS GOOD a day as yesterday was, today is turning into a spectac-
ular pile of shit. Partly because after our emotional talk, followed by a
lot of sex, Gwen and I got very little sleep last night. Mostly though
it's because I got overconfident and brought up child support over
breakfast.

It didn't go well.

And now my dad has barged into my office, which can only mean
my day is about to get even worse.

"William," he says as he lowers himself into the chair across my
desk. There's no hint of his mood or intent in his tone.

"Dad," I reply without looking up from my laptop, content to wait
him out rather than ask what he wants. It's a petty pleasure, no doubt,
but one I have no intention of giving up.

"I wanted to stop by and congratulate you on yesterday's results.
It's shaping up to be a tight race between Kim, Carpenter, and
Hennessey."

That gets my attention, and I look at him over the top of my screen. He wants to congratulate me? It's obviously a trap. "Hennessey is the only one who matters. Carpenter isn't a threat."

"We'll see." Dad folds his hands in his lap and frowns, as if I'm making a grave mistake discounting Carpenter. As if he actually wants Kim's campaign to be successful.

He's working behind the scenes to help Brett Whitaker and if I were him, I'd be pulling hard for Carpenter. She'd be the easiest one for Whitaker to beat if he actually unseats the incumbent president in the Republican primaries. He needs Kim to lose.

"Yup, we will," I agree, because there isn't much else to say.

"You're letting yourself get distracted, Junior. You aren't focused. You need to fire the girl. She's—"

"What Gwen is, Dad, is not up for discussion," I interrupt.

He knows her name but didn't use it for a reason. Women are objects to him, a pretty accessory or a place to put his dick, nothing more. Or, in the case of my mom, a way to elevate his own social status. It would never occur to him that I actually like and respect Gwen, nor does it matter that she's the mother of my child. It doesn't even matter that she's damn good at her job, and from the agency's perspective, that's the only thing that should matter. This is about fucking with me, and I won't allow him to use her that way.

"Are you coming to dinner tonight? Your mom was lamenting this morning that she hasn't heard from you in more than a week," he says, changing the subject to poke at another sore spot.

Between all the travel for work and hanging out with Tristan when I'm home, I haven't made it to my parents much lately. I've been negligent about calling mom too, and I don't even have a good excuse for that, except that I've grown tired of her pleading with me to make peace with my dad. It's not fair to hold that against her; there's a lot she doesn't know, but with everything else, it's one more thing I don't have the energy to deal with right now. "Probably not. I promised Tris we'd spend some time together before I leave again tomorrow." I don't expect my dad to understand my shifting priorities. He was never one of those put-your-children-first kind of dads. Mom will get it, though, but I need to call her.

"I don't know why you're bothering with that, but you could bring him. Your mother and Alex want to meet him."

Mom and Alex want to meet Tris. Not Dad though. It still shocks me sometimes that they can't see what an asshole he really is, that they're fooled by the thin veneer he wears for them. It's just easier to assume I'm the problem, I guess. "Not yet, but maybe—"

I'm interrupted by a soft knock on my door, which swings open a moment later to admit Gwen. She takes three steps into the room and halts, having noticed my dad. He's giving her a hard stare, the kind that says *you don't belong, get out*, and for the briefest second she hesitates, her cheeks flushing. But then she straightens her shoulders, focusing her attention on me. "I'm sorry to intrude but I wanted to let you know the school just called. Tris is sick, so I'm going to pick him up and take him to the pediatrician."

"Is he okay?" Unfamiliar concern sweeps in to replace my anger and frustration. It's not that I've never cared if other people were sick before, but this is different. It's visceral, fueling a sense of worry unfamiliar in its intensity.

"I'm sure he's fine, but I'll let you know after he sees the doctor."

Her cool confidence should be reassuring, and it is, a little. But worry still nags at my gut, and I have to force myself to ignore the temptation to interrogate her for a list of his symptoms. That wouldn't accomplish anything except delaying Tris getting to the doctor and probably pissing Gwen off.

Opening the top drawer of my desk to retrieve my keys, I offer them to Gwen. "Why don't you take my car? It'll be easier than the Metro and more comfortable for him."

"But—"

"Come on, Gwen, you know I'm right." I shake the keys at her as I add, "When I finish here, I'll take the train to your place so I can check in on him and pick it up, all right?"

Gwen hesitates for just a minute then nods, and I toss her the keys. With a promise to text me when she knows more, she leaves.

As soon as the door closes behind her my dad, who was remarkably silent in her presence, starts in again. "You're a fool, William. That girl is going to take you for everything you're worth."

Right, Dad. That totally makes sense. Obviously, that's why she spent twenty minutes this morning calling me every four-letter word she could think of while refusing to take a dime from me.

My anger bubbles up, spilling over before I can stop it. Jabbing my finger at the recently closed door, I glare at him. "Get. The. Fuck. Out."

He nods and rises, satisfied to have provoked my anger, but when he reaches the door, he stops with his hand on the knob. His tone is calm, conversational even, as he says, "You're too cunt-drunk to see it, son, and I get it. But you shouldn't trust her, not after the way she treated you the first time around. That brat of hers probably isn't even yours."

"But I should trust you? You've got to be fucking kidding me right now." My incredulity is the only thing preventing me from getting up and physically removing him from my office. After all the years of anger and animosity, it's a wonder we've never laid hands on one another before, and today isn't going to be the day we start, no matter how gratifying it would be.

"Just trying to give you the benefit of my experience. You can do with it as you wish," he says coolly with an indifferent shrug.

"Your experience has nothing to do with this."

"You keep telling yourself that, William, but we aren't so different." And then he's gone, the door slamming behind him.

CHAPTER 29

GWEN

DRIVING Mac's Lexus is nerve-wracking. It's the first time I've driven in over six months, traffic is a nightmare, and my anxiety is only made worse by the fact that it's his car. He let me drive the Corvette a few times, mostly when he'd had too much to drink, and I was too young and stupid and overconfident back then to be intimidated. That's no longer the case, and I have a pit in my stomach the whole time. He was right, though—having his car is a lot easier than the Metro with a feverish, puking kid.

"If you get puke in your dad's car, I will murder you, Tris." We've just finished at the doctor's office, and I'm helping him with his seat-belt for the trip home as I issue my threat.

"Dad wouldn't care. He's way cooler than you." Tristan gives me a weak smile, obviously not too sick to still take delight in giving me a hard time.

"Dad, is it now?" I tease, giving him a sidelong look as I pull out my phone to text Mac. It isn't the first time he's called him that, but he's

212

doing it more and more and it raises the small hairs on my arms every time.

This is working.

But Tristan just shrugs, his pale cheeks turning ruddy.

"All right, give me just a second to let him know what the doctor said, and then we'll get you home and in bed."

Gwen: Apparently this year's flu shot isn't as effective as they'd hoped.

Mac: Poor kid. Does he need anything? I can stop at the store on my way over...

"Hey, Tris, your dad wants to know if you want him to bring you anything after work?"

"He's going to come over?" The smile that lights up his face makes my heart clench. Not trusting myself to speak, I nod, and Tristan asks, "Pizza?"

That's enough to pull me out of my sentimentality and I shake my head. "Hard pass as long as you're puking. Any reasonable requests?"

Tristan considers that for a moment then says, "Do you think he'll still come if I don't need anything?"

"I'm sure of it."

"Then I guess I'm good."

Gwen: He couldn't think of anything. I'll let you know if he changes his mind.

Gwen: Also, I've been informed that "Dad is way cooler" than me.

Mac: That is not breaking news.

Gwen: Jerk. We're on the way home now so you can come on over whenever you finish up.

Tristan sleeps the whole way home. Luckily, I'm able to score a parking spot near the entrance to our building, because he barely rouses enough to stumble up the stairs to our apartment. I'm struck by an unexpected pang of longing as I watch him struggle up the stairs and into bed, pining for the days when he was small enough that I could sweep him into my arms and carry him. Despite enjoying the freedom his age has granted me, there are things about having a little one I still miss.

Once he's tucked into bed and snoring softly, I busy myself with cleaning. Not that the apartment is messy, but I need something to distract me from Mac's impending visit. He's met Tristan and me here a few times when we were all going out together, but he's never been inside our apartment and it's hard not to focus on its flaws, the primary one being that it's much too small for the four of us. After seeing his townhouse, there's no way our shabby little apartment can live up to his standards.

By the time Mac shows up, Olivia is home from school, and Willa and Dr. Neuhaus—Diane—are in the kitchen making dinner. I have a feeling now that the cat is out of the bag, she will be around a lot. Their company was a good distraction while I was waiting, but now that he's here, I realize all the bodies just make the place seem smaller.

"Uh, come on in. It's a little bit hectic here at the moment, everyone—"

"Mac!" Willa interrupts, coming out of the kitchen with a wooden spoon in hand to greet him. "Dinner is almost ready. Can you stay?"

"I wouldn't if I were you. Willie's a terrible cook," Olivia offers from her spot at the kitchen table where she's doing homework.

"I don't want to impose. I just wanted to drop some stuff off for Tris and see how he's doing," Mac says graciously, raising the two grocery sacks he's carrying.

"Don't be silly." Willa rushes forward to take the bags as she adds more quietly, "Olivia isn't wrong, but Diane is helping with dinner and she's a good cook."

All I can do is shrug helplessly when Mac looks at me. "You're welcome to stay if you want."

"All right," he says, offering Willa a hesitant smile before turning back to me. "Is he awake?"

"Probably not, but he threatened to puke on me if I didn't wake him up when you got here so…"

Mac chuckles, following me across the apartment to the short hall that leads to the bedrooms. I pour all of my nervous energy into chewing my lip, afraid he'll notice the worn carpet, the dingy paint, the single bathroom and the too-few bedrooms.

When I open Tristan's door, he turns his head on the pillow, his dull eyes brightening when he sees Mac. "You came!"

"Of course I did." Mac smiles and takes a seat on the edge of Tristan's bed. "I brought you some Vernor's and graham crackers and—"

"Pork rinds?" Tris asks with more enthusiasm that I would have thought him capable of at the moment.

"Uh, no. Remember the no-puking rule?"

"Yeah, okay, I guess that's fair," Tristan grumps.

"When you're better, okay?" Mac asks, smoothing Tristan's sweaty hair away from his face. Tristan nods, and he goes on. "I figure you'll be out of school for a couple days, so I brought you a couple of books and a movie in case you get bored."

"What movie?" Tristan asks, his flushed face gleaming with interest.

"It's called The Sandlot. Have you seen it?"

"No." Tristan shakes his head. "What's it about?"

"Hmm, baseball, a crazy dog, all kinds of good stuff. It was one of my favorites when I was your age."

"So it's an old movie?" Tristan narrows his eyes, not too sick to be suspicious of anything pre-2010-ish.

"He still hasn't forgiven me for E.T., which is apparently lame," I offer from the doorway.

"Oh, well, I can't blame him for that," Mac says, offering Tristan a conspiratorial grin. "Trust me, you'll like this one."

"Okay, I'll try it," Tris concedes, but it doesn't appear as if his expectations are very high.

"Dinner's just about ready. Do you want to see if you can hold down a little chicken noodle soup?" I ask.

"Did Aunt Willie make it?" Tristan glances between us with a skeptical frown.

"No, it's the canned stuff," I reply, trying not to laugh.

"Sure, okay then." Tristan nods with obvious relief.

When we all gather around the table, it's hard to say who is more surprised when Tristan asks if he can sit in Mac's lap. All the adults in the room share stupefied looks until Mac finally sits down and pats one knee.

"All right, but no breathing on my food, patient zero."

"What's 'patient zero' mean?" Tristan asks as he clambers into his dad's lap.

"The person who gets sick first and infects everyone else," Diane explains, taking her seat.

"Livie, put your book away. You know there's no reading during dinner," I chide her as I set Tristan's bowl of warmed soup in front of him.

She rolls her eyes but complies, and Willa asks, "What's so interesting anyway?"

Eager to talk about her most recent fascination, Oliva explains, "It's a biography of Justice Ramirez. I'm thinking about writing my final paper for AP English on her. She's really amazing, you know?"

"No," Willa answers flatly. Although her interest in political issues the other day surprised me, obsessing about a supreme court justice's life story is still a bridge too far for her.

Diane is interested, though, and they spend several minutes discussing the justice. When there's a lull in the conversation, Mac steps into it.

"Let me know if you decide to write that paper about her. I could get you an interview with her if you're interested in—"

"You know her?" Olivia interrupts with an awed gasp.

"I know—or know how to get to—just about everyone who matters in this town," Mac answers.

"Oh. My. God. You are my hero. Of course I'd want to meet her.

That would be… Wow… I can't even…" Olivia trails off, staring at Mac, wide-eyed and unblinking. The charming bastard. If I'm not careful, my whole family will decide they like him better than me. He's already won Tristan over. It's only a matter of time before the girls follow.

During the meal, Tristan falls asleep in Mac's lap, and it would be far too easy to let myself get carried away imagining nights like this becoming a regular occurrence. Especially after our conversation on his terrace. Neither of us explicitly said we want this to change, to be more like a real relationship, but it feels like we're heading in that direction, and I'm…I think that's what I want. Maybe.

But God is it terrifying.

While I help Willa clean up, Mac carries Tristan back to bed. When he returns twenty minutes later, I set aside my dish towel and walk to the door with him.

"He made me promise to call every day I'm gone," Mac informs me with a pleased smile.

"I'm sorry, but I don't think I should go tomorrow. I'll have to catch up with the campaign when he's well enough to go back to school. Hopefully, it will only be a few days and—"

"I figured, Gwen," Mac interrupts my babbling and puts his hands on my shoulders. "It's fine—you should be with him. I'll have Cece send you some pictures from the road, and you can keep up with your social media fan club from here."

"Okay," I agree, smiling at his teasing about my fan club.

"I'll miss the fuck out of you, though," Mac whispers so the others won't overhear.

My cheeks warm, and I have the incredible urge to burrow into his chest and let him hold me. Anything to delay his departure, because now that dinner is over and Tris is in bed for the night, I have no reason to ask him to stay and I really, really don't want him to go. "Yeah, you'll miss something," I joke in hopes of hiding my overly mushy thoughts.

"I will miss that, but not just that." Mac dips his head, grasping my chin with one thumb and forefinger. "I'm going to kiss you goodbye now, and I don't want to hear one goddamn word of complaint about your sisters, or Tris, or anything else, okay?"

Yes, yes, kiss me!

Pushing up on my tiptoes, I lean toward him, inviting the kiss. Because even though I know I should say all those things anyway, I can't bring myself to do it. Not when I want this kiss just as badly as he does. Maybe more.

"Good girl," Mac praises me with a lazy smile before brushing his lips over mine.

It's a soft, lingering kiss. So tender it reminds me a little of my very first kiss, although it's so much better than that sweetly awkward experience was. In ninth grade, Tommy Shaw was a rank amateur, well-intentioned but clueless. But Mac? He's the Mozart of kissing, playing my mouth as if he's memorized every note of the most exquisite song, a duet only he and I can play together.

"I'll call you tomorrow," Mac promises, his lips still brushing my cheek as he holds me close. I nod, and Mac releases me, giving me one final heated look that tells me he doesn't want to go any more than I want him to, and then he's gone.

Breathless and confused, I turn away from the door with my fingers over my lips, trying to hold on to the feel of that kiss. Finding both of my sisters staring at me with smug expressions—and Diane pointedly not looking at me—I'm jolted out of my dreamlike trance of the last few minutes.

Fuck, they saw that? What the hell am I supposed to say now?

But Willa fills the silence for me, her smile growing wider as she says, "Yeah, it's definitely not like *that.*"

"Oh, shut up," I snap, stalking into the kitchen to finish the dishes.

CHAPTER 30

GWEN

TRUE TO HIS WORD, Mac called every day, but that wasn't the only thing he did in his absence.

When Willie and Olivia came down with the flu two days after Tristan, Mac sent them both flowers. A bouquet of Gerber daisies in every conceivable color for Olivia and an equally colorful bunch of tulips for Willa. It was hard to say if he just got lucky or if the perceptive bastard had somehow guessed their favorite flowers, but that night when he called to talk to Tristan, they both insisted on thanking him. The amount of fawning praise they—and especially Olivia—heaped upon him was embarrassing, and he ate it up with glee.

Two days after that, just when I started to hope I'd escaped the plague, I too succumbed. By that point, Tristan was feeling well enough that he was the one who answered my phone when his dad called that evening. Too busy puking, I didn't speak to Mac, but the phone was passed around between Tristan and my sisters. Apparently, everyone wanted their chance to talk to him now.

The next day, another bouquet arrived, this time two dozen red roses. Olivia snatched the card out of the box before I could get to it, squealing with delight when she read it aloud.

Get well soon, baby. Can't wait to see you again. -Mac

When Mac's housekeeper showed up on our doorstep later that afternoon, the fanciful chatter between my sisters only grew worse. And it was awkward, because until I answered the door in my ratty bathrobe, emergency puke bucket tucked under one arm, I hadn't even known Mac had a housekeeper. But there she stood, loaded down with decades-old Tupperware, introducing herself as Juana and explaining that Mac sent her to take care of us.

Juana returned every day to provide us all with healthful home-made meals, clean up after us, and even do our laundry. She was a saint, and she kept coming back, despite my protests and our continued recovery, until finally I gave Mac a very detailed and explicit threat to his family jewels if he didn't call her off. He laughed and said he knew I was bluffing, because he was confident I was just as fond of his balls as he was, but Juana reduced her visits to every other day after that. It was a partial win, and at this point I'd take what I could get.

Now it's two weeks to the day since Tristan first got sick, we've all fully recovered, and I'm waiting in the lobby of a hotel in Salt Lake City for Cece to meet me with my room key so I can drop off my bags before joining the rest of the team. But waiting around with nothing else to do is never a good thing, and it's especially bad right now because I have nothing to distract me from thinking about Mac.

"What do you suppose it means that he's being so nice to me and Willie?" That's what Olivia asked early this morning while she sat on my bed watching me pack. I didn't answer her, not because I didn't know the answer but because I did, and I had no idea what to do about it.

Back in Ann Arbor, our relationship was a huge risk for someone as cautious as me. But it feels even riskier now, not just because we have a kid together but because this time, my heart is definitely getting involved.

"Hey."

I'm startled by Mac's voice, partly because I was so lost in thought but also because I was expecting Cece. I really should have known better, though. "Hey, yourself." Rising from my chair, I give him what I hope is a confident smile. "Do you have my key?"

"No, you'll have to get that from Cece later," he admits with a widening grin. "But I have *a* key and a few minutes."

Yeah, after two weeks apart, I definitely should have expected this. "Good, because we have some things to talk about," I say, ignoring the butterflies swarming in my stomach.

"Do we?" Mac asks, both brows raised as he grabs my bags.

"We do." When the elevator doors close behind us, he gives me an expectant look, but I shake my head. "Not until we get to the room."

"This sounds like a conversation I'm going to like."

"I wouldn't count on that if I were you." Despite my words, my tone lacks conviction, because I enjoy bantering with Mac. Worse, there are frantic little butterflies—no scratch that, it feels more like a fish out of water violently flopping around in my stomach—in anticipation of being alone in a room with him again.

As soon as we've reached the room, he drops my bags, shedding his coat and tie and herding me toward the bed with nips and kisses. Too weak to resist, and just as eager as he is, it isn't until I'm on my back, legs spread wide as he rubs the head of his cock against my clit, that I remember I still have things I want to say.

"Mac, I was serious before... We need to talk." I gasp out the words, but my hands are on his ass, trying to pull him closer even as I say them.

Lifting his head from my breast where he was licking and sucking my nipple, Mac asks, "Are you going to tell me I'm not allowed to touch you anymore?"

"No, but—"

"Great, then anything else we can multitask," Mac says as he shifts over me, lining himself up and rocking forward, entering me with a single hard thrust.

"Oh, God... So good..." I gasp and Mac picks up a slow but steady pace that sets my body humming.

"Jesus, I want to fuck you so hard that housekeeping will need a crowbar to pry you out of this mattress," Mac grumbles close to my ear, but he maintains his almost-lazy tempo.

"Yes, that, please do that." Locking my legs around him, I arch my back in an attempt to force him to go harder.

"Next time." He bites my earlobe, tugging it between his teeth before lifting his head and adding, "You wanted to talk, and you can't do that very well if I'm shoving your face into the mattress."

"I can't do that very well now," I admit with a helpless laugh, because the words are little more than a moan.

"Try." Mac chuckles, rubbing his nose against mine.

"Okay." I close my eyes and drag in a deep breath in an effort to concentrate on what I want to say rather than the way my pussy is stretched around his thick cock as he gently thrusts against me. My voice is almost steady when I finally say, "Your attempt to charm my sisters was entirely transparent."

"Did it work?" Mac asks with one brow quirked and a mischievous smirk.

But I'm unable to answer, because he chooses that moment to give me one hard, driving thrust, and I cry out, my muscles tightening in anticipation. He doesn't give me more, though, instead settling back into his easy rhythm and biting my chin before prodding me again for an answer.

"Did it work?"

"Yes, it fucking worked, you asshole. They adore you. They can't shut up about how sweet you are. How romantic you are. It's fucking maddening, because they don't know you like I do, and you are neither sweet nor romantic." There are a lot of words I would use to describe Mac, many of them complimentary, but those two are not on the list. They aren't even in the same universe as the list.

Without warning, he stills, both brows rising as he says, "I may have oversold it. I was aiming for thoughtful."

"Oh, bullshit. You were just trying to get me where you want me," I complain while squirming under him, urging him to move again. It's the only explanation that made sense to me. It was a charming manipulation, winning me over through my sisters. What, exactly, he's trying to win me over to? I'm not sure, but whatever it is, I don't like that he's using my sisters to do it.

"Not sure why I'd do that." Mac's gaze drifts lower, lingering on my breasts long enough to make them feel heavy and achy with awareness, then lower still to where our bodies remain joined, his erection hard and throbbing inside me. "I've already got you exactly where I fucking want you."

"Sweet-talker," I huff and make a feeble attempt at rolling my eyes.

"Did it ever occur to you that I realize now what a dick I was to you on our first go and I'm trying to do better this time?" Mac asks, his brows furrowed as his eyes meet mine again.

No, no, that didn't occur to me and now that he's said it, I'm more confused than ever. He's just admitted the very thing I feared and, confronted with his unvarnished truth instead of just my own speculation, I don't know what to do. He's trying to be better. Does that mean he wants *us* to be different? Better? More?

And is that what I want? Yes. Yes, it is. The only real question is if I'm brave enough to take a chance on him. On us.

His warm brown eyes search my face, studying my expression. He must recognize my sudden confusion, because he lowers himself over me and starts to move again, his face in my hair as he whispers, "Don't think about it now, baby. Just be here with me."

And I listen, because despite my unsettled emotions, the one thing I do know is that's what I want too, to be here in this moment with Mac.

CHAPTER 31

MAC

ONE OF THE things that's surprised me about sharing a room with Gwen on the road is how much I enjoy getting ready together in the mornings. Brushing our teeth side by side before showering, usually together. Shaving while she dries her hair and puts on her makeup. Leaving her to finish while I drink a cup of coffee and scan the mornings headlines on my tablet, reading out loud for her anything important or that I think she might find interesting. When she's finally finished in the bathroom, we get dressed together. She picks out my tie, and I zip her dress or help her with that fiddly button that frustrates her so much on her favorite lavender blouse.

It's goddamn domestic, and a month ago I'd have scoffed at the idea that I might like it. Because even though we've been sharing hotel rooms for a while now, it took the absence of our comfortable routine for me to notice what a satisfying way it is to start my day.

God, the last month has been brutal, though. Between our disparate schedules leading up to Super Tuesday and everyone—well, everyone but me—getting sick afterward, I'm fucking starving for

Gwen. Yes, we had sex as soon as she arrived yesterday and again when we finally made it back to our room last night. And sure, there was lazy, sleepy sex this morning before we rolled out of bed. Doesn't matter; none of it matters. I cannot get enough of her.

Except…that's not precisely the truth, or at least not the full truth, because it isn't just about sex. The whole time we were apart, there was a constant knot in my stomach that was at its worst in the quiet moments when I missed her most, but never eased until she was standing right in front of me. Now I still have this nagging buzz in my gut that won't settle until I see Tris again, but it's familiar. Somewhere along the way over the last couple of months, I've learned to miss him and accepted the fact that things aren't quite right when we're apart. But this thing with Gwen? That's new, and I'm not sure what to make of it.

All I know is I can't take my eyes off her and I hate it if she gets more than an arm's length away from me. I'm smart enough to realize it's irrational and ridiculous, but I'm evidently not smart enough to figure out what's prompted this sudden change. Maybe it's just an unexpected consequence of our dozen years apart and the way she took off the first time. That sort of makes sense, doesn't it?

"There's something else I wanted to talk to you about," Gwen says, interrupting my thoughts.

"Lay it on me." Reaching for my shaving cream, I glance at her in the mirror and find her turned toward me, one hip against the counter and arms crossed over her chest. Okay, maybe this isn't a conversation we can have while I shave.

"Juana," she says with a frown once I've turned to face her.

"What about her?" I ask, mimicking her posture. Not that it really matters how she answers, because this is not a negotiation. There will be no compromise. She's keeping Juana whether she likes it or not, and Juana will remain on my payroll not hers.

"How long will you demand she keep coming to our apartment?" She makes it sound so unreasonable, like I'm forcing the poor woman to work sixteen-hour days, seven days a week, for pennies a day.

"Forever." I pause, rubbing my lip as I give it more thought, then amend my initial response. "Eh, I think she's in her late fifties. Forever or until she retires. And when that happens, I'll replace her."

"Why?" The flash of anger in her eyes is unmistakable, but I have zero fucks to give about it. Not this time.

We still haven't had a real conversation about money. Every time I try to raise the issue, even in an abstract or tangential way, she gets pissed off and shuts down. Then they got sick, and I sent Juana because I was worried. No ulterior motives; I just wanted to help. But then it occurred to me that between Olivia and Tristan and all the travel, Gwen's life is a circus even on the best of days. She could use the help on a regular basis. So could Willa, who has cheerfully stepped up, even though she's under no obligation to do it, and keeps all the balls in the air when Gwen is on the road. If Gwen won't accept my money—and seriously, what the fuck is her problem?—she's damn well going to have to learn to accept things like this.

"Because you won't allow me to help in the way I should be helping," I explain, my words clipped with frustration.

"I don't need anyone's help." It's her stock answer, one I've already heard a dozen times.

"I know that." With a heavy sigh, I consider my words carefully before continuing. "I am not, and I would never, question your capability. You are a fantastic mother and you have done an incredible job with Tristan and your sisters and yes, you could continue to run yourself ragged doing it all, but aren't you tired? Wouldn't it be nice to have a little help?"

"No."

Well, okay then. If I could just understand why she's so damn resistant to letting me help her, it would be easier, but none of it makes a damn bit of sense, and my frustration only fuels my irritation. "And what about Willa? What do you think she'd say if I called and asked her if she wanted Juana to keep coming?" That is met with stony silence, because she knows damn well what Willa would say. Sensing my advantage, I press on. "You realize you let Willa do more for you and Tris than you let me, right? If you're not just paying lip service to the idea, if you really want me to actually be his father—"

"I have never done anything but encourage your relationship with Tristan," Gwen interrupts, standing taller and holding her chin high, full of righteous indignation.

"Except let me help support him." Even to my own ears, my voice is remarkably calm, but there's no give in it, no doubt or uncertainty.

This is the bottom line. She wants me to be Tristan's dad, but only on her terms. And maybe there are a lot of men out there who would fucking love her terms, but I'm not one of them. I will not be the jackass who's only there for the good times. I'm not going to be a half-assed father like I had. I may have been denied nearly eleven years of his life, but now that I know about Tris, now that I love him, there's no halfway, and Gwen will have to find a way to make peace with that.

Her startled expression indicates she's never considered it from that angle before, but she doesn't say anything, instead just nodding stiffly.

"Juana stays," I say, softly but firmly.

Another stiff nod. "Fine. But that's all."

"Fine. For now," I agree, mostly because this feels like a win and I don't want to push her too far too fast. Maybe if I give her some time to think about this, she'll realize I'm right.

We stare at each other for a long minute, both taking stock of where we're at and how we got here. Finally, muttering under her breath, Gwen turns back to the mirror. "Stubborn asshole."

"Sorry, didn't catch that. What did you just say, control freak?"

I have to bite back a smile when she gives me a sidelong look in the mirror, humor sparking in her eye among her other still raw emotions. Yeah, we'll be all right. This is how Gwen and I have always been. We might fight and fuck like it's the end of the damn world, but we'll figure it out.

Turning back to the sink, I grab my shaving cream for the second time this morning. I've smeared it halfway over my face when Gwen's breath hitches, and something clatters on the counter. Giving her a quick glance, mostly because I'm curious what she dropped, what I see makes me stop abruptly and give her a double take.

She's staring at herself in the mirror, eyes wide and unblinking.

Her cheeks, moments ago flushed with the heat of battle, are now blanched, her mouth pressed into a firm, worried line. "No, no, no, no," she's stammering, waving one shaky hand in my direction as if to keep me at a distance, and her breathing is coming in short, rapid bursts. By all appearances, she's on the verge of a panic attack.

Grabbing a towel and wiping the shaving cream off my face, I consider growing a beard. Maybe this is a sign from the universe. "Gwen, baby, what's wrong?" I ask when I've tossed the towel aside.

But she doesn't respond, at least not to me. She's still talking under her breath and slapping one hand down on the counter, feeling around for something. "This can't be happening. No, just... Goddammit...what the fuck am I going to do? Shit!"

"Honey, I want to help you, but you need to tell me what's going on." It's like talking to a brick wall. I doubt she even hears me, and it's starting to freak me out.

She doesn't try to stop me when I take another step closer and put a tentative hand on her shoulder, but she doesn't acknowledge me either, at least not until she's found what she was searching for. Then she turns to face me so abruptly she stumbles into me and I have to steady her with both hands as she shoves her open pack of birth control pills in my face.

I don't understand what she's trying to show me. Judging by the stickers with the days of the week across the top, today's pill is halfway pushed through the foil backing, because I guess she was about to take it when she flipped out. I'm no expert on the pill, but everything looks fine to me. All the pills before today are gone, and there's five more after today. "I don't know what you're trying to tell me." Except once I say the words out loud, dread coils deep in my gut, because I think maybe I do.

"My period should have started yesterday." She sticks the pack of pills in my face again and grabs my bicep with her other hand, squeezing hard like she's trying to physically force me to understand.

"Okay, but that happens sometimes, right?"

"N-not to me," Gwen stutters and glances down at her phone on the counter, checking the time. "The l-l-last time I was late is probably eating a bowl of Cheerios with Olivia as we speak."

She's speaking English, and the stutter is distracting but not that bad; I should be able to understand what she's saying. But I can't. It's like the words are getting stuck in a sludge of molasses somewhere between my ears and my brain.

Despite her own distress, she must sense my trouble, because the pack of pills tumbles to the floor and she smacks my bare chest with both palms, the loud slap startling me more than the sting. "Mac, are you fucking listening to me? Because I'm, like, ninety-nine percent sure I'm pregnant." Tears are spilling down her cheeks and she's shaking so hard I'm surprised her teeth aren't chattering.

I reach for her, intending to pull her against my chest and tell her—

Wait. What did she just say?

"I... You... What?" Apparently, it's my turn to stammer incoherently, but I'll be damned if I can come up with anything better.

"I'm pretty sure I'm pregnant."

This time I understand her.

Mac and Gwen's story continues in Unexpected, coming August 11, 2020. Pre-order your copy now!

Gwen

Just as Mac and I have found a sort of routine in our unorthodox relationship, our world is rocked with shocking news—I'm pregnant. Not exactly ideal timing, given how busy the firm is on this high-stakes Presidential campaign, not to mention Mac's tenuous new connection with our son. As we deal with all these complications, I'm learning how to compromise with Mac so he can be a bigger part of our children's lives—and despite my efforts, I'm falling in love with him. But when I discover Mac's been keeping huge secrets of his own, I begin to realize how precarious our relationship really is...and now I have to protect my heart at all cost.

Mac

One blurry photo of a blue plus sign is all it takes to throw my life in turmoil. I'm already struggling with doubt about fatherhood, consumed with fears that I'll turn out just like my old man. I'm determined not to let my newfound family down, though. But when campaign scandals start hitting too close to home, I'm suddenly faced with important decisions about my future with my family, my career, and Gwen.

ABOUT THE AUTHOR

Liza Gaines grew up in Michigan before moving to Virginia in 2007. She misses her family and the Great Lakes but has otherwise fallen in love with her adopted home state.

A dedicated reader, Liza often has her nose in a book. She also enjoys cooking, baking, knitting, and watching terrible science fiction movies with her husband. Their small farm in Fredericksburg, Virginia is home to an ever-expanding menagerie that currently includes three dogs, five cats, two horses, and three goats.

For the latest updates and sneak peeks:
http://www.lizagaines.com/newsletter